Prescott Jane

THE RIGHT SIDE OF WRONG

by
PRESCOTT LANE

Copyright © 2021 Prescott Lane
Print Edition

Editing by Editing4Indies

This is a work of fiction. All characters, organizations, and events portrayed in this novel are either products of the author's imagination or used fictitiously. All rights reserved. This book or any portion thereof may not be reproduced or used in any manner whatsoever without the express written permission of the author, except for the use of brief quotations in a book review.

TABLE OF CONTENTS

Prologue	1
Chapter One	2
Chapter Two	11
Chapter Three	26
Chapter Four	32
Chapter Five	35
Chapter Six	42
Chapter Seven	48
Chapter Eight	53
Chapter Nine	56
Chapter Ten	59
Chapter Eleven	62
Chapter Twelve	76
Chapter Thirteen	78
Chapter Fourteen	82
Chapter Fifteen	87
Chapter Sixteen	92
Chapter Seventeen	96
Chapter Eighteen	101
Chapter Nineteen	103
Chapter Twenty	111
Chapter Twenty-One	118
Chapter Twenty-Two	124
Chapter Twenty-Three	134
Chapter Twenty-Four	139
Chapter Twenty-Five	142
Chapter Twenty-Six	150

Chapter Twenty-Seven	152
Chapter Twenty-Eight	160
Chapter Twenty-Nine	166
Chapter Thirty	170
Chapter Thirty-One	173
Chapter Thirty-Two	179
Chapter Thirty-Three	188
Chapter Thirty-Four	196
Chapter Thirty-Five	199
Chapter Thirty-Six	202
Chapter Thirty-Seven	208
Chapter Thirty-Eight	214
Chapter Thirty-Nine	218
Chapter Forty	224
Chapter Forty-One	227
Chapter Forty-Two	231
Chapter Forty-Three	234
Chapter Forty-Four	240
Epilogue	246
Also by Prescott Lane	250
Acknowledgements	251
About the Author	252

PROLOGUE

PAIGE

Promises.

Every promise that was ever made to me has been broken. That's why I've never made one myself. I never want to break one. All that's about to change. I'm about to make the most important promise of my life.

It's not to my husband on my wedding day. It's not to a boss or a best friend. No, this one is more important.

It's to the little newborn boy in my arms. And unlike wedding vows that can be undone by a judge, this one I won't ever let be broken. This is my promise to keep.

"I'll do whatever I have to. Your life will be better than mine."

CHAPTER ONE
FIVE MONTHS LATER

PAIGE

His arm tightens around my waist. God, how much cologne does he have on? Not that it matters, it's not enough to mask the smell of whiskey and old man that seems to radiate off him. That's really not fair. He's not that old, just old compared to me. I'm only twenty, and he's got to be at least sixty.

I flash him a smile. He's paying for my company this evening, so it really doesn't matter how old he is or what he smells like as long as the evening ends with a wad of cash in my hands. Rumor is, he likes his girls young, brunette, and blue-eyed. Rumor also is that if he really likes a girl, he'll set her up with a place, a car, a spending account. Tonight is an interview of sorts.

His hand slides to my ass, not caring who sees. In fact, I'm sure that's the point. He wants everyone at the party to see. Bile rises to the back of my throat, but I swallow it back down with a smile. It's all a lie—the smile, the dress.

Lies can be big or small, but they don't always have to come in words. Only amateurs lie with words. Master liars like me can lie with a smile, or a laugh, a forced tear. My smile says I'm happy. My eyes say I love you, but that's not the truth. I smile to hide the pain. My eyes sparkle because they are on the brink of tears. I don't need words to lie. I lie to survive. I lie to keep a promise.

"Fetch me a drink, sweetheart," he says.

Another fake smile earns me a pat on my ass as I walk away.

Making my way through the crowd, I let my body relax a little, giving myself the hundredth pep talk of the night. I know it could be much worse. Think seedy hotels and kinky fetishes.

The line at the bar is long, which is a blessing. I need the extra time to convince myself to stay in this game. I run my hands down the red chiffon fabric of my dress. It's easily the nicest thing I've ever had against my skin. A present from him for me to wear tonight. Some would think it's a sign of his generosity, but I know better. This man wants to control me. From the way I wore my brown hair to the makeup artist he sent to make sure my blue eyes didn't overshadow the red lipstick he wanted me to wear to match the dress, he's the master. I'm the plaything.

Everyone here is dressed to the nines—sequin dresses, high heels, jewels—and I fit right in. No one would know I'm "working" tonight. I wonder if there are any other girls like me here? It's a bit ironic that this party is a charity event to support the arts in the greater Nashville area when I'm probably the one who needs charity the most. There's an auction for a bunch of frivolous junk that no one needs.

It's not that I don't think the arts are important. Not long ago, I was a college student. I love books, history, museums, but I love having food on my plate, clean clothes, and a roof over my head more. I thought I'd escaped this life. College was my ticket out of poverty, public housing, and watching my mom snort, smoke, or shoot up anything she could get her hands on. I never wanted to be like her. I wanted out. I worked hard in school despite often not having the supplies I needed. I was going to use my brain, not my body, to make a living. What do they say about the best-laid plans?

Everyone else seems to be having a wonderful time, drinking and dancing, smiling and laughing, but I'd rather be anywhere else. I'm not here for fun. Nothing about this is fun. A woman doesn't decide to sell her body, her time, her soul for fun. She doesn't come to it until she's out of options and no other choices remain. It's not something you do lightly. It's not something I thought I'd ever do, but I don't do it for me. I do it for the only member of the male species I'll ever love—that little baby boy.

All the women here look so in love with their dates, their husbands. Girls like me don't get the luxury of love. Yes, love is a luxury. It's not a right. It's a privilege not all of us are afforded.

"Having a good time?" a deep, rough voice asks from beside me.

I look up at the man who's suddenly appeared by my side. In my heels, I'm easily six feet, and he towers over me. He's one of those big guys—the type you just know has to have his suits custom made. I'm pretty good at sizing people up. One look at this guy tells me he's used to getting what he wants. I give him a polite smile. I can't afford to give him more than that.

"My father has good taste. I'll give him that," the stranger says. My head whips up. Family is not part of the deal. He extends his hand. "Slade Turner." I reach to shake his hand when he slips his hand over mine, pulling me close. Unlike his father, he doesn't reek of whiskey and old age. "I've seen your type before. I know you're just after his money."

Straightening my spine, hoping my stilettos give me a boost, I say, "Yes, I am." This tall, broad beast of a man jerks back just enough for me to notice. But I don't throw him off his mission for long. He leans closer, his mere presence forcing me to look at him. "You want all of his money for yourself?" I ask with sass.

"I don't need his money."

"Then mind your own business."

The bastard actually smiles at me. "I'll let my father know you needed to leave early."

"I'm not leaving."

He motions with his hand to another man I hadn't noticed standing just a few feet away. Roughly the size of a house, he's bald, and his eyes are so dark they look like a moonless night. "Make sure she gets home."

"Your father invited me. I'm not leaving," I snap. No way am I losing this gig.

"He hasn't paid you yet?" Slade asks, glaring at me.

My heart starts to thump. It's one thing for him to think of me as a gold digger, but it's another for him to suspect me a whore. In truth, it's just semantics. Gold digger, prostitute, escort, whore—they all mean the same thing. All words meant to degrade women and maintain power over us.

It's not the first time anyone's ever looked at me like I'm trash and worthless, but that doesn't make it any easier.

He turns to his friend. "And make sure to pay her."

The sound of poverty bleeds through the window of my one-bedroom apartment. You know the sound—the sirens, the gunshots in the distance, the cries and screams of women and children. I've never spent the night in a rich neighborhood, but I imagine it's serene with a humming of birds or insects in the background. Perhaps even the traffic of taxis in big cities like New York.

Dumping the contents of my wallet on the table, I hear the clang of the two pennies I have to my name, literally. Apparently, I can't even sell my body correctly. I really needed that trick tonight. I would've hated every second of it, but I would've done it. We need it. Bad. I'd do anything for that sweet little boy asleep in the next room. Anything.

I hate to resort to working a street corner, but I may have no choice. I made a promise to that baby boy, and I won't let him down. No matter what it takes. That's what I promised him. Glancing down at my oversized gray sweatshirt and sweatpants, I'm hardly the picture of sex appeal.

More the picture of my true self, working two and three jobs while trying to take care of a baby. And it's barely paying the bills. If I'm going to get my head above water and make enough money to go back to school, I've got to take the next step. That's what tonight was about. And that self-righteous prick had to ruin it. Or he saved me, depending on how you look at it.

The truth is, I left. I could've put up a much bigger fight, made a scene, refused to go, found his father and finished what I started, but I didn't. Now I have to pay for that decision.

At least I have the chiffon dress. That should earn me a pretty penny at the consignment shop. When people think of Nashville, they think about country music, honky-tonks, and The Grand Ole Opry. Of course, that's part of it, but like every big city, there are neighborhoods like mine.

Dangerous neighborhoods.

But my address isn't the real danger.

There are a lot of bad things in this world. I grew up with most of them in my own house. Drugs? My mom is an addict. Prostitution? My mom's profession. Abuse? I've endured my share. Hunger? More days than I care to think about. I've survived it all.

The real danger, the thing that can take anyone down, is hope.

If you don't hope, your heart doesn't get broken. If you don't hope, you aren't disappointed. The first lesson I learned as a child was the only person I can rely on is me. Hoping my mother would get clean and take care of me broke my heart more times than I can count. Hoping someday someone would rescue me from the hellhole of my life only kept me waiting.

No one was coming.

I had me.

Hope can go fuck itself.

Heavy footsteps pound through the hallway, the kind of footsteps that only a man's weight produces. A single gal living alone in this kind of building tends to become an expert in said footsteps. I know the sound of 4A's regular on Monday night. The sound of 4B's abusive boyfriend. The weight of the elderly gentleman who visits his grandchild in 5C. But these footsteps are new. A new client for 4A?

They stop right outside my door.

A rapid swoosh sounds as an envelope slips under my door. Leaping to my feet, I grab it, ripping it open to reveal five crisp hundred-dollar bills. The exact amount I was due for tonight.

Son of a bitch!

Without another thought, I fling the door open, finding Mr. Nosy, Slade Turner, sauntering back down my hallway. The friend he had bring me home must have given him my address. He stops but doesn't turn to me. Guess trash like me doesn't deserve the courtesy. I wad the envelope and bills into a tight ball and throw it with everything I have, which is pretty sad. It's paper, so it doesn't go very far.

I might be poor. I might be trash in his eyes, but I don't take money that I haven't earned. That will come back to bite you in the butt every time. No one, not even family, gives you something for free. Strings are always attached whether you see them or not. The wad of money lands close enough to him that he gets the message.

Nonchalantly, he bends down, picking it up and turning to me. God, I'm so pissed, my chest rising and falling rapidly, my fists in tight balls at my side. "I don't want your damn money!" In one stride, he's towering over me with that smug smile that makes me want to smack him. "I didn't take the money when your goon offered it. What makes you think . . ."

"Goon?" he repeats, fighting back a smile. "Who uses the word *goon*?"

Is he really questioning my vocabulary right now? "What else should I call him? He's huge. Barely said two words to me."

"His name is Jon, and I'm sure he didn't mean to scare you," Slade says.

"I wasn't scared."

"Of course not," he says, taking hold of my wrist and dropping the wadded-up cash into my hand. "Stay away from my father."

"You get that you can't control me, right?"

He leans forward, but I hold my ground, refusing to give him an inch. "My father will chew you up and spit you out."

"And I'll let him."

I hear him inhale a swift breath right before a little cry starts from the other room. With surprise in his eyes, he darts his gaze to my bedroom door. Not now. While I was at the party, I had him at a twenty-four-hour day care I sometimes work at. It's not far from here, but now he's off his schedule. The cry gets a little louder. The walls are thin, so I can't let him cry for too long without disturbing the whole building, but it looks like my guest isn't going to excuse himself.

Without a word, I walk backward toward my bedroom door, my eyes glued on the blue eyes of Slade Turner. How did I not notice their color before? They're so clear, almost like sapphires.

Shaking my head, I disappear into the bedroom. I'm only gone about thirty seconds, but when I step back into my living area, Slade has stepped just over the threshold of my door. On my hip and cuddled into my side is a complete chunk of baby love. You'd never think we are so poor by the looks of my little guy. "You should go," I say. "I need to get him back to sleep."

"You live here with him alone?" Slade asks, shutting the door behind him.

My fight or flight response kicks right in, and I angle my body, shielding the baby, my eyes darting for something to use as a weapon. Slade must sense my panic because he holds his hands up.

"I just meant, where's his father?"

"None of your damn business," I snap.

"Fuck," he says, looking at the floor like he's searching for something. "I mean, you don't have a roommate, family, or anyone else helping you? Protecting you and him?"

"We're fine. We're perfectly safe," I say.

"The stoned guy passed out in the hallway tells a different story," he says with a hint of a smile playing on his lips.

"We all can't have a rich daddy."

"I'm not judging you," he says, his voice soft.

"Yes, you are. You judged me from the moment you saw me at the party. You've just got more ammunition now."

"No, now I have more of the story," he says, holding out the money again. "Please take it."

"I can't," I say, holding the baby closer. "I didn't earn it."

"Some kind of prostitute principles?" he asks.

Our eyes meet as a fire of anger fills my chest. If he wasn't such a prick, he'd be swoon-worthy—okay, he still is. But I can't be distracted by his hard chest or those piercing blue eyes. Just because he's hot as hell doesn't mean he's not an asshole—just a hot asshole. Those are the most dangerous kind.

I could use that money. I should take it, but no one gives you something for free. Those bills would mean I owed him, and with no idea what the repayment will be or when it will be expected, the risk is too high. "Something like that. Now get out of my apartment before I call the police."

He reaches into his back pocket and pulls out his wallet. I'm expecting another wad of bills, but instead, he places a business card on my rickety coffee table. "I have my own business separate from my father. I can help get you a real job."

"What will it cost me?" I ask.

"Can't be more than you were willing to give away for five hundred bucks, can it?" he asks, holding my glare. "You should really charge more."

It's late, I'm tired, and my eyes lower to the ground for a second. "Why do you care?"

"I don't," he says. "But I want you away from my father, so I figure I'll get you a real job and . . ."

"Your father came to me," I say.

"I'm aware of how it works."

"Yeah, you seem to have all the answers," I say sarcastically.

"At least we agree on that," he says with a smile before motioning toward the business card. "This is the part where you thank me for helping you and getting you off the streets."

"I'm not on the streets," I bite out, "and I haven't accepted your offer."

His blue eyes narrow just a tad. "You will, for two very important reasons." Before I can open my mouth to tell him to go to hell, he flashes me a full smile, making my heart pound. "For one, you don't seem to have a whole lot of other options. And you're holding the most important reason."

He's got my number, and he knows it. I was ready to sell my body to his father for this little boy. I'd do anything to give him a better life and keep him safe.

But sex for money is a straight-up transaction. A cut-and-dried deal. Yes, you might need to negotiate the terms of the sex, but what Slade is offering is different. It's much more dangerous. It's the unknown. And I get the feeling he doesn't play by anyone's rules.

"What skills do you have?" he asks. "Other than being beautiful."

Our eyes meet with a different kind of heat this time. That was the last thing I expected him to say. I'd expect something more along the lines of, *"Other than blow jobs and spreading your legs."*

"I've worked retail, fast food, mowed a few lawns."

"Mowed lawns?" he asks, amusement in his voice. "Anything recently?"

"On the weekends, I clean office buildings at night. And during the day, I work a couple of shifts at a day care. They let me bring Finn, so it works out well."

"His name is Finn?" he asks, reaching toward me before stopping himself. "What about you? What's your name?"

"Paige. Paige Hudson."

CHAPTER TWO

PAIGE

It only took me two days to yield to the will of Slade Turner. Well, two days and a double homicide on the second floor of my apartment building. After my call, Slade wasted no time sending a car for Finn and me. Yes, Finn. The car was equipped with a rear-facing infant car seat. He may be a pretentious prick, but that was a nice touch.

Of course, Finn loved it. Since I don't have a car, he never actually had a car seat. He kicked and cooed and put on quite a show. I have no idea what today will bring because Slade didn't tell me what position he had in mind for me. He simply asked me to meet him. That brought some anxiety, but I doubt it's anything too risqué since I'm bringing the baby along.

This is a gamble, one where I don't know the stakes. But when you're holding a losing hand, you either fold or bluff, and I'm no quitter.

Looking down at my jeans and two sizes too big sweater, I'm hardly dressed for a job interview, but it's the best I have. Finn, however, looks adorable in his baby jeans and onesie with a firetruck appliqué on it. You can find really cute baby clothes in consignment stores. I think it's because babies grow so fast. They wear something for three months max before they outgrow it. At least that's the way my little guy is.

I'm not sure what I expected today, but I certainly didn't expect to leave the city limits of Nashville. After almost an hour, the city's bustling streets have given way to the long, winding roads of the country. No longer flanked by sidewalks and skyscrapers, the stretch of road is now guided by wood fences. Occasionally, you can see a big, beautiful house in the distance settled back among the trees. Everything is green with hues of yellow mixed in. The sky is such a rich shade of blue it almost looks purple.

I've lived in cities my whole life. I wonder if it's easier to be poor in the city or the country? They probably don't have soup kitchens or public housing out here, but it's beautiful. Beauty doesn't fill the belly, but it feeds the soul. I grew up looking at cracked concrete and run-down buildings. Even the so-called "green" spaces were overgrown and filled with trash and litter.

I guess what they say is true. The grass is greener on the other side.

Turning, we pull up to the gates of a ranch. There are stone pillars to pass through, but no sign. Usually, these places have names, but there's nothing. An egotistical man like Slade probably would've named it after himself. Maybe I just missed the sign.

The driver, Jon, the same *goon* who brought me home the other night, slowly rolls down a long stone driveway, and the most beautiful home I've ever seen comes into view. It looks like a cabin, only it's one a millionaire would live in. I take that back. It almost looks like a church with its steep-pitched roof and windows that stretch across the entire front section of the house from the porch to the roofline, which is at least two stories high. Hopefully, my job isn't to clean those suckers!

"This is where Slade lives?" I ask.

"He has a place in the city, so he's usually just here on the weekends," Jon says, eyeing me in the rearview mirror.

I avert my eyes, taking in the landscape of rolling hills on a canvas of green as far as the eye can see. "Look, Finn, horses," I say, pointing out the car window. I'm clearly more excited about them than he is.

The car slows to a crawl, stopping in front of the house. I'm unbuckling Finn when Jon opens my door for me. Grabbing the diaper bag and the baby, I step out into the crisp and clean air. Apparently, the rich even have better air quality.

Jon heads for the front door, snapping me from my oxygen envy, and I follow him into what can only be described as the most luxurious treehouse. Windows line the back of the house as well, showcasing acres and acres of rolling hills and trees, making it seem like I'm floating in the forest.

"This way," Jon says.

I follow him, my eyes still on that view, barely glancing at the wooden beams making up the vaulted ceiling or the incredible furnishings. We step through a butler's pantry and into a kitchen, if you can even call it that. It's huge. The wooden beams extend in here, and the ceiling is just as high. The cabinets look crafted out of old vintage wood, and the island is bigger than my bed at home.

Jon walks over to a beautiful woman with bronzed-colored skin and eyes that match. He kisses her on top of the head, then gives her belly a little pat. "Paige, this is my wife, Catrine."

"Oh my! Look how cute he is," she says. When she gets to her feet, a pronounced baby bump comes into view. "I'm having a boy, too. What's his name?"

"Finn," I say as she picks up his chubby little foot, giving him a little tickle. "He's five months old."

She smiles up at me. "Jon and I can't agree on names to save our lives. I think we'll be calling this little guy Chewie forever," she says, making me laugh a little. "Jon's a *Star Wars* fan."

"When are you due?" I ask.

"Eight weeks left to go," she says, "so I'm glad you're here. I can't keep up with the place anymore. And once little Chewie comes, I'll be staying at home with him."

"The job is out here?" I ask, my heart sinking.

Smiling, she says, "Yeah, basically, I run the house day-to-day. Since the maid quit last week, I've been doing some light cleaning, too, but it's getting hard. Besides that, I just answer the phone, get the mail and the groceries, make sure the stable hands are tending to the horses, pay them every week, and help plan some events for Slade's company. I'm going to be staying on as long as I can to help you learn the routine. And maybe you can help me not be scared to death of pushing this kid out."

She starts to laugh, and Jon gives her a little hug. I can't believe I ever thought Jon was a goon. He's hardly scary, and the two of them together are disgustingly happy. And they're both being so nice to me. Jon knows I was at the party with Slade's dad, but clearly, Slade hasn't told them everything. I doubt they'd want me around then.

"Why don't you show Paige around?" Jon says.

Adjusting Finn on my hip, I say, "I'm sorry, but there's no way I can take this job."

Catrine looks at Jon in confusion. I guess she thought this was a done deal. She asks, "Why?"

"I don't have a car. And no public transportation comes out this far, so . . ."

"Jon, did you tell her *anything*?" Catrine asks, shaking her head. "Slade has a room ready for you and Finn."

"A room?" I ask. "He expects me to live here? With him?"

I feel my heart doing these weird somersaults in my chest. Is this some Cinderella story to him? Where the rich man swoops in and saves the poor girl? Is that what I am? I guess, in Slade's eyes, it would be more like *Pretty Woman*, where the rich guy saves the prostitute. Well, I've got news for him.

She lightly strokes my arm. "He's hardly here. Just come see the room."

"Do you live here?" I ask.

"No," she says.

"Does the hired help normally live here? Or am I the first?"

Finn starts to cry and fuss. God, sometimes I wish I was a baby and could just scream whenever I feel like it. Jon wraps his arm around his wife. "You'd be the first."

Now I get Slade's game. He thinks I'm moving in here to be his full-time plaything. Well, no one owns me. Adjusting the diaper bag on my shoulder, I say, "I'd like to go home, please."

"Sorry I'm late. Is there a problem?" I hear Slade's commanding voice and turn, finding him lingering in the doorway. He's dressed in a white T-shirt and jeans, completely opposite from the suit he wore at the party. It's kind of hard to decide which way he looks better, not that I'm thinking about that.

"Let's give them a moment," Jon says, leading Catrine toward the door.

She turns back to me. "Would you like me to take the baby? We could show him the horses."

I glare right into Slade's blue eyes. "Thank you, but I won't be staying."

They walk out without further interruption of our staring contest. Slade's blue eyes spark, clearly enjoying our little game. Finn squirms in my arms, his back arching, before releasing the most explosive sounding poop you've ever heard, forcing me to lose. Slade slips his hand to his mouth, trying to cover up a smile, but it's too big to contain.

"The joys of motherhood," he says, chuckling a little.

"Yeah, one of many," I say, looking around for a place to change him.

"Come," Slade says, motioning with his hand. Either I follow him or risk poop leaking from the diaper. It's not a hard choice.

I follow Slade down a little hallway, and he opens a door, stepping aside for me to enter. But I freeze at the threshold. This, apparently, is "my" room. A huge bed with a fluffy white comforter dominates the room. There's a crib in the corner, a rocker, and a changing table complete with diapers, ointments, and wipes.

Slade sticks his hands in the pocket of his jeans. "Hope it's alright. I could put Finn in his own room, but you two were sharing a room at your place, so I just figured that would be best. Thought you both would be more comfortable together."

"That's very thoughtful," I say, taking a step inside. Maybe I misjudged him and the situation. He obviously isn't thinking about fucking me or making me his personal plaything if he put Finn and me together in a room.

Placing Finn down on the changing table, I start to clean him up. I've never done this on a changing table before outside of public bathrooms. At home, I usually just put a pad down on the floor. And as if I wasn't self-conscious enough, Slade is leaning against the doorframe, watching my every move.

I give Finn's tummy a little jiggle, loving his cute little innie belly button.

"I really do need someone here to take over for Catrine. There are no ulterior motives. I'm not paying to sleep with you. In fact, if you work for me, then you're retired from all that shit," Slade says.

He really likes to boss people around, but that's one order I can live with. I snap Finn's onesie, holding up the dirty diaper. "I've got enough other shit to handle." Slade smiles a little, and I realize I did that on purpose. Made him smile. I like his smile a little too much.

"What about your father?" I ask, seeing a vein bulge in his neck. "I mean, does he come here? I just want to be prepared if I'm going to run into him."

"No. I can count on one hand how many times he's been out here. We aren't particularly close." I nod, placing Finn on my hip. "Before we go any further," he asks, "do you still want to leave?"

"There's something you should know first," I say.

One of his eyebrows rises as if he thinks he already knows everything he needs to know about me. What could be worse than what he already thinks? "What's that?"

"I don't do windows," I say, trying not to smile.

He chuckles, giving Finn's belly a little tickle. "Your mommy has a smart mouth."

Our eyes meet for just a fraction of a second before I break the connection. "What else should I know?"

"First," he says, walking me to a panel on the wall, "the alarm. It's imperative you keep the alarm on, especially at night." He gives me the code, making me arm and disarm it several times to make sure

I have the hang of it. It's funny. He lives on this massive estate, where I'm sure no one will bother him, but he has a state-of-the-art alarm system. In contrast, no one in the run-down slum where I lived, where you actually might need the police, has an alarm. No one could afford it.

Slade leads me around the house, giving me a little tour. Five bedrooms, four bathrooms, an office, a library, a workout room. More space than one man could possibly need, and I haven't even seen the outside of the property.

Slade's bedroom is all the way on the opposite side of the house. It would be entirely possible for him to be here and us not even see each other. I'm sure that's the way he'll want it. He's used to living alone, and he's definitely not used to having a baby around.

He opens another door, this one leading into a garage. His black Land Rover is parked inside next to a silver Mercedes sedan. That's all I can tell you. I know nothing about cars, especially when they start naming them with numbers and letters. E class, S class, 5 series. X this, G that. Who can keep up? I miss cars that had actual names, like the Volkswagen Beetle. Everyone knows what that is.

He points at the keys for the Mercedes hanging on the wall. "For you to use for errands, groceries, that sort of thing."

"You want me to drive that?" I ask, unable to remember the last time I actually drove a car and having never driven anything that wasn't partially held together by duct tape.

"Why not? We'll install the car seat for Finn. Part of your job is to shop and—"

"I know," I say. His lips purse in a tight line, clearly not used to being interrupted when he speaks. "It's just so *nice*. I'll have to park a mile away to make sure no one dings it with a shopping cart or anything."

His forehead wrinkles up. "You'll do no such thing. You'll park as close as you can since you'll have Finn with you." He closes the garage door. "Is this all too much for you with Finn?" he asks. "Once Catrine leaves, it will just be you here. Can you keep up with this with a baby around?"

"Of course," I say. "It's nothing more than any stay-at-home mom does." As soon as those words are out of my mouth, I regret them.

"We aren't playing house," he barks. "This is a job. I would assume someone with your background would know that."

"Of course," I say, steadying myself. "That came out wrong. I just meant I can handle it. And you won't even know Finn and I are here."

A walk of the outside property completes the tour—a pond and pool but no other houses in sight. "Most of the stable hands have left already. Catrine will introduce you to them another day."

The gorgeous stable is painted a crisp white with dark green trim. Why anyone would paint a stable white is beyond me since it's not a very practical color for hay and horses. I have a baby, so we think about these things. As far as I'm concerned, everything should be distressed and the color of dirt.

And I'm not going to make the mistake of calling this place a barn. It's a stable. A barn can hold anything—equipment, animals, grain—but a stable is the home of horses. And this one looks like it could house at least twenty. These horses live under better conditions than most people I know. "It's beautiful," I say as both Finn's and my noses wrinkle up.

Slade chuckles slightly. "Still smells like horse shit, though."

Smiling, we walk through, and I quietly read the names on each stall door to Finn. *Scotch, Bourbon, Gin, Brandy.*

"You named all your horses after alcohol?" I ask. Even though it's a few weeks until my twenty-first birthday, you don't grow up in this state without knowing your Tennessee whiskeys. No matter how poor or how rich you are, we all have that knowledge in common.

Slade walks over to one stall, where a beautiful stallion sticks his head over the gate. "And this is Whiskey," Slade says.

I watch Slade's hand comb through the horse's dark mane. He's beautiful—pure muscle, but he's got the world's longest eyelashes. This horse is exactly what a real-life hot man would look like. They draw you in with their dark hair and muscles, their eyes making them look charming and sweet. Then they stomp you to death.

Slade and his horse are both handsome devils, not that I'm admiring anything other than the horse. Slade's eyes land on mine, catching me staring, but they don't scan my body. He doesn't look anywhere but at my eyes, and I pray he can't see my soul or read my mind. My secrets have to stay hidden. Finn squirms and fusses slightly, breaking the connection.

"So," Slade says, clearing his throat. "Salary."

We start walking back toward the house, discussing my salary, which is to say, he tells me what it is. I was so shocked I couldn't speak, anyway. And to have room and board on top of it is surreal. It's all happening so fast.

"I have some paperwork for you to fill out. I'm adding you to my company employees. That way, you can get medical and dental insurance," Slade says.

I can't help it when my eyes start to well up. Quickly, I wipe them. Taking care of a baby costs a lot of money, and one big chunk of that change is doctor's appointments. Never in a million years did I expect insurance. I plant a little kiss on Finn's bald head. I'd promised him a better life, and it's happening.

Most of my childhood memories aren't good. I wonder what that means, what your first memories say about you. How would I be different if my memories were of laughter, love, and happiness? I don't have those, but Finn will.

Of course, I'm aware this could just be some sort of setup. It is too good to be true, but I have to risk it for Finn. I'll just keep my guard up.

Walking behind him, I notice how tall and broad Slade is. It's been a long time since I've noticed a man like this. When you're worried about where your next meal will come from, that tends to cut down on your man ogling time.

"What is it you do, exactly?" I ask.

"Real estate development, mostly," he says, pausing for a second. "And breed a few of the horses."

So he basically buys land, develops it into things he thinks we need, then either sells it or sits back and rakes in the profits. "But you stay in the city during the week?"

He nods. "I'm here most weekends. But I don't expect you to wait on me or cook for me. Since you'll be living here, there aren't set hours. I just expect shit to get done. When it's done, then your time is yours. Use the pool, ride if you want, whatever. But know that if I need something, then I expect you to drop what you're doing and be there."

"I understand," I say, catching his eyes again. "I was wondering. Why are you doing this?"

"You don't trust people, do you?" he asks, holding my gaze.

"It's been my experience that it's best not to."

"Mine, too," he says quietly, his eyes roaming my face.

"So why?" I push. "I'm no one to you. Why go to all this trouble to help me?"

"Did you ever consider I'm not doing it for you?"

Finn? I guess it would be hard for anyone to see a baby grow up the way we were living. Still, most people would just hand you a dollar and move on.

"The reason isn't important," he says.

I guess he's right, but I still want to know. Something tells me now is not the time to push the issue, so it's probably best to let it go. What does it matter anyway? "When do I start?"

"Now," he says.

"Now?" I say, unable to hide the shock in my voice. "But my stuff. I need to pack up my things and forward my mail. Tell my neighbors. That kind of thing."

"Jon will arrange to get your things brought over. I don't want you going back there," Slade says.

"I need to let them know where I am," I say.

"The hooker on the fourth floor keeps track of your movements?"

This man can't seem to decide if he wants to be a nice guy or a complete dickhead. But he does have a point. It's not like I have concerned neighbors or even friends. Poverty and single motherhood take away time from friends, as well as admiring the opposite sex. "I'll just call who I need to," I say. The rent is month to month, so I don't have to worry about breaking a lease or anything. People come and go all the time. But I will need to call the few people I do work for, like the day care, and let them know I've found other employment. It's always best to leave on good terms in case you need to come crawling back. And I've got no idea how this thing with Slade is going to go.

"Anything else?" he asks. "Questions? Catrine will be back tomorrow to help with the transition."

I want to look confident, so I smile brightly. "Thank you," I say. "The room. The stuff for Finn. That was really very sweet."

He simply nods and walks straight back inside the house.

I have to check the garage to see if Slade's even still here. This is going to take some getting used to.

The quiet.

I was right. The nighttime sounds different for the rich.

Finn is down for the night. At least, I hope so. He's usually a good sleeper, but being in a new place might mess him up. My stuff has already arrived. There wasn't much—a few boxes of clothes and shoes, toiletries, books, and toys. I had Jon donate the furniture and what few kitchen items I had. It was all pretty much garbage, anyway. I wasn't going to pay to have it stored somewhere. Tiptoeing into the kitchen, I realize I'm starving. I haven't eaten. It just feels weird to go in Slade's refrigerator and eat something that I didn't buy myself.

Luckily, I had baby food in the diaper bag for Finn to eat for dinner and enough formula. But I definitely have to hit the grocery up tomorrow. Placing the monitor down on the island, I rest my hand on my stomach when it lets out a loud growl. I'm being silly because he told me to make myself at home.

I wonder if that includes the use of his computer. My phone is so basic it doesn't even have internet. With my new salary, I just might be able to take a night class here and there. I need to check to see what's being offered next semester and the cost, class time, etc. I'll ask Catrine tomorrow about internet and computer use. If I'm going to ask for that, I should at least be able to eat a piece of fruit or something. I open the refrigerator. There's actually not much there—a few eggs, juice, yogurt.

I hear footsteps coming down the hallway. Even if we weren't the only adults in the house, I know the sound of the weight of his body already.

"Anything good in there?" he asks.

I hold the door open a little wider. "Not from the looks of it."

"Damn," he says, leaning in over my shoulder to take a look. His body towers over mine, so close I can smell the faint scent of his shampoo. "You should know this about me. I like my food. Meat and potatoes. None of this salad and yogurt shit."

I can't help it and start laughing. "Good thing I'm not in charge of cooking for you. I'd make you eat your vegetables."

"I'd like to see you try," he says as if daring me.

"I happen to do a very good airplane impersonation. It works wonders in the infancy crowd," I say, trying to make sure my voice doesn't sound flirty. Flirting with the boss isn't part of the job. It doesn't matter how handsome he is.

"Christ, you're going to fill my fridge with green shit, aren't you?"

"Yep, and you're going to love it."

Shaking his head, he opens the freezer portion. I swear I see his lip pout at the lack of beef inside. It reminds me of Finn when I don't get his bottle made fast enough. Guess all men are the same.

I grab the carton of eggs. "I was just about to make myself some eggs. Want some?"

"I meant what I said. I don't expect you to wait on me."

"I'm making them anyway," I say. "It's no extra work."

"Fried or scrambled," he says, trying to hide his smile. "None of that hard-boiled stuff."

"Scrambled," I say.

"In butter?"

"Not likely."

He groans. "Tell me there's bacon."

"Didn't see any," I say, getting started on the eggs. "I'll run to the store tomorrow. Why don't you make me a list?"

He starts moving things around in the refrigerator in a desperate hunt for bacon. "I'm heading back to the city tomorrow, so just get what you need. Catrine has the credit card for the house and will show you how to do the checks and stuff."

I give him a little nod, watching him kneel to look in the bottom of the freezer. It looks like he's literally praying for pork. While he's distracted, I grab some green onions, quickly cutting them up and tossing them in the eggs. "Where are the plates?" I ask.

He gets up, reaching into a cabinet for two plates and handing them to me. "Drink?" he asks, taking down two glasses, as well.

"Just water," I say.

He pours the drinks, placing them down on the island, then reaches for forks and rips off a couple of paper towels from the roll by the sink. "Tell me you aren't one of those people who uses paper towels as napkins?" I tease.

He glances down at his place settings. "They're the same things."

"No vegetables, and now this?" I say, scooping the eggs onto the plates.

He rolls his eyes at me, and I place the eggs down in front of him. Immediately, he starts to move the eggs around on his plate like a kid trying to avoid eating his food. "What's this green shit in my eggs?"

I burst out laughing. "Didn't you like *Green Eggs and Ham* by Dr. Seuss?"

"Maybe if I had the ham."

"Just try it."

"You've been in the house less than a day, and look what's happened already." He lifts the fork, smelling it, then closes his eyes and takes a slow bite.

"Yes, it's all part of my clandestine plan to make you eat green." He looks over at me, surprise in his blue eyes. "It's good, right?"

Smiling, he shoves a huge bite in. "Yeah, not bad."

I take a little bite, watching in amazement at how fast this man can eat. "I was wondering if there's a computer I can use?" I ask quietly.

Without looking up, he says, "The Wi-Fi password is . . ."

"No, I need a computer. I don't have one, and my phone only calls and texts." He looks up, and for once, he's speechless. He has no idea what it means to be poor, and I had it better than most—a roof over my head, no matter the chipped paint. "I only want to use it for school. But if it's a problem, I can just go to the library and use one there."

"Paige," he says softly. It's the first time he's used my name today, and it comes out with a tenderness I wasn't expecting. His head shakes. "Catrine will show you the computer. You're welcome to use it. You're in school?"

"Well, no, not right now. I had to take a break with Finn and everything, but I want to go back. I'm about halfway to getting my bachelor's."

"What did you study?"

"Nursing." I take a deep breath, revving up for the monologue that's coming. "Originally, I wanted to go to med school, but it takes a long time, so I was thinking I'd get my nursing degree, then maybe go back in a few years and . . . I was actually hoping to maybe take a night class next semester if that's alright. I could leave Finn with a sitter. Not here, of course. Maybe just take one class. That's why I wanted the computer, to see what's being offered. I promise it wouldn't interfere with my work here. It's probably stupid to bring this up on my first day. It's just with the salary you'll be paying me, I can finally afford to take some classes again." I stop to take a breath, quickly opening my mouth to continue my argument, but he simply holds up his hand.

"You just started working here, and this is what you're thinking about?" he asks.

Of course, he's right. I should be thinking about this job, not bettering myself to leave this job. Getting to my feet, I start to stress clean. You know, when you clean to avoid? "Forget I said anything. I should've waited."

The baby monitor lights up with a deafening scream. Without looking back, I leave my plate in the sink and head toward my room. "New place. He's probably a little confused about where he is. I'll clean up first thing in the morning."

I don't give him time to respond before rushing to my room.

CHAPTER THREE

SLADE

This has to be one of the strangest nights I've ever had with a woman. She gets me to eat green shit, berates my choice of napkin, then rushes off to a screaming baby. What the hell am I doing?

I've been asking myself that same question ever since I saw her walk in on my father's arm. One look at her and no way in hell was that happening. I've watched my father's parade of women most of my life, and I've mostly kept my opinions to myself. What a man does in his bedroom is his business. If the woman is willing, and the man is willing, then I don't give a fuck, but one glimpse of Paige changed all that.

She's beautiful, all my father's women are, but none of them has ever made my head turn, my heart skip a beat, and my dick stand up and take notice. Even as I approached her that night, I had no idea what I was doing other than saving her from my father. I could've left it at that, but instead, I went to her shithole of an apartment. Then the job offer and shopping for Finn.

I don't do all that for a woman because she's hot as fuck. She is, but that's beside the point. I don't do serious relationships. And I've certainly never done anything like this before.

Love at its best is fleeting; at its worst, it's a weapon.

Even if I wanted to take that bullet, Paige is almost ten years younger than me, was with my father, and appears as gun-shy about love as I am. I've never done the whole love thing. Luckily, the woman usually waits for the man to be the first to make such a declaration. For most women, there's a time limit on when a guy should say it. If you're approaching a year and haven't uttered that word, the writing's on the wall, which is fine by me. If you're unlucky, and the woman happens to say it first, well, she's signed her own pink slip.

I've lived my life by that. No falling in love. No big commitments like living together. Again, what the hell am I doing with this young single mother in my house?

All I know is that I want to protect her and Finn. The why isn't important. I'm making up everything else as I go along.

I've always been the type who follows my gut, and I've never been afraid to take a risk. For the most part, it's worked for me. You don't get where I am in business at the age of thirty by playing it safe. But there's risk, and there's downright stupidity. And nothing can make a man more stupid than a woman.

Any reasonable person would think I'm insane for bringing Paige and Finn into my life and my house. Lucky for them, I live by my gut. Following instinct versus reason has landed me in hot water before, but those times are rare. If my mind and my gut disagree on the next course of action, I usually go with my gut. This is definitely one of those times.

"Finn." I hear her voice and look down. She's left the baby monitor in the kitchen. Reaching down to turn it off, I graze the button with my finger, but hearing her sweet voice stops me. "It's okay. Shh!"

I know I shouldn't listen. I should turn the damn thing off or, better yet, take it to her, but I don't.

"What are we doing here, buddy?" she says quietly, the baby settling at her voice. "I promise I won't mess this up. What was I thinking, asking about school so soon? No more of that. I need to be happy with what I've got. You, this job. That's enough. That has to be enough. No more selfish dreams. I'll save every penny. You won't ever have to give up on your dreams or watch them die."

I listen to her talk him to sleep, promising him over and over that she won't mess this up, promising him a good life, a home. It's a mantra. One I'm sure she's said before. It's the most selfless declaration of love I've ever heard.

Most "I love you's" come with conditions. Forget what wedding vows say. The phrase "I love you" is always followed by an unspoken "if." I love you if you stay beautiful. I love you if you provide for me. I love you if you don't screw up. You'll love me if I'm perfect. You'll love me if I do what you say and want. The list is endless.

It's a lie, a farce, a fucking fairy tale. I don't plan on ever getting married, but if I did, my future wife would have to vow to love me when I'm an asshole. Don't think there's a woman alive ready to take on that life sentence, and I don't blame her. Forever and women should not be thought of in the same sentence, but somehow, against all common sense, I have a young woman living in my house—a young single mother, to boot.

As soon as I saw her walk in on my father's arm, something shifted inside me. It's a wonder it wasn't felt on the Richter scale. I've seen my father use women before—countless times. I never stepped in, never interfered. Paige is the first.

The decision was that quick. It almost wasn't a decision at all. In business and in my personal life, that's usually how I know I've done the right thing. If I can go to sleep at night without giving something another thought, it's almost a guarantee I've done the right thing. The night I met Paige, I slept better than I have in years.

"We will be happy," she says, and I know I'll do anything in my power to make that possible. "Content."

I hate that word, *content*. I know it's about being happy with what you have and where you are, but if everyone lived that way, then nothing new would ever be discovered. What happened to drive and ambition? It's obvious Paige has it, already looking forward to school and classes. That's not someone who's "*content*." To be content is to accept your lot in life. I didn't drag her out of that shithole of an apartment for her to be content.

I dragged her out of there so that *I* could be content, find peace, and maybe absolution. But so far, it's not working.

Something happens to a man when he turns thirty. You go from most of your friends being single to being married or in serious relationships. I'm not saying there aren't any single guys over thirty, but the numbers are dwindling. I'm in danger of extinction.

Even I now have a woman and baby living in my house. How the hell did that happen?

I didn't stick around to try to figure it out and headed back to Nashville before the sun was even up. Work is always a good excuse.

No, babe, I can't tonight—working.

Can't stay the night—early meeting.

Those verses are in any single guy's bible.

My phone rings, and I hit the button for the Bluetooth feature, hearing the biggest traitor of all's voice. Jon is more than my employee. He's my best friend and has been for as long as I can remember. We vowed to live the bachelor life, but that all went out the window the day he met Catrine. It's actually my fault since I'm the one who introduced them. Twenty-one and he was a goner. It took him a little longer to lock it down, but I knew she was it for him before he even did.

Why is that?

Why can others see things so clearly about us before we can?

"Want to tell me what the hell all that was about yesterday?" Jon asks.

I know he's talking about Paige and Finn, but one of the benefits of guy friends as opposed to relationships with women is that we don't really have to share shit. It's not part of the bro code. Clearly, Catrine has gotten to him. His man card is in danger of being revoked.

"You mean the golf course project?"

"I didn't say a word when you asked me to get her away from your father," Jon says. "Even though you've never cared about your dad's extracurricular activities before."

He's wrong. I've cared. I know exactly why my dad is the way he is. Jon keeps talking, but the open road has all my attention. There are miles of road stretched out before me and miles I've traveled, but no matter the distance, some journeys never seem to end.

"Catrine really likes Paige," Jon says.

I didn't share Paige's "profession" with Jon. He knows my dad likes younger women, so I didn't feel the need to share that information with him. I'm glad I didn't because I don't want anyone to have any preconceived notions about Paige. Although, I'm sure he has his suspicions.

"Good."

"She's an attractive woman," Jon says, stating the obvious. "The baby's cute, too."

"Your point?" I ask.

"Wondering if you would be taking such an interest in this woman if she was ugly?"

"I hired you, didn't I?" He bursts out laughing. "She needed a job, so I gave her one," I say. "That's it."

"Okay," he says. "But I also know how you are once you decide you want something. Once you set your sights on something, you're unstoppable."

"Jon . . ."

"The Rose Bay Hotel," he says, reminding me of a development we did together.

"That turned a profit."

"Four years"—he laughs—"no one wanted that shithole, but you made up your mind, and there was no changing it. Took four years to complete."

"One time."

"How about the Mockingbird Club, the Cotton Mill Mall, the . . ."

"So I like a challenge," I say. "That has nothing to do with this situation."

"I'd say a single mother is a big challenge," Jon says.

"You forget, all your examples were in business, not in my personal life."

"Do I need to start naming women?" Jon asks. "Because that list is pretty long. It's the same thing. When you decide you want a woman, you go after her. The only difference is, you don't keep her around as long as you would a strip mall."

I chuckle, and I know he's right. "I hired Paige to do a job. There's no deciding anything."

"Not yet," he says. "Just remember, a baby ups the ante."

"I know," I whisper.

CHAPTER FOUR

PAIGE
AGE 5

"Paigey Poo, be a good girl. Go outside and play in the rain," Momma says. "I have to work."

She smells funny.

She sounds funny.

She even looks funny.

I smile.

Momma likes it when I smile.

She opens up the front door to our apartment, and a man walks in.

He smells worse.

He looks scary.

I grab Momma's leg, but she kicks it. "Outside."

The screen door closes behind me, and I hear Momma laugh, and I smile.

Momma's happy.

It's good when Momma's happy.

Tip, tap, tip, tap —*my toes splash in the puddle outside our door. The mud squashes under my toes, and a raindrop falls through the hole in my T-shirt, landing in my belly button.

I like the rain. No other kids are outside. People run, trying to avoid the rain, but I'm lucky. My momma lets me play in it. I have the best Momma.

My wet hair sticks to my face, and I push it back, turning my head up to the sky and opening my mouth to let the rain fall in. I lost my front teeth. Both of them. Makes it easier to catch the raindrops.

They slide down my tongue. I like the taste of rain. It's better than the water from the sink in our kitchen that doesn't even work half the time.

I wish it rained more. I'd never be thirsty.

Holding my arms out wide, I spin around and around, holding my mouth open, drinking the rain. Around and around.

Dizzy in my head, I fall to my bottom, laughing. More people should play in the rain.

"You look like a pig rolling in slop," a boy yells at me.

I look up, seeing him smoking, his front door wide open. Our apartments are across from each other. Momma says he's trouble with a capital "T." I don't know what that means. But I don't like being called a pig, so I get up and walk over to the window of our place.

I shiver, and tiny bumps pop up on my skin. The old lady who used to live next door called them goose bumps. I've never seen a goose, but I don't think they have bumps. She was a funny lady.

Raindrops slide down the window. The water kind of looks like that finger painting I made one time with Momma. Taking my finger, I chase the drops down the window, hoping the tiny one will win the race to the bottom.

My tummy wiggles in my stomach, making a loud noise. I lift my shirt, looking down at my skin, waiting to see it do that again.

One, two, three . . .

I count the bones on my body. I can count all the way to one hundred, but I don't have that many bones. My stomach starts moving, vibrating. It hurts.

I let my shirt down. It hangs wet and feels too heavy now. Pulling open the screen door, I walk inside, pushing my hair out of my face. It's cold.

"Momma," I cry, making my way to her bedroom door.

With a pool of water dripping at my feet, I push open the door. Momma's sitting on the scary man's lap with her shirt open. He's holding her as she bounces up and down.

No jumping on the bed. That's the rule.

"Momma, I'm hungry," I say.

"Jesus, Paige!" she screams. "I told you to play outside!"

The man lifts her off his lap. "No, don't go," Momma says.

"Feed your kid," he says, throwing some money down on top of a stack of bills already on the nightstand.

Smiling, she leans over and kisses him. "Be right back."

Then she turns to me, pointing out the door. "I'm hungry," I say again.

She picks me up, holding me away from her body, and marches into the other room. "I'm working," she says, her teeth showing. She tosses me down on the sofa, my wet clothes making a squishy sound. Then she picks up the TV remote, flicks it on, and goes back to work.

I turn my head to the TV. The man on the show is making biscuits.

CHAPTER FIVE

PAIGE

It's the first day of my new job, so I'm up early, dressed, and ready to go. Finn is up, dressed, and fed, so it's time to get started. Despite what I told Slade yesterday, this isn't going to be easy with a baby. Unlike my tiny apartment, this house is huge. I can't see or hear Finn from one side of the house to the other without the monitor. Plus, I'm not used to him being that far away from me. It's not in my nature to leave him to play in his crib while I go do something in another room. I worry too much about him and get nothing done anyway, so it's best to keep him close.

Perhaps I need to invest in one of those baby carriers I can attach to myself. Or maybe a playpen would be better. I don't want to clutter Slade's house up with baby stuff, but I could take it down and move it to my room, out of the way, when I'm not using it. I hate to start spending money already, but I'm going to need something. Maybe a consignment store would have one.

With Finn on my hip, I head into the kitchen to clean up from last night's midnight snack, not wanting anyone to wake up to my mess. Plus, I want to be ready to go and prove I'm up to the job. Unfortunately, the kitchen is already cleaned, and Catrine is already here working on the island. It's not even seven in the morning. There goes my good impression.

She flashes me a smile. "Morning."

"I'm sorry if I'm late," I say.

"You're fine," she says. "Slade needed to go back to the city. He left early."

"Oh," I say, looking down at Finn, knowing we'll be all alone tonight. We've been alone in that crappy apartment almost every night of his life, so why does this feel so strange?

"Want to go over the schedule?" she asks, and I nod. "This is just how I do things. You'll find what works for you. With you staying here, you'll have more flexibility than I do."

We spend the next couple of hours going over stuff, everything from the computer, which is in Slade's office, to where the cleaning supplies are stored and how to work the sprinkler system. We walk the property, and I meet a few men who work with the horses. Her phone constantly dings with texts. The first few times, she smiles and answers. The next series of times, she ignores them. When they start to come faster, she picks up her phone and sticks her tongue out at it.

"He usually doesn't blow up my phone like this," she says, taking a seat at the kitchen island, clearly uncomfortable in her state of pregnancy. "He's a good boss. Low key."

"Those are all from Slade?" I ask, fixing a bottle for Finn.

She nods, typing out a message. "Well, one was from Jon checking on me."

"Anything I can help with?" I ask.

She shakes her head. "I'd say no since every message is about you."

"Me?"

She flips her phone around, showing me the messages, all asking if she told me this or that. Reminding her to show me how to use everything from the garage door opener to the coffee pot.

"He must think I'm an idiot," I mumble.

"More likely, he just can't stop thinking about you," she says, raising an eyebrow.

"Oh no," I say, shaking my head vehemently. "It's not like that. We aren't together. I'm nobody to him. Just an employee, like you."

She smirks at me. "If you say so, but I don't know a man alive who goes shopping for cribs and changing tables for a woman who's *nobody*."

"You didn't do that? I just assumed it was you," I say, taking a seat and giving Finn his bottle.

"Not me," she says, patting her belly. "He didn't even ask for my help."

I think about how perfect the room is and how he covered every detail. What thirty-year-old single man has a clue about diaper rash creams? Why would he bother? Go to all that trouble? No man does that, not even for nookie. No vagina in the world is magical enough to make a man do all that. There's always another woman to move along to, one with less baggage.

"Still, I know he's not interested in me like that," I say.

"Because you're friends with his dad?" she asks.

My armor goes on at record speed. Slade told her? I never asked him not to tell anyone I was "working" that night, but I didn't expect him to blab it all over, either. "You know how we met?"

She shrugs. "Yeah, Jon told me you met at a party. That you are a friend of his father's. Slade hates his father, so I was surprised he'd hire a friend of his dad's." She looks me up and down, smiling. "That is, until I saw you."

Breathing a sigh of relief that she doesn't know everything, I feel my skin warm. "Standing next to you, I look like a servant girl next to some goddess."

"A whale of a goddess." She laughs, patting her baby bump. "What did you do before this?"

"Odd jobs," I say, which is the truth. "I was in college before I had Finn, so I'm hoping to go back and take some classes."

Finn starts babbling, causing milk to bubble up all around his mouth and ooze down into the fat rolls of his neck. Placing the bottle down, I prop him up on my shoulder, and before I can even pat his back, he burps, laughing at the same time.

"Can I hold him?" Catrine asks. Finn hasn't been held by many people. His doctor, nurses, the occasional babysitter, but for the most part, it's just been him and me. Still, he's a friendly baby, and Catrine is the sweetest person I've met in a long time. After wiping Finn down, I hand him over to her, then start to clean up his bottle. "He's five months?" she asks.

"Yeah."

"You lost your pregnancy weight already. I hope I'm that lucky."

"You look great. I'm sure you won't have a problem," I say.

"I'm going to breastfeed. I hear that helps. Did you try breastfeeding him?"

Glancing over my shoulder at her loving on him, I say, "He's always been on formula."

"And he seems to like it," she says, tickling his chunky baby belly.

"His pediatrician says he's almost off the charts for his weight," I say with a proud smile.

"Who's his doctor?" Catrine asks. "We are interviewing pediatricians now."

"He sees . . ."

Her phone dings again, interrupting us. "Good grief," she says with an eye roll.

"What does Slade want this time?" I ask.

"To make sure you know where the grocery store is."

I didn't see the point in both of us going to the grocery store. Despite Slade's lack of confidence in me, I knew I could do that on my own. So I loaded Finn up and did the shopping. And no matter what Slade said, I parked far away. The last thing I needed was to dent the Mercedes. I even splurged on a new playpen for Finn. I couldn't resist. When I saw the baby store right across the street from the grocery store, it seemed like a sign. By the time I got back, it was late in the afternoon, and Jon had returned to pick up Catrine. Despite my first impression of him, Jon seems to be a big old softy, at least when it comes to his wife and unborn son, smiling at her, doting on her. They're very sweet together. I haven't seen much of that in my life. Dysfunctional, yes, but not sweet.

Jon helped me bring the groceries in, but I assured him I could put them away on my own. Accepting help from anyone is hard for me. In my experience, people don't do things for you without expecting something in return. That goes double for the male species of the population. A part of me still wonders what price I'll have to pay Slade Turner for this job and when he'll come to collect.

Catrine gives me a full-on hug before she leaves like you would a friend. It's been a while since I've had friends like that, and it feels good. She says, "Tomorrow, I have my checkup at the doctor, so use it as a cleaning day. I left you a note on the kitchen island. My number's on there in case you need anything."

"Thank you."

"I left a package on the island for you, as well," Jon says, wrapping his arm around his wife, then they head out for the night.

As soon as they're gone, I place a blanket on the floor in the kitchen and put Finn down on his stomach with a few toys. He likes tummy time and can get up on all fours now, doing this little rock back and forth. He doesn't go anywhere, and I'm thankful. I'm not ready for him to crawl yet.

Keeping one eye on Finn, I make quick work of putting everything away. Well, as quick as I can while trying to figure out which cabinet is which. The next order of business is the playpen. Luckily, I don't need any additional tools to put it together. By the time I finish everything, get Finn and myself fed and bathed, I'm exhausted, but in the best way tired can feel.

Tired because I worked hard, not because I worried hard.

Tired because for the first time in months, I feel like I can be tired. I'm allowed.

With Finn fast asleep in his crib, I sink down into the oversized sofa and grab the remote control. I can't remember the last time I watched some mindless television. It takes me a few minutes to figure out the buttons, but I go straight to the Cooking Channel and zone out when I do. The cooking show host demonstrates how to make the perfect steak on the stove, not a grill. This must be kismet since my new boss is a meat and potatoes man, so I happily watch, making mental notes. And I almost die laughing when they make green beans as one of the sides. Of course, they also make potatoes, but I won't tell Slade that.

A noise startles me from my happy place, and I dart up. I can't see a thing out of the windows. It's pitch dark outside without the benefit of streetlights like in the city. I'm sure there is outdoor lighting, but damn if I know which switch it is. This house has more light switches than I've ever seen, and some of them do things other than turn on and off the lights—some control ceiling fans and another the garbage disposal. Yet others seem to have no purpose, or else I haven't figured it out yet.

The noise comes again, and this time, I can tell it's coming from the kitchen. It sounds like a phone ringing faintly, but I know it's not my ring tone. Flicking on the light, I wait and listen. When it rings again, the package Jon left wiggles just slightly. I'd forgotten to open it.

Tearing open the box, I find a brand-new smartphone, tablet, and laptop computer. A small note rests on top.

Paige Hudson, M.D. has a nice ring to it.

It's not signed, but I know who it's from.

Holy crap! Why would he do this? I don't usually find men this confusing, but Slade has me not knowing which way is up.

Looking down at the missed call, I see it's Slade's number. He's the only contact number saved in the phone. I wonder why he was calling. To make sure I got the gift? Does he need something? Should I call him back? Or just text? I have to thank him, and that deserves a phone call. But this is a lot. I can't keep this, right? I mean, buying things for Finn is one thing, but for me? There has to be a catch.

Trapped in my internal debate, I shouldn't be surprised when the phone rings again, but I still jump slightly. My boss needs something. I should answer.

"I'm very grateful for the gifts. Thank you, but there's no way I can accept," I say when I answer.

"Well, hello to you, too," he says with a hint of mischief in his voice.

"I don't want you to think I'm not appreciative. I am. But it's too much."

Ignoring me, he asks, "How was your first full day?"

"It was fine," I say, blowing out a deep breath. "Are you listening to me?"

"Yes, and I'm choosing not to respond."

Two can play that game. "Did you need something?"

"Just checking on you and Finn. Your first night alone in the house. I wanted to make sure everything is okay," he says.

"We are fine."

"Alarm on?" he asks.

"Yes," I say, even though I can't remember doing it.

"You sure?"

I glance toward the panel on the wall. Sure enough, he's right. I forgot to set it. Quickly, I hit mute on my phone so he won't hear me activate it. "Yep."

"Good."

"I can't keep this stuff," I whisper.

"Thought you'd be used to getting gifts from men, given your previous occupation."

A tear rolls down my cheek, and I wipe it away. "Leaving all that behind, remember?"

I hear him exhale into the phone. "I need you to have a reliable phone, not that flip thing you use."

"I'll keep the phone, but I need the other stuff to go back. I can use the computer here."

"If that's what you need," he whispers. "Good night, Paige."

He doesn't wait for me to respond before hanging up. My new boss completely confusing. One minute, he's sweet, and the next minute, he doesn't hesitate to throw my past in my face. I wonder if he'll ever look at me and not see the woman he met on his father's arm.

CHAPTER SIX

PAIGE

I toss and turn all night long. The quiet of the country should settle me, but it doesn't. When you've lived on the edge for so long, it's hard to trust the stillness. Most people relish doing nothing at the end of the day and look forward to the peaceful slumber. I think that's why everyone advocates meditation these days. They enjoy the solitude. It settles them.

For me, it's the opposite. Quiet is waiting for the other shoe to drop. The stillness of the night is waiting to be broken by the sounds of gunshots or the creak of my bedroom door because one of my mom's tricks thinks I'm part of the bargain. Quiet is what you hear right before someone smacks you to the ground, and everything moves in slow motion. There is no safety in the night, no protection in the stillness. At least when it's loud, you expect what's coming and can be ready. It's when you're hit unexpectedly that it hurts the most. That's what the quiet is for me—unexpected. I'd rather hear the asshole's footsteps as he approaches my bedroom door, so I can grab the knife I keep under my pillow.

At least out here, there's a lot of room to pace, so I don't have to worry about waking up Finn, who easily sleeps through the night. Guess the quiet agrees with him.

∼

Exhausted, I begin tackling the list that Catrine left for me, having to stop frequently to play with Finn or give him a bottle. I move his playpen into each new room I clean. It's a bit of a pain taking it up and down, but I'm not about to complain. Catrine texted that she'll be later than she thought, which sucks because there's one room I don't want to clean—Slade's bedroom. That seems much more private than, say, vacuuming the rug.

I wait until Finn goes down for a nap, attach the monitor to the waistband of my jeans, then head to the other side of the house. Rustic double doors lead inside the only bedroom over here. The kind of doors you'd imagine leading to a secret garden, but it's more likely a garden of sin.

My hand lands on a real glass knob like you'd see in an old house. It's cool under my fingertips. I push open the door, and even though it's the middle of the day, the room is dark. I reach for the light switch, and even that doesn't fully illuminate the room. The walls are a deep gray, the wood floors just as dark, and the fact that the curtains are drawn isn't helping matters.

Everything about this room screams that a man lives here. And not just any man but a man with something to hide. Chills run down my spine, and goose bumps cover my skin as I step across the room, anxious to pull the curtains back to fill the space with light and scare back the shadows.

The curtains are heavy and huge, stretching all the way from the floor to the ceiling, which is at least twenty feet high. It actually takes some effort to pull them open, but when I do, the entire room transforms, and the view—nothing but trees and sky—is magnificent. Why would he ever close these curtains? I could stand here for hours just staring, but I don't. There's work to be done.

Catrine told me if his bed is made, he doesn't want the sheets changed. Lucky for me, it's neatly made today. Cleaning someone's house is a little bit like snooping. It's like they give you permission to be nosy as long as it's disguised as dusting. It gives you the excuse to look at pictures, pick up mementos, perhaps see a note lying around or a prescription bottle, but I don't find any of those things. Nothing in here tells me anything about Slade Turner, not even what books he likes to read. Nothing.

Perhaps under the bed? I take my job very seriously, and that would entail sweeping under the bed. But I strike out there, too. Not even a dust bunny with a secret to tell.

"Hello, hello, hello?" Catrine's voice chimes through the house.

"In here," I call out.

She walks in, looking adorable in her maternity jeans and T-shirt. "I'm so sorry I'm late."

"No worries. How are you and Chewie?"

Before she can answer, I hear Finn start to cry through the baby monitor. "Crap, I probably woke him with my yelling," Catrine says. "Sorry. I'll go get him."

"You sure?"

"I need the practice," she says, already heading out the door.

"Please grab his bottle from the fridge!" I yell out, unsure if she heard me.

When she comes back in, she's got Finn cradled in her arms with the bottle in his mouth. "How am I doing?" she asks, doing a little twirl. "You know, I've never fed a baby. How is it that I'm having a baby but never actually fed, changed, or bathed one?"

"You're a natural," I say. "Somehow, you just figure it all out."

"I don't know how you do it all alone," she says. "I'm so scared, and I have Jon."

"It's amazing what you can do when you don't have a choice."

I can see the curiosity in her eyes. She wants to know about Finn's dad. *Who is he? Is he in the picture? Why did he leave?* The questions are like cartoon bubbles over her head. I always did love bursting people's bubbles, so I say, "Only room left to clean is the master bathroom. You want to clean the toilet, or should I?"

Honestly, there is no way I'd let her bend over to scrub the tub, shower, or toilet, but it got her off topic, which is what I wanted. She holds Finn while I do the cleaning, and we just chat. It's nice and distracts me from the fact that I'm cleaning all the places that Slade uses when he's naked. Plus, Catrine is the type of person who, as soon as you meet, you just know that the two of you will be friends. She's honest and funny, and we hit it off. And as with any two women, you put them in a room together, and within an hour, you'll know everything from her menstrual cycle to her celebrity crush. Hers is Dwayne Johnson. Mine is Henry Cavill. And since she's pregnant, her cycle is a non-issue at the moment.

That becomes our pattern over the next few days. I do a lot of work, and she does a lot of directing, which is the way it should be. I need to learn, and she needs to say goodbye to this job. Plus, she's great with Finn, which helps me out a lot. By the time Friday afternoon rolls around, I'm feeling good about everything. The only problem is I can't fall asleep here. Every night it's the same. I watch the Cooking Channel, then I turn off the Cooking Channel. I toss and turn for a couple of hours, then I turn the Cooking Channel back on. I've tried sleeping in different rooms, and I've tried sleeping with the television on as background noise, but nothing works.

I'm not settled. I've been here almost a week, so I should be settled. The job is going well, and Finn is happy. Catrine and I are becoming good friends, and I'm sure that will continue even after she leaves, but I can't relax into my new life. Too many secrets and lies from my past are waiting to sneak up and bite me in the butt, I guess.

Slade hasn't called me again. That's one part of the job I haven't taken over for Catrine. He calls and texts her, but not a peep to me since he called on my new phone. I have to wonder if I insulted him when I didn't accept the computer and tablet. They were gone the next day. I guess Catrine took care of them.

Catrine says he's only calling her because she's working on some event for him. Her last big project before she leaves—the opening of a golf course or something. Still, I wonder if it's more than that.

The last order of business before the weekend is to pay the guys who help with the horses and manage the stables. The main man is an older gentleman who looks like he could've played the part of Robert Redford in *The Horse Whisperer*. And the fact that his name is Tom, just like the character in the movie, only adds to the fun. His helper is his grandson, Clay, who works here in the summer and around his school schedule during the school year. He's about eighteen and does all the grunt work, like cleaning the stables. I think it's just the sweetest thing seeing granddad and grandson working together. Tom oversees a couple of other guys, too, but Catrine says they don't ever come up to the house. She really only sees them on payday or if she takes a stroll.

Catrine hands the envelopes with their checks to Tom, who's latching a stable door. "He's beautiful," I say, admiring the horse's shiny coat. His eyes look almost black, his mane thick and dark.

"You've got good taste," Tom says. "Whiskey is a fine stallion."

"Can I pet him?" I ask. "I've never been around horses." He reaches his hand over the opening, and the horse comes right over. He takes my hand and places it on the horse's neck. "Look, Finn," I say. "Horsey."

Finn doesn't seem too impressed by my bravery, simply sticking his hand in his mouth. "Be a few years before we can get you up on a horse," Tom says, taking Finn's hand. "We had Clay up by the time he was four. Now he's winning ribbons all over the state."

"*Granddad*," Clay mumbles, walking toward his grandfather. He glances over at me, smiling.

Tom throws his arm around him. "I'm just proud of you, kid."

"We should get back," Catrine says. "Have a great weekend."

"You come by anytime you want a ride," Tom says.

We turn, walking back through the stables. "I think somebody has a crush on you," Catrine says.

"Tom's more interested in the horses, I think."

"Not him," she says, laughing. "Clay! The poor boy was almost drooling."

"The only one drooling was Finn. Besides, he's what? A senior in high school?" I ask, not that it matters. I'm not interested.

"Freshman in college," she says. "Besides, aren't you only twenty?"

"Yeah, and with a baby," I say, hiking Finn up on my hip.

"Clay's cute," she presses, bumping my shoulder lightly.

"Again, baby on board."

She laughs. "Okay, so you like 'em older."

I pause in my step for a second. Did Jon tell her about Slade's father? Did Slade? But she simply continues walking and talking. I think she was just making a joke. At least I hope so.

Her phone dings, and she pulls it out. "Speaking of older men. Slade."

Slade's hardly older. He can't be more than thirty. "Everything okay?"

"Yeah, he's not coming in this weekend."

"Oh, did he say why?" I ask.

She shakes her head. In the pit of my stomach, I wonder if it's me.

CHAPTER SEVEN

PAIGE

I've had this whole big house to myself for two days, and it's felt like years. Partly because it's rained on and off the entire weekend, so we couldn't really go outside. I'm nervous enough to drive his Mercedes in beautiful weather, so I wasn't about to go for a joyride in a monsoon, leaving us stuck inside. And while I love Finn, he's not exactly good conversation.

This thing is, I don't do relaxation well. I've been stressed out for so long, I don't know how to just sit and do nothing anymore. I think that's why I can't sleep. I'm used to worrying myself to sleep, and here, there's not a whole lot to worry about. Sure, I can worry about stupid little things, like my hair or if a certain celebrity couple is really breaking up, but nothing compares to my worries before, like how we are eating or how I would pay for Finn's checkup. Those are the worries that exhaust the mind, body, and heart.

Most women my age worry about guys and clothes and careers. My job is set, my clothes could use some work, and the only guy in my life is Finn, who's presently lying on my chest as I veg out to my favorite channel. He had a big day today. He actually crawled a little. I screamed so loud, I probably scared him so much he'll never do it again. Granted, it was just a few inches, but it's one for his baby book. I wrote it down and took a picture of him on my new phone. We had a celebratory dinner of mashed banana, then he conked out.

I wipe my face. Today was a happy day, so I shouldn't be crying. I should be calling my family and telling them, bragging to my friends, sharing this big news with somebody, anybody, but there's no one. I thought to text Catrine but felt silly.

Picking up my phone, I see only one other person in my contact list.

And something tells me he couldn't care less.

After another restless night, Finn and I are up with the sunrise. The rain has stopped. It's a new day. At my old place, we never played outside. We didn't have a park nearby, not that it would've been safe anyway.

It's time to start some new habits. My plan is to go for a walk, see the horses, or maybe even explore the woods every morning before Catrine shows up and the workday begins. We're usually up early, and Finn loves it outside. I haven't done this enough with him.

Grabbing an apple from the refrigerator, we head out to see the horses. I open the back door, and the loudest, most aggravating sound I've ever heard fills the house. Finn starts screaming, and I hold his head to my chest, attempting to protect his little eardrums from exploding. Slade wasn't kidding with this house alarm system. It could wake the dead.

Rushing to the alarm panel on the wall in the other room, I enter the code to disarm the damn thing. The blaring sound stops, and I blow out a deep breath, giving Finn a little kiss on top of his head. Shaking my head, I don't remember arming the system last night, but perhaps the sleep deprivation is getting to me, and I just don't remember doing it.

Settling myself and Finn, I wait for a few minutes to see if the security monitoring company calls. I think I deactivated it quick enough that they won't call, but it's best to stick around and make sure. The last thing I need is for the police to show up.

After a few minutes, I say to Finn, "Let's try this again."

With the apple in my pocket, we head to the stables. The weekend rains have left the ground wet and muddy, soaking my tennis shoes. A slow fog rolls over the land. The morning sun calls it back, seemingly disappearing with each step we take, like a curtain being pulled back. It's quiet, calm. Even the horses aren't making any noise. Whiskey is the first to poke his head out of his stable. His big brown eyes look like they're happy to see me. Only Finn has ever looked at me that way in the morning. "He must smell our apple," I say to Finn.

We step closer. I'm still a little scared, having never been around animals much. And Whiskey's huge. You see horses from a distance or on television, and you have no idea how big a horse really is.

Slowly, I lift my hand, making sure to keep Finn angled away. There's no one else here this morning to guide me, so I'm extra careful. Whiskey simply lowers his head and waits. I bring my hand down to pet him, and he stays completely still as though he can sense my nerves. Even when Finn starts to wiggle and coo, Whiskey doesn't move. It's only when I move back that he lifts his head.

Taking the apple from my pocket, I'm unsure how to feed it to him. I stare down at it for a second, remembering what I used to do for a piece of fruit. Now I'm about to give it to this horse. Reminding myself that was my old life, I simply drop the apple to the ground in Whiskey's stable.

"Not really supposed to do that," a voice says behind me.

Startled, I turn, seeing Clay walking toward us with a saddle on his shoulder. "Sorry, I didn't know."

"I won't tell," he says, grinning. "They're all on strict diets, especially this guy. He's being bred soon." I give him another nod before starting to head out. His eyes stay on me as I walk toward him. When we pass, he says, "Paige, right?"

"And Finn," I say, lifting him up slightly. This guy is *young*. Granted, he's probably only a year or two younger than me, but I've lived a life he's only read about or seen in made-for-TV movies.

He places the saddle down, reaching out and taking Finn's little hand in a real gentlemen's handshake. "Got yourself a little cowboy there."

"Maybe," I say, starting to walk again.

"I'm here most mornings if you want to ride or just give the horses a walk or something."

"I've got Finn," I say. "I can't really . . ."

"I can hold him," he says. "I'm the oldest of ten."

"Ten?" My eyes widen, and I take a little step back toward him. It's nice to talk to someone after a weekend with no adult company. "Finn just crawled for the first time yesterday."

He smiles, approaching me. "He'll be ready for his first riding lesson any day then."

"Probably should get him out of diapers first." I laugh. "Speaking of, I think he might need to be changed."

"I'll walk you back," he says.

"We'll be fine," I say, not wanting to encourage him in any way. He gives me a tight smile and a slight nod. I think he got my message.

"Is it true?" he asks, his voice soft. "What everyone is saying about you and Mr. Turner?"

"What are they saying?" I ask, completely unaware that I'd be the topic of conversation.

He holds his hands up. "I didn't believe it."

Stepping in his direction, I whisper-shout, "*What's* being said, and *who's* saying it?"

"The guys," he says. "I mean, all of a sudden, Mr. Turner brings a pretty young girl with a baby to live in his house. Everyone thinks you are . . ."

"They think we're together?" I ask. "I'm working. Plus, Slade hasn't even been here since I started. If we were a couple, wouldn't he be here?"

He shrugs. "I'm just repeating what the guys are saying. They think maybe Finn is his."

"Oh my God!"

He reaches for my arm. "Not me. I didn't think any of it was true."

"Good, because it's not."

"Shit, I'm sorry," Clay says. "I shouldn't have said anything. Can we just start over?"

"As friends?" I ask pointedly.

"Sure," he says. "It's nice to have someone close to my age out here. I'm planning my class schedule, and these guys are talking retirement."

I'm not entirely sure I can believe that he's just looking for a friend, but I figure it can't hurt anything to be friendly. "Where are you in school?"

Over the next week, Finn and I settle in to a nice little routine. We walk to see Whiskey in the mornings. Most of the time, Clay is there. We talk classes, majors. He has no idea what to major in, still lives at home, and hates his English lit professor. For those few minutes every day, I feel my age. Well, minus the baby on my hip. Then I retreat to the house, my job, and being Mommy to little Finn. I still haven't perfected sleeping in this big house. I still haven't seen my elusive boss again, but we're safe, fed, and I've got a couple of new friends in Clay and Catrine. Life is good.

CHAPTER EIGHT

PAIGE
AGE 10

School is the best. Not only do they have a library full of books that I use to escape my god-awful life, but I get a free lunch. It's a win-win. I'm one of the few kids on free lunch. Most of my classmates bring their lunches. They have fancy lunch boxes with matching Tupperware to keep everything neat and organized. Their containers are labeled, their napkins neatly folded. Some even get little notes from their mom or dad every day. My mom's never even asked me what I ate for lunch, much less packed me a brown bag.

Case in point, today is field trip day. I was the only kid in my grade that didn't go. I didn't even bother asking my mom to sign the permission slip this year. I've been down this road before. Field trip days mean bringing a lunch from home. Not gonna happen.

Year after year, I've been the kid who "forgets" their lunch on field trip day, forcing the other kids to share their gourmet brown bags with me. Well, not this year. This year, I just didn't bother having my permission slip filled out—or I should say, I didn't bother forging my mother's signature. What's the point?

Besides, since all the teachers are on the field trip, I get to spend the whole day in the library. Not a bad deal. I was stuck eating with the grade above me, but I'm used to eating alone anyway.

I often wonder if parents are just stupid. God knows, my mom isn't the brightest. But I'd think the parents of these other kids would be smarter than to pack carrot sticks and fruit in their kids' lunches. Don't they know all that goes in the trash? That works for me, though.

I snuck out of the library with a restroom pass to make a quick trip to the cafeteria after everyone left. Some people would think it's gross to take an orange out of the trash, but the rind is going to get peeled off anyway. And some people probably don't have to worry about what they're going to eat for dinner.

Opening up my book bag, I casually stroll by the trash can. Some idiot actually threw away their peanut butter cracker pack. Carrot sticks, apples, oranges, bananas, and boxes of raisins are all mine for the taking. It's a good day. Most kids hate this kind of "healthy" food, but not me. Did you know you can buy a single banana for less than fifty cents? That's a pretty cheap breakfast.

"What are you doing there?" a voice questions softly.

Clutching my book bag shut, I turn to see one of the seventh-grade teachers. She's young and pretty and new this year, so she probably isn't aware of my free lunch status. I can use that to my benefit.

"What have you got in that bag?"

"Nothing," I say, holding up my bathroom pass. "I was just . . ."

"Open your bag," she says, crossing her arms over her chest.

Slowly, I open the bag, an orange bursting free and rolling on the floor. Her mouth falls open, and her eyes dart to mine. "Are you taking food out of the trash?"

"It's such a waste," I say, my voice sounding smaller than I want it to. "They threw it out."

Her eyes go soft. She must have a good life. A life where compassion and empathy are strengths, not weaknesses. In my neck of the woods, compassion gets you killed.

"What's your name?" she asks.

"Paige."

"Honey, are you . . . ?"

I start to laugh. "Oh, no. You thought this was for me?" I giggle some more. "Goodness, no. It's just, my mom and I drive by this homeless guy every day on our way home from school. You know how they hang out under the bridge by the interstate?"

"Yes," she says. "So sad."

"Well, we see this one guy every day. He has a dog."

"I think I've seen him," she says.

This is too easy. "I just saw all this good, nutritious food going to waste, and I thought, why not take it to him?" I'm lying. I've gotten good at lying. It's better to lie than have Child Protective Services called. All kids in my neighborhood know that. "I'm sorry. I didn't mean to take anything that didn't belong to me. I just thought it shouldn't go to waste."

"This is very sweet of you."

"So I can take it?" I ask with a sweet smile. She nods, holding her finger up over her lips like it's our little secret. Dinner is served.

CHAPTER NINE

PAIGE

One of the best things about this job is I can wear anything I want. I could probably stay in my pajamas all day. So even though I'm doing a little work on the computer today, I'm dressed in a simple white tank top and cutoff jeans. With a baby around, messes are frequent, and they usually end up on me, so simple is best.

Catrine walks into the office. I would never say she was waddling, but let's just say her gait is looking more and more cumbersome. She glances over at Finn asleep in his playpen. "Slade called. There's some problem with Whiskey. I'm going to walk to the stables."

"I'll go," I say. "You should be taking it easy."

"Slade said the same thing," she says. "But I . . ."

Getting to my feet, I say, "I love that horse. I'm going."

"Thanks. I'll watch Finn," she says, sitting down on the sofa.

Ten to one, she's napping right along with Finn when I get back. Throwing on some boots, I head straight for the stables, seeing a group of men all huddled together, seemingly in some deep discussion. They look like they are plotting an international coup, concerned looks on their faces, rigid postures. The stables are usually relaxing, a place to unwind and escape. Whatever is going on here is the complete opposite of that.

Clay turns, seeing me coming, and starts for me, holding his hands up.

"Is Whiskey alright?" I ask, feeling a lump in my throat. I know nothing about horses, but remember some old stories where they shot horses who got sick or injured. I won't let that happen.

"He's fine," Clay says as I march right past him, needing to see for myself.

The sea of men part, and Slade's blue eyes land on me. Correction, they pierce right through me. Clearly, he wasn't expecting me. Well, *tough*.

Ignoring him, I walk over to Whiskey's stable. His ears are flicking back and forth, his front hoof clawing at the dirt. Something has him upset. I start to reach for him when Slade's hand lands on my forearm. "Don't. He may bite."

"You're upsetting him," I say. "All these people."

"You know horses now?" he asks, raising an eyebrow.

"I know this one."

Keeping his eyes on me, he motions with his hand, and everyone starts to scatter. "You, too," I say to Slade.

"Not a chance."

Rolling my eyes, I take a deep breath and reach toward Whiskey. His head whips side to side, his hoof pawing the dirt. I just wait. Waiting is a gift, a gift we don't give each other enough. Waiting to hold the door open for someone. Waiting for the perfect moment to kiss someone for the first time. Oftentimes, we hurry these moments. We hurry through our lives. But today, for Whiskey, I wait.

After a few minutes, he steps toward me, placing his head under my hand, and I give him a nice rub. "Hey, boy."

"Are all men putty in your hands?" Slade asks with a grin.

I laugh a little. "I think my charms only work on Whiskey."

"I don't know about that," he says, his eyes narrowing on Clay, who's watching me.

My heart starts to pound, my knees go weak. "I wouldn't do *anything* to screw up my job here," I say quickly. "Clay is just a friend."

Slade's magnetic blue eyes shift back to me. "Why are you here? I told Catrine there was no need to come out here."

"She was worried, and she's so uncomfortably pregnant, she didn't need to trudge all the way out here in the mud and dirt.

Besides, I love Whiskey. Finn and I come see him every day."

His eyes shift back to Clay. "I didn't know that."

"Nothing to know," I say. "Is Whiskey alright? He's not sick or anything?"

"No." Slade starts to pat him with me, his long fingers slipping under Whiskey's mane. "He should be a happy guy. We're breeding him with a thoroughbred mare today. Instead, he got aggressive."

"Maybe he doesn't like her," I say jokingly.

He doesn't chuckle. Instead, he just looks down at me. "Or maybe he likes it rough."

Unable to tell if he's serious or making a joke, I swallow hard. Turning my face to Whiskey, I say, "What's the problem? I'm sure I can help."

"Whiskey is a prized stallion. Other breeders want foals with him. They pay big money."

"How much?"

"Fifty thousand."

"You're kidding?"

His head shakes. "Breeding fees for some stallions can go as high as two or three hundred thousand."

"I had no idea."

"Told you. You were charging too little," Slade whispers. "You and Whiskey are in the same profession."

He can take me out of the slums and give me a respectable job, but he'll always think of me as a whore. I pull my bottom lip between my teeth, focusing the pain there, then reach for the latch on the stable.

"What are you doing?" Slade asks, grabbing my waist.

I glance down at his hands on me, and he quickly moves them. "Taking him for a walk." I turn my eyes to him. "He'll do what he needs to do. He just needs some time to come to terms with it."

CHAPTER TEN

SLADE

With my arms folded across my chest, I watch Paige. She must've walked Whiskey around the pond three or four times already. He looks more settled, relaxed. She did in twenty minutes what my stable guys haven't been able to do all morning. I can see her lips moving and wonder what on earth she's saying to my horse. He probably knows more about her than I do.

I've been asked a dozen times how much longer by my colleagues, but I simply brush them aside. The truth is, I have no idea. I've left my gigolo horse in the hands of my prostitute maid. Who the hell has any idea what's going to happen?

And I'm not the only one interested. My stable hand, Clay, hasn't stopped watching her, either. She looked downright petrified when I pointed it out, like I'd fire her on the spot. So despite the fact that I've been a total asshole to her since she started, she still wants this job. I can't stay away from my own house forever. I hired her, for God's sake, so why am I avoiding her?

"Clay," I call out.

He walks to me, glancing back and forth between where Paige is walking Whiskey and me. "Yes, sir?"

"You like working here?" I ask without looking at him.

"Yes, sir."

Turning my eyes to him, all I say is, "Good."

Message received.

He stands there for a moment, and I turn my eyes back to Paige and Whiskey rounding the curve of the pond. I don't have to say anything else. The threat is more than implied. I catch Paige's eyes and step toward her. She motions in the direction of the riding ring.

He's ready.

Watching two horses go at it takes about as long as taking a piss. The whole courting, mating ritual is only a little over a minute, so slightly longer than a piss. Too bad that relationships between men and women aren't so straightforward. And Whiskey was a professional. Everyone is busy congratulating each other, which is slightly absurd considering we all just stood around and watched horse porn. Well, everyone but Paige.

As soon as Whiskey mounted the mare, Paige turned back to the house. And if I didn't know better, I'd think I saw her wipe her cheeks a few times. I pull out my phone, texting her.

Stop.

I see her pull out her phone, but she keeps walking. So I try again.

Thanks for your help today. Please wait.

This time she stops, glancing back at me over her shoulder. Even from this distance, I can see her flushed cheeks. As quickly as I can get rid of everyone, I make my way over to where she's waiting, frozen in the field with her back to me. It only takes one look at her to remember the exact reason I'm avoiding her.

I can't see her face, but she still looks beautiful standing there, her brown hair moving with the breeze, mud splashed up on her long legs, those jean shorts hanging low on her hips. Damn!

Why do I have to be an ass man? And why does hers have to be fucking perfect?

When I'm close enough, I say her name, only to hear her whimper a little. "What's wrong?"

She turns to me, her eyes wet with tears. "Will you ever not think of me as a whore?"

I don't mean to, but my step falters. I did this to her. I'm responsible for her tears. Is there anything worse than knowing you've made a woman cry? "I don't think of you that way."

"You take every chance you get to make a jab about me. It's very clear what you think about me. I have no idea why you hired me."

"I told you why I hired you."

She just rolls her eyes. "This was a bad idea," she says. "I should've never come here."

She's right about me taking jabs at her, but she's not right about the reason. It's not that I think that way about her. It's my way of reminding myself that she's off-limits. I found her on my father's arm, for Christ's sake. I have to keep that in the forefront of my mind, or the next place I'll take her will be in my bed. "The last thing I want is to hurt your feelings," I say, my hand reaching for hers but stopping just short. "I was coming over here to thank you."

"It does hurt," she says softly. "People assume girls like me don't have feelings. But the truth is, we probably feel things deeper than other people."

"I'm sorry," I say, and I truly am. I'm trying to save this woman, not hurt her further. "No more comments." She looks up at me from under her wet lashes. I can see all the people who have lied to her right there in that one look.

"I better get back to Finn," she says.

CHAPTER ELEVEN

PAIGE

Some things you can prepare for, and some things you can't. Slade Turner is in the latter category. He's as unpredictable as he is hot. Okay, yes, the man is hot. But he's also cold and cunning, and knows how to cut me down to size in one swipe of his tongue. Bad example, I shouldn't be thinking about his tongue. At least I told him how I feel. I'm not going to stand for being degraded every chance he gets. If he wanted a verbal punching bag, he hired the wrong girl.

Opening the door to the house, I'm also unprepared for what I find. Catrine is on the floor, laid out with Finn next to her. He's eating his foot, and she's struggling to lift her leg. They both are in a fit of laughter. "What's this?" I ask, giggling.

Finn's head immediately pops up, recognizing my voice. "He thinks it's funny when I try to eat my toes, too," Catrine says. "But once I got down here, I couldn't get up."

"Let me help you."

"No," she says. "Watch Finn."

He's laughing the cutest little baby giggle as he slams down one hand, moving forward a little. I move a little closer so he doesn't have that far to go. A string of drool hangs from his bottom lip, leaving a little trail as he crawls to me. It's not fast. For that, I'm grateful. But he makes it all the way to me. Picking him up, I smother him in kisses, not minding the drool.

"I hope Chewie likes me that much," Catrine says, still lying on the floor.

"He'll love you," I say. "You'll be able to eat your toes together."

She laughs. "Can you help me up now?"

"I've got it," Slade says from the doorway behind me. I turn, and he gives me a small smile. "If Jon saw you down there, you know he'd flip his shit."

She rolls her eyes, holding her arms up for him to help her. "Finn and I were playing. He's starting to crawl," she says, getting to her feet. "Show him. It's the cutest thing. He looks like a little bear cub. His stomach almost touches the ground."

Slade glances at me. His blue eyes look different—friendlier. "This I have to see," he says.

He looks sincere, like he really does care. And Catrine was so happy and excited. This is the moment I wanted a few days ago and never had, so I'm going to grab it. I place Finn on the ground, then move over by Slade and kneel. Slade does the same, flashing me a small smile.

"Crawl to Mommy," Catrine says.

With one huge squeal, he's off again. Only this time, he's a little faster. Maybe I shouldn't be encouraging this? "That's it, Finn," I say, giggling and holding my arms out. Only he crawls to Slade instead.

"Hot rod," he says, smiling down at him. But Finn doesn't stop, moving into his lap. Slade looks over at me. "Um . . ."

"It's alright," I say. "You can hold him."

"I'm not sure I can," he says, and I see the panic setting in. "I've never held a baby before."

Catrine and I both burst out laughing, a little twenty-pound baby bringing a two hundred and something pound man to his knees. Slade isn't a man you'd expect to see nervous. He's controlled, guarded. But Finn has knocked that all out in one little crawl. Slade looks like a man who might be used to having people on their knees, perhaps even crawling, but not like this.

Scooting closer to them, I say, "He's not an infant anymore, so it's a little easier, but he does wiggle, so you've got to have a firm hold on him."

He picks Finn up, but under his arms, holding him out away

from his body. My poor little guy is dangling in the air. Finn's face wrinkles up, his lip popping out. Slade moves to hand him to me. "You're doing fine," I say, encouraging him to bring Finn to his chest. His eyes meet mine. "Hold him close."

"That's what he likes?" Slade asks, his voice low and hungry.

My throat suddenly dry, I whisper, "Yes." I stroke Finn's little bald head as he nuzzles into Slade. "You've got it."

"Are you staying the weekend?" Catrine asks Slade.

His eyes don't leave mine when he says, "At least one night."

"Want me to run to the store?" she asks.

Slade gets to his feet, still cradling Finn. "It's alright. If we need to, we'll go ourselves."

Catrine flashes me a look, but I'm not sure what's come over our boss, either. "Since we're all here, should we discuss the party for the opening next week?" Slade asks.

Slade's been involved in developing a new golf course and club just outside of Nashville. The grand opening is set for a week from now. Catrine is the go-between for the party planner and Slade.

"I'd like Paige to take over for you on this one," Slade says, sitting down on the sofa with Finn. "You'll be off soon, so she should learn the ropes."

"I don't know the first thing," I say, surprised by his sudden display of confidence in me. "Slade, I don't want to mess this up."

Catrine tosses her hands up. "The party planner does most of it. Just think about it like when you were a kid and had a birthday party. You need food, dessert, entertainment. Easy."

"But I . . ." Choking back my words, I reach for Finn, but Slade holds up his hand, motioning that the baby is now comfortably resting on his chest. No longer able to fight back the barrage of emotions in me, I push on my eyes, my hand running through my hair.

Slade sits up just slightly. "Catrine, give us a minute."

She looks at me first, and I give her a little nod that I'm fine before she disappears into another room. "If this is too much, then I'll find someone else to coordinate," Slade says.

"No, no, I'll do it," I say, not wanting to do anything to put my job at risk. Sitting down beside him, I stroke Finn's little foot. Slade just waits, watching me. He's my boss. He deserves an explanation and to be reassured I can handle it. Softly, I whisper, "I've never had a party before, so I'm not sure what I'm doing. But I can figure it out."

"Never?" he asks. I shake my head. "A cake, balloons, presents?" Another head shake. "Not one ever?"

Looking down, I'm not sure why I'm ashamed of that, but I am. How pitiful and pathetic I must seem to him. But that's the truth. Most of the time, no one even remembered. My birthday could come and go, and no one would even wish me a "Happy Birthday," much less get me a card, cake, or a gift.

"Well, you'll need to learn because I see a lot of race car parties in this little guy's future," Slade says, pushing out a smile.

I look up at him. Finn in his arms, playing with the stubble on his face. I've never seen Finn in a man's arms before, outside of his doctor. "I grew up in the system, in and out of foster care," I say. "My mom lost custody because she did drugs and was a . . ." I just can't say it. "Her pimp tried to recruit me when I was barely fifteen. When I refused, he beat me up, and the police got involved. That's when I was taken from her for good."

"Where's your mom now?" he asks.

"Not sure."

He leans up slightly, reaching out, but doesn't touch me. "I need to ask you something. It's not a jab, but I need to know." I give him a little nod. "Is there anyone? A pimp or a madam that might be looking for you?"

"No," I state firmly.

"What about Finn's dad?" he asks.

"No."

"Was he one of your clients?"

"Give him to me," I say, almost ripping Finn from his arms and flying to my feet.

"Paige," he says, standing up and rubbing the sides of my arms. "I only ask because if there's someone you need protection from, I can help. You're safe here. You both are."

"I'll handle the party," I say.

"Do you not know?" he asks quietly. "Who his father is?"

My hand whips across his face with such force that it leaves my palm print on his cheek. I suddenly realize what I've done. I just hit my boss. It's not the first time I've hit a man, but it's always been to fight back or fight them off. What have I done? Regret shoots through my veins, and my body starts to tremble and shake. "I'm sorry. Dear God, I'm sorry."

His hands come up, and I instinctively cower, sheltering Finn while bracing for the impact. "Paige," he says softly.

I don't look up, still covering Finn, waiting.

"I'm not going to hit you," Slade says gently. "I would never."

It takes me a second before I find the courage to turn my eyes up to him. One look into his handsome face, and God help me, but I believe him.

Slowly, he reaches out again, running his hands through my hair before doing the same to Finn's bald head. His touch is soft and tender. No man has ever touched me like this. Ever.

"I don't know who *my* father is," I sob quietly. "Because my mom was a prostitute." His blue eyes hold mine, that ugly truth not scaring him away, which makes me open up more. "When I was very little, I used to imagine him as some sort of hero who would come and rescue me." I shake my head. "Stupid. A man like that is no better than my mother."

His lips curve up in a small smile. Maybe he agrees with me. The woman always gets the bad rap for being a whore, but what about the men who pay for that service? Are they really any better? As far as I'm concerned, they're worse. At least the woman is honest about what she does. The man is probably sneaking around on his wife or girlfriend. And don't even get me started on the boys will be boys nonsense. Having a penis is not an excuse for bad behavior. Finn will know that.

"Your face," I whisper, my fingers grazing his red cheek. "I'm sorry."

"It's fine," he says. "But I wasn't passing judgment on you."

"I just can't talk about it. I want to give Finn a better life and not think about all that bad stuff."

"I know," he whispers. "More than you think I do."

Something in his eyes, his voice, makes me believe he does get it. My eyes well up, and I gently hold his cheek in my hand. "It's so red."

He inches closer to me. "It's alright."

I'm not sure what comes over me. The only thing I can think about is making it better. Clearly, I'm taking this mommy thing to new levels, and I lean in and softly kiss Slade's cheek. It wasn't more than what people casually do when they greet each other, but when I pull back, there's a desire in his eyes, the heat filling up the space between us.

Finn reaches up and smacks *my* cheek this time. I catch his little hand. "Good to know he's on my side," Slade says, giving him a little tickle. "Us men have to stick together."

"Oh great," I say. "When Catrine leaves, I'll be outnumbered."

He flashes me a wicked grin. "I like those odds."

Let's recap—in the past five minutes, I've slapped my boss and kissed him. On the cheek, but still. Maybe it was better when he was never here.

Catrine pops her head in my bedroom door and asks, "Hey, you alright?"

"Yeah, thanks for checking."

"Don't worry about the party," she says. "I'll help you. We'll get it done."

"You've done a lot of these for Slade?"

"A few," she says. "They're always a lot of fun. Although I have no idea what I'm going to wear to this one because I'm so huge. We'll have to do some shopping. Maybe drive into Nashville."

I look down at my shorts and tank top, unable to remember the last time I did any shopping at something other than a resale shop. "That would be fun."

"Do you have anyone to watch Finn?" she asks. "We could get our nails done, too."

"I really don't," I say. "I've been meaning to try to find someone nearby."

"Well, we can just take turns holding him."

It's just the kind of frivolous stuff I shouldn't spend money on, but going out and having fun is part of having friends. I can splurge a little.

"Okay, so I'll be back on Monday morning, and we'll get to work," she says, heading for the door. But she turns back and laughs. "Don't take any shit from Slade this weekend. He may own the house, but we run it."

I can hear her giggling all the way down the hallway. Quickly, I change Finn, then head into the kitchen to get his dinner together. It doesn't involve cooking, but it does involve a huge mess. I swear I need a hazmat suit to feed this child. Usually, I don't mind, but Slade's here at least for the night. He may not approve of our lack of table manners in his house.

Even though I'm still struggling to sleep, I've gotten used to being here alone at night, so I'm not quite sure how to act when I walk into the kitchen and find Slade holding up a clean baby bottle.

"Sorry, I should've picked that up," I say. "I'm sure you didn't plan for baby stuff to take over your house."

"It's fine," he says, opening a cabinet. "You can just put his stuff in here. If you need more room, just move some stuff around. This shouldn't be like you're living out of a suitcase."

"It's not. We're comfortable here."

"Good. And when he's ready, we can move him into his own room." He takes Finn out of my arms. "You'll need room for your trucks, won't you?"

"Maybe he'll like books or art and not trucks," I tease.

"Your mommy has lost it. Trucks, sports, horses, and women, and not in that order," he says, poking Finn's belly and making him giggle.

"Oh good Lord," I say, opening the refrigerator. Finn immediately starts wiggling around in Slade's arms.

"Damn, kid," Slade says. "You like to eat, just like me."

"Yeah, but he's having avocado and banana," I say, grabbing what I need.

"No," Slade says. "You can't feed him that. He's a growing boy."

"What would you have me feed him? He has no teeth."

"Bacon?" he says, grinning. I take Finn from his arms, looking up at his smile. Slade's very charming when he's not being an asshole. He's got one of those smiles that I'm sure gets him anything he wants. "At least mix some bacon grease or sugar in with that."

"Stop it!" I laugh. "He likes it."

"That's because he doesn't know any better. Give him some ice cream, and he'll never eat that shit again."

Rolling my eyes, I sit down with Finn in my lap. He's so excited he's squirming all around, making it hard for me to get the lids off the baby food. With Finn's pediatrician's approval, I started him on solid food as early as I could, around four months. He was ready, and it's cheaper for me to make my own baby food.

"You need one of those baby chair things," Slade says, taking Finn back from me.

"A high chair?"

"Yeah," he says, sitting down with Finn in his lap. "You're ordering one of those tonight. This is too hard to do by yourself."

"We do alright," I say.

"I know that," he says, cutting through my defensiveness. "Alright, let me see if you're telling the truth about him liking that green crap."

"You're sure? It can get a little messy." He just shrugs, so I get a small spoonful of avocado. Finn is so excited, his arms and legs moving a mile a minute. Somehow, I get the first spoonful in his mouth. His chubby body does this little wiggle in delight, and Slade bursts out laughing. "Told you."

"Told *you*, poor kid doesn't know any better."

I'm rolling my eyes hard, which might explain why the second spoonful ends up on the floor. "Finn," I scold gently. This time, when the spoon comes close to his mouth, he grabs it, helping me shove it in.

I've done this enough times to know I'm not getting that spoon back, so I grab another baby spoon. This is where the real fun starts. Finn takes another bite, then sticks his spoon in his mouth, pulling out a lovely heap of mashed avocado and baby drool. I try to catch it, but it drips on Slade's jeans. Trying not to laugh, I reach over to wipe it away. His blue eyes watch my hand gently swiping his leg. "We get just as much on the floor as we get in his mouth," I say, looking away.

Placing the avocado on the table, I pick up the container with the banana. Finn tries to slap my hand away, but I'm on my game this time. "Banana," I say. "You like bananas."

"Demand bacon," Slade whispers in Finn's ear.

I tilt my head, giving him a coy smile. "Maybe you should show him how good it is?" I say, holding the spoon up to Slade's mouth. Pursing his lips, he shakes his head, but little Finn looks up at him and holds up his own spoon.

Slade barely opens up his mouth wide enough for me to shove the baby spoon in. "Mmm," I tease, nodding my head.

"Mmm." Slade mimics me, acting as if he loves it. Finn reaches up, trying to stick his little fingers in Slade's mouth to pry it open. Laughing, Slade grabs the spoon from me. "Okay, your turn."

He gets the biggest scoop of bananas possible and holds it out for me. Our eyes lock again, and I slip the spoon in my mouth and swallow. His eyes watch my mouth, my neck, my tongue as I lick my lips. Suddenly, I'm very hot.

"Umm, I should clean up. It's close to Finn's bedtime, and I still need to bathe him and give him a bottle."

He watches me as I wipe up the floor and the counter before whipping off Finn's bib. I'm like one of the vampires in *Twilight*, moving lightning fast. When I'm done, I take Finn from his arms. "Guess I should clean up, too," he says.

"Me, too," I say, motioning to the stains on my shirt.

"Want me to watch him for you?"

"That's okay. I usually wait until he goes to sleep, or we just bathe together."

"Lucky boy," he says playfully, but his eyes say something totally different. Unable to think of a witty comeback, I head for the door. "Paige," he calls, causing me to turn around. "You didn't eat."

"I do that once Finn's asleep."

"Then I'll see you in a little bit," he says, giving me a hopeful grin.

Finn almost falls asleep in the bathtub. The poor little guy is so tired. If he gets up at all at night, it's usually just once. But lately, he's been sleeping a good ten to twelve hours a night. I get him down a little later than usual, then grab the baby monitor and head toward the kitchen. I'm starving.

Glancing down at my knee socks, shorts, and T-shirt, I wonder if I should've put something else on. It's a little weird to wear my nightclothes in front of Slade. I kept my bra on, but there's nothing normal about your boss knowing what you sleep in. Minus the socks. I don't sleep in the socks, but the floors here can be cold.

Maybe the cold feet are about something else or someone else. I step into the kitchen, seeing Slade at the stove. He's changed, too, wearing baggy sweatpants and a white T-shirt with no socks. But his sweatpants look much better on him than my shorts look on me. I shouldn't be noticing that.

He looks back over his shoulder at me. "Tonight, we have steak."

"Smells good," I say, unable to remember the last time I had steak. "But we need some sides."

"Learn that on those cooking shows you watch?" he asks. I freeze, my feet unable to move. Told you these floors are cold. He glances back at me. "Paige?"

"Are there cameras in the house?" I ask. "Are you watching me?" He steps away from the stove, his blue eyes giving nothing away. "Answer me."

"I'm just confused," he says. "Where is this coming from?"

"How'd you know I watch the Cooking Channel?" I ask.

He gives me a little shrug. "When I turn on any television in this house, that's the channel that comes on. I've never known Catrine to watch cooking shows, so I assumed it was you."

My body starts to thaw. "Sorry."

He turns back to his meat. "There's something like three hundred channels. So what's up with you watching cooking all the time?"

I move closer. The steaks look almost done, leaving me no time to make any real side dishes. Opening up the refrigerator, I pull out the spinach salad I made earlier. "It relaxes me."

"Maybe you should forget medicine and become a chef, or start your own business making organic baby food." He throws me a smile over his shoulder, seeing me pouring the salad on two plates. "No green stuff tonight," he pouts.

"But this one has bacon on it," I say, only it comes out flirtier than I intended.

This time, I set our places at the island with real napkins. It's strange to have a routine with him after two meals, but we move around the kitchen like we've been in here a hundred times together. We sit and eat. He even tries the salad. Well, he picks the bacon out and says he tried the salad. We both clean up, and I try my level best to ignore the electricity between us. I wonder if he feels it. It's like we orbit around each other, instinctively knowing where and how the other one is moving.

I realize I don't know much about my new boss. He's sexy, handsome, rich, works hard, likes horses, and hates vegetables, but not much else. I guess it's fair. He doesn't know much about me, and most of what he *does* know he doesn't really *know*. Still, I find myself curious.

"I was wondering . . ." I stop myself, but it's too late.

"What?" he asks, leaning against the kitchen island.

"I don't know much about you," I say, realizing this is risky. Asking him about himself opens me up to questions.

"You want some sort of get-to-know-you session?" he teases.

God, he's handsome when he smiles. "Favorite color?" I ask with a grin.

"Green," he deadpans.

"It is not!" I laugh. "Tennessee Titans or Nashville Predators?"

"Football or hockey," he says. "Tough one. I've got season tickets to both."

"Country music fan?"

"This is Nashville. Kind of have to be." I wrinkle my nose. "No?" he asks.

I shake my head. "Guess I'm a rebel."

"Me, too," he says.

"Give me one example," I say.

"Hired you," he says. "That's not playing it safe."

"Guess not," I say. "You like to live on the edge?"

"I like to make my own decisions," he says. "If I fail, then at least I did it my way."

"Me, too," I say, our eyes meeting. Somehow this well-off bachelor and I are more alike than I could've imagined.

"Is that why you don't work with your father?" I ask, knowing I'm pushing the limits. Favorite color is one thing, but family is a whole other level. "I know he's some big finance guy or something."

He nods. "Owns his own investment firm. I'd never work for

him. I started working when I was fifteen and saved, not wanting a cent from him. Went to college, double majored in business and construction engineering, then took out a huge loan to do my first real estate development when I was around your age, right after I graduated."

"Risky," I say. "What was it?"

"You know that ice skating rink and go-kart track out on Interstate 24?"

"That place is always crowded. You did that?"

"Yep, even worked there for a while to make sure things ran smoothly. Built the business, then sold it for a pretty penny. Used the profits to finance my next build and so on."

"Wow," I say. "You seem to love it."

"There's something about taking a piece of land or an old, run-down building and . . ."

"Rescuing it," I say, thinking he's done the same thing with me.

"Seeing the beauty in what others can't," he says, his voice low.

The heat in the kitchen suddenly went up a few thousand notches. "I'm just gonna . . ." I head toward the den, and he does the same. But I stop at the entrance. Usually, I plop down on the sofa, but I can't do that now. I don't even know if I should sit on the same surface as him. "I'll see you in the morning," I say.

"No cooking show tonight?" he asks.

I shake my head. "Good night."

"Paige," he says, "sleep well."

I smile, thinking there's no hope for sleep. This house is a curse to my REM.

"Aren't you forgetting something?" he asks. The confusion must show on my face. "The alarm," he says.

"Oh right," I say, crossing the room to activate it.

"Have you been arming it every night?" he asks.

"Yes," I lie, unsure if I've activated it at all since the last time he reminded me. I need to develop a new habit of setting it.

He gets up, walking toward me. The man is mammoth. It's not

just his physical presence. It's more than that. Everything about him overwhelms me. "Why are you lying to me?" he whispers.

"This job is important to me," I say. "I swear, I'm setting it when I go out to the store and stuff. I just forget at night. I mean to set it before I go to bed, but I'm not really sleeping."

"I'm not mad," he says. "You're out here all alone. The alarm is important to keep you and Finn safe."

I nod. "How'd you know I was lying?"

"The same way I know you're lying about the Cooking Channel relaxing you," he says, tilting my chin up softly with his fingertips. "Look at me."

I look up at him from under my lashes, and the truth starts to spill out of me. One look into his blue eyes can do that. "Lots of times, I'd go to bed hungry," I say. "My mom didn't always buy food, but we always had the television. You'd think those shows would make it worse, but they didn't. I'd sit and watch and pretend all that food was for me."

His eyes close, and his head does a little shake. He looks like that breaks his heart, but the way his hands clench into fists, he looks more pissed off than anything, like he just wants to hit something—hard.

And I'm still not sure how he knew I was lying. I've got to do better. I've got bigger secrets to keep.

CHAPTER TWELVE

PAIGE
AGE 11

"Mom, do you have to go tonight?" I ask, hoping she'll remember.

"Your mom's my best girl," her pimp says.

I shouldn't know what a pimp is. I just turned eleven. Today, in fact, not that anyone remembered.

"Someone has to pay the bills," she says, snorting the little white line on the coffee table. There goes the electric bill.

I look over at the stack of bills on the counter, then glare at the man before me. He brings her "the good stuff." Normally, a needle in her arm does the trick, but when he needs her to do something particularly awful, he brings her the powder.

Wonder what it is tonight?

I don't really want to know. Because it will be me that has to take care of her after. The bruises, the withdrawal—I'll hear all the apologies. The lies.

He takes my mom by the hand, then places his other hand on my shoulder. "One day."

My breathing increases, my chest rising and falling quickly. "Mom?"

"What?" she snaps.

"Never mind," I say, looking at my feet.

She giggles a little, then reaches down and pinches my cheeks. Yanking my head away, I stick my tongue out at her.

"That's a rude thing to do to your mother," her pimp says as if he's some sort of moral authority.

With defiance in my eyes, I stare him down and stick my tongue out at him.

He crouches down, reeking of body odor and shit for brains. "Do that *again."*

My knees tremble, but I will not let him own me like he owns my mother. No man will ever own me. I cock my chin up and stick my tongue out as far as I can.

Before I know what's happening, he licks my tongue, ramming his tongue down my throat. I can't breathe. I can't break away. His tongue fills my whole mouth, moving around, darting in and out. The taste of his bad breath overwhelms me, and I start to gag, forcing him to release me.

Though I have tears in my eyes, my mother only laughs.

He takes hold of my ponytail, pulling me closer. "First kiss?"

"No," I lie, tears streaming down my face.

He chuckles, and I know I need to learn to lie better.

"All your firsts," he whispers. "They'll all be mine."

CHAPTER THIRTEEN

SLADE

She's lying to me. I'm lying to her. Some would say that's no way to have a relationship with someone.

To me, it's the only way.

The more time I spend with her, the more I realize I need to spend less. But fuck me, I don't want to. My brain knows this is a bad idea. I've got a con list a mile long on why I need to stay the hell away—age difference, my father, her past, my past. But it doesn't matter. None of it matters when my dick throbs at every little thing she does. I swear, she could sneeze and make me come.

That's true, but it's also another lie. They're piling up. The cold hard truth of it is that I don't just want to fuck her. I fucking like her and want to get to know her. This woman who's ten years younger than me. This woman who would sell herself to feed her child. This woman who wants an education, a career. This woman who insists I eat vegetables.

She's changing me. I can feel it. Which is exactly why I'm showering then getting the hell out of Dodge this morning. One night with her almost did me in. I tossed and turned all night long. I know she didn't have a picturesque childhood. Who did? Not me, but when I think of the things she had to endure—mad as hell and heartbroken are the two emotions that seem to cover it. She had no one. No birthdays and no one loving her or protecting her. I know that's why she loves Finn the way she does.

Some of us learn how to love by *not* being loved.

Fucked up, but true.

All the more reason I have to protect her and Finn. The problem is, they might need protection from me.

Closing my eyes, all I see is her in those shorts and those damn socks she wore last night. She was beautiful the first night I saw her, all dressed up in high heels and makeup, but that's nothing compared to the way she looks all relaxed and smiling. I like her better in knee-high socks than a thigh-high slit dress any day.

I step into my shower, the feel of her lips on my cheek still new—her mouth so soft and sweet. Lowering my head underneath the raging water, I place my hands on the shower wall, my dick hard and so fucking heavy that it hurts. I've resisted doing this since I met her, refusing to think of her to get me off. But screw it.

As I grip my dick, flashes of her play in my mind like lightning—her mouth, her tits, that tight little ass, her tongue sweeping across her lips. I pump hard and fast, wanting it to be her pussy instead of my hand. Wanting to see my cock pounding into her, hearing her moan, wanting to know what she sounds like, looks like when she comes all over my dick. Has sex ever been that way for her? Was it always work? God, I want her to know the pleasure I can give her, shatter her world as I come deep inside her.

"Christ," I grunt, releasing all over my hand. But I don't open my eyes as the fantasy of lying in bed with her after satisfying her holds me hostage. I want to make her so tired, so relaxed that she finally sleeps. And I want that in my bed.

"Slade!" I hear Paige screaming.

And it's not the pleasurable scream I'd imagined a few minutes ago. Quickly, I rinse off, hopping out of the shower and wrapping a towel around my waist.

I hear her scream my name again. Only this time, I recognize that it's more of a yell—the yell of a pissed-off female. Those are unmistakable.

She bangs on my door. "How could you?"

What the hell? Wonder what I did? I could hide in here like a little chickenshit, but that's not my style. It will be too much fun to play with her when she's all worked up. Besides, this is my house. When I open my bedroom door, she's standing there seething. One her hand on her hip, her chest rising and falling quickly, and the other holding the baby monitor. Guess she didn't want Finn to witness her outburst.

"Good morning," I say, smiling.

Her eyes narrow, but she can't stop them from wandering down my body. That's it, babe, take a nice, long look. My dick starts to come alive under the fire in her blue eyes, and my towel isn't doing much to hide it. Good. If we can't be honest about everything, at least we shouldn't lie about what we do to each other.

She raises her finger at me. "Did you threaten Clay's job?"

"Did he tell you that?"

Her head tilts a little. "Not exactly."

"Well, what did he say?"

"He said he likes his job here," she says.

"That's good to know," I say, grinning at her.

"I know you threatened him," she storms at me. "Maybe it was just implied, but I know you did."

"I have a policy against employees dating," I lie. What's another one?

"What about Catrine and Jon?" she asks, thinking she caught me.

"They were already married when I hired Catrine," I say, and it's the truth.

"So employees can be married, but not dating?"

"Jon is my oldest friend," I say. "It's different. I can't have employees dating and breaking up and bringing all that to work."

"We weren't dating," she says, her voice growing soft. "He was my friend."

I hate the sadness in her voice. This was never my intention. "And he's not anymore?"

She shrugs. "You know how I take Finn to see the horses in the morning. Clay would usually meet us there. We'd just talk. This morning, he blew us off and would barely talk to me. He hardly even looked at me." She looks up at me. "Did you do that?"

"Paige, you have to know he didn't want to be just your friend."

"Did you do that?" she yells.

"Yeah, I did," I bark. I expect her to yell some more, but she turns and starts to walk away. "Paige?" I reach out, catching her by her elbow.

She looks up, her eyes wet with tears. "I don't have a lot of friends," she says. "It's hard when you're trying to take care of a baby. I was just trying to start over." Her head shakes, and she pulls away, disappearing down the hallway.

I'm an asshole. It's official. The thing is, I don't regret saying what I did to Clay. He needed to know she's off-limits. I do regret that it ended like this. My intentions were selfish, I know that, but I never wanted to hurt her or make her sad. That's the last thing I want.

CHAPTER FOURTEEN

PAIGE

Catrine and I have been out most of the day, meeting with the party planner and going over the menu, flowers, band, and various other details for the opening of the golf course. Not much of a party girl myself, I wasn't sure I'd be any good at planning this sort of thing, but now that I've seen everything, I'm actually kind of excited about it.

The clubhouse at the golf course is the venue, and after doing a walkthrough of the space, I know it's going to be wonderful. The place is so beautiful, I could serve them baby food, play nursery rhymes, and give diapers as party favors, and it would still be a great party.

I've never been anywhere like it. I only saw the golf course's greens from a distance because I was more focused on the clubhouse. The woodwork is exquisite—a hand-carved spiral staircase leading up to a viewing area, two bars, and windows offering a view of the beautifully landscaped course.

We have everything handled from the food, to the band, to the table arrangements. That narrowed our to-do list to finding something for Catrine and me to wear, so we decided to stop at a little boutique dress shop on the way home. She's only weeks away from giving birth, so I knew she was stopping at this store for me. There wasn't a maternity dress in sight.

So presently, I'm in my underwear in a dressing room as Catrine shoves dresses at me over the door. A blue sequin number comes flying at me. "I said nothing with bling." I laugh.

"Finn picked that one," she says. "He says it matches your eyes."

"Finn can't talk." I giggle, not adding the fact that he was fast asleep in his stroller when Catrine shoved me in here. She's been pushing him and picking out dresses for a good half hour now. Poor Finn, it's hard to be carted around all day and still get your naps in. But he's a trooper.

"Try it on," she says, and I know she's taken a seat outside to wait. Stepping into the dress, I know this isn't the one before I even have it over my hips.

"I felt a distinct chill in the house when I walked in this morning. Something happen with Slade?" she asks.

"When does something *not* happen with Slade?"

"You two should just screw and get it out of your systems," she says.

I pull the door open to the dressing room so fast, I forget I'm not zipped up. "Why on earth would you say that?"

"Please," she says, motioning with her hand for me to turn around so she can zip the dress. "The sexual tension between you two is off the charts."

"No, that's just hatred and disgust."

She laughs, then wrinkles her nose at the dress. "Jon thinks the same thing I do."

"If Slade's so into me, then why does he stay gone all the time?" I ask, hoping to shut her up.

"A couple of reasons maybe," she says. "You're a lot younger than him. And he thinks he wouldn't be good for you."

I step back into the dressing room, closing the door, but we continue to talk through it. There's no one else in the dressing rooms to hear us. "The age thing is just stupid. I'm sure that wouldn't stop him," I say. "But why would he think he's not good for me?"

Catrine doesn't know about my upbringing, but Slade knows some of it. Why would he not be good enough for me? He's handsome, successful, and surely has no problem finding women.

"You haven't been around long enough," she says. "Slade's complex."

"How?"

"He's just very guarded. No one is close to him, except maybe Jon. I'm not sure anyone else knows who Slade Turner really is," she says.

"What about his family?" I ask, feeling slightly hypocritical. I don't like to talk about my past. I shouldn't pry into his, but for some reason, I care. I know I shouldn't, but I do. Besides, I should know who my employer is, who I'm sleeping down the hall from.

"His mother is dead. And he can't stand his father. No one else I know of."

She throws another dress over the door. This one is black, and something about the illusion neckline piques my interest. You think you know what you're seeing, but you really have no idea. That's me in a nutshell.

Slipping it on, I say, "So he's private. That doesn't mean anything."

"Maybe," she says. "Or maybe he's got things he doesn't want anyone to know. Especially a young, sweet single mom."

Nothing he's hiding could possibly be worse than what I am. Donning the black dress, I open the door. The look on my friend's face tells me this is definitely the one.

She raises an eyebrow at me, saying, "Just know when Slade wants something, he usually gets it."

The truth stirs deep inside me. I want him to want me.

Catrine goes home for the day, and I head back to Slade's. It's hard for me to call it home. Such a simple word carries a whole lot of meaning. Is home a building? A place? Is it where the people who love you are?

I've always thought of home more as a feeling. In fact, I think the word home should be an emotion—the best emotion. Imagine if someone asked you, "How are you feeling today?"

Like I'm home.

People say all the time that they want to be loved, feel love, find love. They search their whole lives for it.

Really, they're searching for a home. The place where they are accepted for who they are. Sheltered and protected from the outside world and all the things that bring them harm.

I never had that. I hope that's what I'm giving to Finn. I hope that when I hold him, he feels *home*.

Pulling onto the property, I find myself searching for a sign again. This place has to have a name.

Shithead Slade's Sanctuary or *Twat Turner's Town*.

Yes, I'm still pissed at him. The truth is, I'm hoping Slade is long gone. I know that's bitchy. It's his home, not mine, but I'm still pissed he did what he did to Clay. I can handle my own relationships and friendships without him interfering.

Why did he feel the need to do that?

He promised me no more jabs, but he must think he needs to protect his male employees from the whore he has living in his house.

Employee policy. What a crock.

That was just the excuse he came up with.

Slade will always see me one way and one way only. I only have myself to blame for that. You can take the girl off the streets, dress her up, put her in a big house, but she'll still just be trash. As soon as something starts to smell, you know just where to look. He can think what he wants, but I know who I am. Who I really am.

Just once, I wish someone else could see it, too, though.

Slade's car isn't in the garage, so he must've left already. I'm thankful to have a moment to myself. I'm used to my own company, so it doesn't matter how much I love Catrine, I think I'll always be most comfortable alone. It's what I know.

My hands are full with Finn, the diaper bag, my purse, and my new dress as I struggle through the door, hurrying to turn the alarm off before it wakes Finn. Anxious to unload something, I toss the garment bag down on the sofa, then carry Finn to our room, placing him down in his crib. The poor boy is wiped out. He shouldn't be napping this late in the day if I want him to go to bed on time, but I don't have the heart to wake him.

Grabbing the baby monitor and the empty bottles out of the diaper bag, I head to the kitchen and immediately stop in my tracks. A new piece of furniture has been added—a high chair. And not just any high chair. This is the Cadillac of baby high chairs. Immediately, I feel my heart soften. Something is sweet about a man shopping for a baby, especially one who doesn't belong to him. But another part of me, a bigger part of me, is still pissed.

Like a woman on a mission, I march through the house, unsure why other than to try to work out my frustrations. Does he really think he can just buy me something, and I'll forgive what he did?

Of course he does. That's how us whores operate.

His bedroom door is open, and I walk inside. The curtains are open, and I sit down on his bed, looking out the huge windows. Hot, angry tears roll down my cheeks. Why am I letting this man hurt me? My whole life, I've done everything in my power to prevent men from hurting me. I've protected my body, my soul, my heart.

I've never cared what anyone thought of me, much less a man, but even though I hate to admit it, I care what Slade thinks. I don't want him to think badly of me, and it's not just because I need this job. The man makes me absolutely crazy, but he makes me feel a lot of other things, too. Things I shouldn't feel about my boss.

Running my hand across his comforter, I let myself relax on his bed, breathing in the scent of him. What am I going to do?

CHAPTER FIFTEEN

SLADE

As soon as I open the door to the house, I know she's here. The energy in the place shifts when she's here. It's almost like the air gets sweeter. Shoving my keys in my pocket, I glance at the high chair in the kitchen. It's still in one piece. I was a little worried she'd take a hammer to it. But I should know better. She wouldn't be that wasteful.

The house is quiet, too quiet for a baby living here. He must be sleeping. Hopefully, Paige is resting with him. I can't figure out why she can't sleep at night, but she's got to be exhausted. Maybe it's the sounds of the house, nature, or perhaps it gets too cold or too hot. I wonder if maybe her mattress isn't the best?

Contemplating, I head through the house. I was right. She's resting, but not with Finn. She's curled up in my bed, not under the covers but on her side facing the windows. Quietly, I walk over to her. She's out like a light, her soft pink lips open just slightly. This had to be an accident. No way would she walk in here and deliberately take a nap on my bed. But it's the best kind of accident. She looks absolutely exquisite asleep in my bed, just like I knew she would.

The one place she can sleep is in my bed? My grin is too damn big at that thought. A hot woman in your bed will do that to a guy, but this is a different kind of happiness. One I've never let myself feel with a woman. My control is slipping.

She shifts slightly, and I lean away. I don't want to wake her. She needs to sleep. I don't want her to know I've been here. It would embarrass her to know I've found her in here.

Resisting the urge to touch her, to crawl in behind her and wrap her in my arms, I simply take one last look then leave, walking to the other side of the house to check on Finn, who's also fast asleep.

Then I head outside to wait. When I'm sure she's up, I'll come in like nothing at all happened. Like nothing is different when, in fact, everything feels different.

The sun is setting over my land. The sun's rays are captured in the reflection of the pond, the woods already starting to disappear into shadows. The day is settling into night.

I love this time of day. When the stable hands have all gone home, and I'm alone. Only I'm not alone this time. Paige and Finn are inside.

I look back toward the house. It was a run-down, abandoned chapel when I found it. I really bought this place for the land, the pond, and room for horses. I never intended to keep the old, dilapidated chapel. The plan was to tear it down and build new. It would have probably been cheaper to do it that way, but at the last minute, with the demo crew on-site, I couldn't do it.

Instead, it took the better part of two years and a shit ton of money to transform it. A lot of the woodwork and the beams are original. They've all been refinished. The cabinetry in the kitchen is all crafted from old pews. Even the old doorknobs have been repurposed.

Normally, I like things shiny and new. My place in Nashville is just that—sleek and modern. The ultimate bachelor pad, complete with a hot tub on the balcony. This place is different. It doesn't look like it's built for the same man. Maybe I built it for the converted man, the saved man.

Salvation—brick by brick.

The house in the city for the man I am. The house in the country for the man I want to be.

I've never had a woman in this house. Never.

Its walls have never heard the moans of my one-night stands. Its pool has never been the scene of midnight skinny-dips.

My converted church house has never had one single room christened.

This house is a virgin.

A virgin house sheltering a former . . . and her baby boy.

It's hard to even consider Paige in that profession. Stepping into the stables, I unlock Whiskey's gate. He actually looks disappointed to see me. It's clear who he likes more. Can you blame him?

I prefer to look at Paige any day of the week. Wonder if she's up? Patting Whiskey, I pull out my phone. I can check the security cameras in the house from anywhere with an app on my phone.

I know I lied to her about that, but I didn't want her thinking I was spying on her. There aren't any cameras in the bedrooms or bathrooms, and the only time I've checked on her was that first night. If I'm honest, part of it was because I'd just left a prostitute alone in my house, which was cause for a little alarm. I logged on just to check that she wasn't robbing me blind, finding her mesmerized by the Cooking Channel, confirming my initial instinct about her. The other part of me wanted to make sure she and Finn were okay. I called and reminded her about the alarm and haven't spied on her again until today. A few times, I activated the alarm from my phone, but only when it was really late at night, and it was obvious she forgot, but even on those nights, I never looked at the camera. I'm not a creep, but I doubt she'd see it that way.

It only takes a couple of seconds before I see her walk through the den, so I close out the app, lock Whiskey's gate, and head back toward the house.

Wonder if she's still pissed about Clay? Only one way to find out. Heading inside, I hear Finn laughing and follow his little giggle to the den. I find Paige holding Finn up in the air, smelling his rear end and saying, "Stinky, stinky."

I let out a little chuckle, and her eyes fly to me. Guilt covers her face. I don't know how this girl did the things she did. She's not good at hiding things. "I didn't think you were here," she says.

"Was out with the horses," I say, my eyes landing on a bag slung across the sofa. "How'd it go today? You got a dress?" I ask.

Ignoring my obvious and lame attempt to smooth things over, she says, "What's in the kitchen?"

"The high chair?" I ask. "You never got around to ordering one the other night, so I just picked up one."

"Take it back."

"Why? The lady at the store said it was the best one on the market. You wanted a different one?"

"The brand is fine," she says.

"Then what's the problem?" I ask.

"You thinking you can just go buy something, and somehow, that's going to fix what you did with Clay."

Yep, still pissed. Women can hold on to their anger forever. It's so much simpler for males. We just punch each other, and it's over. "If that were true, I'd feel bad about what I said to Clay, and I don't."

"Of course you don't," she says as Finn starts to squirm in her arms. "I thought you'd be in the city tonight."

I can't help but smirk at her. "Thought I should stay and make sure you activate the alarm."

Having her mad at me is not the deterrent she thinks it is. She's probably used to throwing around some bitch routine as part of her tough-girl image, but it only makes me want to make her feel better.

So for every door she slams, I open one for her, even if I'm nowhere near her. For every side-eye, she earns a smile. Every time she ignores me, I think of something else I want to say to her. Basically, the next week is hell for both of us. On top of that, she's been run ragged preparing for the golf course opening.

If she's waiting for me to apologize, she'll be waiting until hell freezes over. I don't feel bad for warning Clay away. He's not what she needs, and there is no way in hell he was just looking for friendship. I saw the way he looked at her. I *know* that look. I look at her much the same, but Paige seems clueless. For a woman who lived the life she did, how can she not know when a man wants her? I thought that was a prerequisite for "working" women?

We seem to be at a stalemate. I won't apologize, and she won't cool down until I do. My mother always called herself a peacemaker. She said she had to be in order to be married to my father. So she was the one who always said she was sorry even though my father was usually the one at fault. She wanted peace at any cost.

I didn't inherit that trait. Obviously, Paige doesn't have it, either. So here we are.

One week into this argument, there's a high chair she refuses to use and a party to attend tonight. I've stayed out at the ranch most of the week, but the opening forced me back into the city last night. Five hundred of Nashville's most influential will be there tonight, so this needs to go off without a hitch. Stepping into my closet, I reach for the garment bag that's home to my tuxedo. I wonder what Paige's dress looks like. All I saw was a very similar bag.

I hope her dress isn't red. I don't want to think about her with my father.

CHAPTER SIXTEEN

PAIGE

The opening of the golf course is tonight, and I'm excited about it. Catrine asked her mom to babysit Finn for me, which was so sweet. I've got a new dress and shoes. All I need is to grab a few more things, and Catrine and I will be headed out to drop Finn off and then go to the party. I look at my dress hanging from the top of my bedroom door. It's floor-length and black, but it's cut low, almost to my navel, and covered in illusion fabric. Catrine said I looked hot and classy, so I trusted her.

The past week has been a whirlwind. Slade was around a lot more, but I tried to keep my distance as much as possible. Falling asleep in his bed had been a warning sign, a big one. I'm too comfortable. I'm too close. If I've learned any lessons in my life, it's that close and comfortable are dangerous. So I stayed busy. Not sure Slade cares that I'm giving him the cold shoulder, but it's better this way. Or at least, that's what I'm trying to convince myself of. Clay's still not really talking to me, and I've just had to accept that. I can't force his friendship, especially if he feels like his job is in jeopardy.

"Paige," Catrine says from behind me, and I can tell in her tone something isn't right. "Slade just called."

"Oh no," I say. "Is there a problem? Did the band flake? Because I'll yank their deposit so fast."

"No," she says, looking down and rubbing her belly bump. "He says I should take it from here."

"What do you mean?" I ask.

Taking my hand, she says, "He said for you to stay here."

"Oh," I say, looking wistfully at my dress.

"I tried to tell him how hard you've been working."

"I understand," I say, not wanting to take any joy away from her. It's not her fault, and this may be her last chance to dress up and have a night out for a while.

Her head shakes. "I'm sorry. You really should be there."

I guess my attitude this week has come back to bite me in the ass. I wanted distance and space, and now I'm getting it. I hope I'm not also getting fired. "It's his party," I say, putting on my bravest face. "Do you have everything you need?"

She nods, giving me an extra-long hug before she leaves. Does she know I'm being fired? Is this her farewell hug? I simply smile at her. Someone with my history learns how to smile through the worst shit. This is nothing, and the last thing I want is for her to feel bad.

When she's gone, I sit down on the sofa with Finn in my lap, giving him a smile. "We don't need a party, a dress, or dancing." Only this time, a tear falls down into the crease of my smile.

Leaning against my doorway, I listen to Finn breathing sweetly, peacefully. It should lull me to sleep, but it doesn't. I've perfected tossing and turning so much it should be an Olympic sport. I reach out, rubbing the fabric of my dress between my fingertips. I should've known better than to hope. Girls like me don't wear dresses like that unless they're bought and paid for by the man paying for our attention. No fairy godmothers are coming at the last minute to send us to the ball. There is no Prince Charming. There's only Slade Turner. And he won't be showing up with a glass slipper to pledge his love. He didn't even want me at the ball.

I feel stupid for dwelling on it. It's silly to be upset over something as trivial as a party. If only I could sleep. I look toward the other side of the house to the only place where sleep was possible. I know he's not coming home tonight. He can stop me from coming to his party, but he can't stop me from sleeping in his bed. My passive-aggressive side takes over, and I walk in that direction.

My eyes flutter open, but it's not Finn's cry that's waking me. Fingers lightly brush my hair from my face. Slade's blue eyes pierce through the darkness. "What are you doing here?"

"Shh," he whispers. "I didn't mean to wake you."

Suddenly, I recognize my surroundings. I'm in his bed. I'm not under his covers or anything, but him seeing me here is bad enough. I'm sure he didn't expect to come home to find the help asleep in his bed. Shit. He wasn't supposed to come home tonight at all. "I'm sorry," I say, starting to sit up. "I just . . ." There's no good explanation as to why I'd be in his bed.

Encouraging me to lie back down, he says softly, "No, I'm sorry. I found out my father was coming to the party. I wasn't expecting him to come, and I couldn't stop him. That's why I asked Catrine to have you stay here. I didn't want you blindsided."

I lean up on my elbow. "I thought you didn't want me there."

"Paige," he says, cupping my cheek. "How could you think that?"

I have to be dreaming. His lips are just inches from mine. "I haven't been very nice to you this week. I thought this was payback."

"No, I was looking forward to seeing you tonight," he whispers.

"You could've called me," I say. "You didn't need to come all the way out here."

"I wanted to see you," he says.

My heart is beating so loudly in my chest, I think he can probably hear it. "Eventually, I'll probably run into your father. I can handle it."

"I can't," he says. His voice is quiet, but the jealousy is loud and clear.

"Slade, that was the first night I was with your father. Nothing happened between us. Not even a kiss."

I see his body relax in relief. His hopeful eyes fall to my lips, and at that moment, all I want is for him to kiss me—to be viewed as a woman and not anything else—but he pulls back. "I should go back to the city. I just wanted you to know what happened tonight."

In what is probably one of the most honest moments I've ever had, I reach for his hand.

He looks down at our hands, then up to my face and says, "You better mean the next thing you say or do."

I'm too confused by what I'm feeling to be sure of anything. Slade is not a patient man. He turns for the door, leaving me alone in his bed.

CHAPTER SEVENTEEN

PAIGE

An entire week passes without a word from him. I can't explain what happened on the night of the party. Maybe it was the exhaustion, maybe it was the night, or maybe it was being in his bed. Who knows? But I almost kissed my boss. And I'd have let him do more than that. Now, I'm not sure how to move past it. Should we talk about it or avoid it? Judging by the radio silence, I guess Slade's choosing the latter. And I'm not going to push a conversation with my boss.

My emotions waver from wishing I'd kissed him to thinking I should have never grabbed his hand. What never changes is the certainty that I'm falling for him, though it's a mystery as to why. He's hot one minute and cold the next. I'd chalk my fascination up to him just being sexy and wanting to know what it would be like to have him kiss me, but it's more. I hate to admit it, but he seems to want to take care of Finn and me. I grew up on fairy tales where the prince always saves the princess. The New Age movies always have some twist where the female characters are strong and can save themselves. I believe in that message. Hell, I am that girl.

Still, having a man want to protect and take care of you, no matter how misguided and Neanderthal-like it is—it gets a girl going. So I'm falling for him despite my best efforts not to, despite the fact I'm bad for him, and despite the fact this is the worst idea in the history of love affairs.

There are too many reasons this is wrong for it to possibly be right.

I'm not going to dwell on it anymore right now. It's a beautiful Tennessee Saturday, but more importantly, it's my twenty-first birthday. Most twenty-one-year-olds might binge-drink or fly to Vegas, but I've decided to give myself my first birthday party. Finn is the only person on the guest list, and he's easy to impress. I might even let him have a tiny bite of cake. He had a rough day, too—his six-month checkup with his pediatrician.

It's so nice she's open on Saturday mornings, which helps working parents out. So while it's my birthday, Finn got a couple of shots today, so I think we *both* deserve cake. Finn and I went to the store and bought balloons, birthday plates, candles, and everything we need to make my first birthday cake. And I'm doing the whole thing from scratch.

Because it's my first time baking a cake from something other than a box mix, I'm keeping it simple—yellow cake with chocolate icing. From start to finish, it takes me about three hours. I know most people could do it in half that time, but most people aren't baking with a six-month-old.

After setting up the decorations on the island, I place the cake in the middle on a little cake stand I found in the cabinet, then pluck Finn out of his playpen. "Alright, buddy, let's get you changed, then party time."

Smiling and already singing "Happy Birthday" to myself, we head to our room. I'm in the middle of changing his diaper when I hear the sound of the garage door opening. It has to be Slade. Catrine doesn't work weekends. I feel myself smiling. Maybe he remembered it's my birthday. It was on the paperwork he made me fill out, so it would be incredibly sweet of him to remember.

I place Finn in his crib, taking a second to brush my hair. I look at myself in the mirror, the stupid grin on my face. The man drives me crazy, but something is between us, and it's time we get it out in the open.

Propping Finn on my hip, I'm almost skipping toward the kitchen. "Slade? I can't believe you remembered."

I grind to a halt, finding a long-legged, raven-haired beauty with a fork in my cake. She didn't even bother to cut it. She's just standing there, eating *my* birthday cake right off the cake stand, sticking her fork in it over and over again. To make matters worse, she's one of those women who oozes sexiness and knows it.

"Who are you?" I ask.

"Kimberly. Slade invited me for the weekend," she says, eyeing me. "You must be the maid."

The weekend? He brought her here to sleep with her, right under my nose. Then I'd have to wash his damn sheets after. "That's my cake," I say, walking over and yanking the stand away.

"Slade told me to make myself at home," she says. "He's just making a phone call. I'm sure he'll want to hear about how rude the help is."

"I don't care *what* you tell him," I bite out.

"Oh, there you are," she says, waltzing over to Slade, who just appeared in the doorway. She snakes her body around him as he flashes her a dirty grin.

Finn wiggles in my arms, reaching out for Slade, and for the first time, he locks eyes with me. He's hurting me on purpose, and I have no idea why. I grab my purse and Finn's diaper bag, walking past them, still pawing each other.

I don't know how I find the strength, but I stop, look him right in the eye, and say, "Today's my birthday, and she ruined my cake."

With tears streaming down my face, I hold Finn, the diaper bag, my purse, and a small overnight bag. It's a lot, but I wasn't about to make two trips. There's no way I can stay in this house and listen to them go at it all weekend. We'll find a cheap hotel for the next couple of nights.

Reining in my tears, I force myself to bury the hurt, like so many things in my life. If life has taught me anything, it's how to stuff emotions. I can't think about all that I've lost because there's always more to lose. I promise myself that I'll have a good cry about it later when all the losing is done and over.

I open the door to the garage, finding the outside garage door open. Slade stands with his head down and his hands in the front pockets of his jeans. My hands are too full to grab the keys, so I place the bags down, then reach for them. His head turns to me. I wipe my hot cheeks, pushing the button to open the trunk of the car, but he promptly slams it shut.

"You shouldn't drive when you're upset," he says.

"I can't stay here," I sob.

"Nothing happened with her. She's gone," he says, stepping toward me. "Just had one of the ranch hands drive her home. She won't be back."

"It doesn't matter."

"But it's your birthday. I don't want you to be alone."

I look him right in the eye. "I've been alone my whole life, even when I was with people. This is no different."

"Paige," he says, softly touching my hand, "let's celebrate your birthday. You can wear the dress you bought for the opening, and Finn and I will take you out."

I just glare at him. "Despite what you think of me, I can't be bought."

"You know I don't think that way about you."

I laugh out loud, shaking my head. "Something almost happened between us the other night, but you pulled away. And then stayed away all week. That was enough of a message, Slade. I didn't need you to do this. I get it. You think I'm a whore, and you don't do whores. Okay, I fucking get it!"

"No, Paige," he says, taking me by the waist. Finn squirms in my arms, feeling the tension, and starts to fuss.

Pulling away from Slade, I stick my finger in his face. "But let me tell you something. That woman was more low-class trash than I'll ever be. At least I know how to use a damn knife and cut a slice of cake!"

Moving past him, I frantically strap Finn into his car seat, throw the bags inside, and slam the door shut. Slade holds his hand over my door, preventing me from opening it. "Just hear me out," he says.

"You hurt me. And worse, you did it on *purpose*. I don't need to know anything else."

"Please, just stay here. I'll go," he says, almost pleadingly. "I don't want you driving when you're upset."

"It's your house."

"My mother died," he says, his voice almost unrecognizable.

This is the closest the man has ever come to opening up to me. I ask, "When? In a car accident?"

His head shakes. "Just stay here."

"Is this why you don't get along with your father? Something to do with your mom?"

I can see the walls go up in his eyes, and he snaps, "Will you please just stay here? I'm leaving. We'll talk when things have calmed down."

All I can manage is a nod.

CHAPTER EIGHTEEN

SLADE

This is what I thought I wanted. I wanted her to hate me. It seemed like a good plan at the time, but what works in theory feels a whole lot different in real life. What kills me is the reason she thinks I did this. Immediately, she jumps to the belief that someone like me couldn't want someone like her. Nothing could be further from the truth.

I've made this drive into the city a thousand times, but this time it seems to be taking forever. Why do bad things seem to last forever, and the good moments are so fleeting?

This push and pull, back and forth isn't good for either of us. Either she stops, or I do. Either she stays mad in an attempt to push me away, or I do something to push her away. Enough is enough. This has to stop. Today is the biggest fuckup I've made with a woman ever. As soon as I saw her, the hurt, I regretted it. I knew I'd made a mistake. I just hope I can come back from it.

Sometimes it takes losing someone to realize all the reasons you shouldn't be together don't matter.

I hate being the asshole. Forever, Paige will think of me as her jerk of a boss who brought home a sidepiece just to rub it in her face. Kimberly didn't deserve to be used, either. Not that I laid a finger on her, but I still used her. So I'm a double asshole. But something tells me Kimberly will forgive me easier, not that I care or that it's even important to me. All I care about are Paige and Finn.

That woman is fully underneath my skin. I haven't spoken about my mother in years, much less her death. Granted, I skirted the truth, but for the words to even come out of my mouth is proof of the hold Paige has over me. From the first moment I saw her at the party, my need to save her, to protect her overpowered me.

I try to tell myself the hurt she's feeling now will safeguard her against a greater one. The problem is, I'm a selfish man.

CHAPTER NINETEEN

PAIGE

I'm still in my pajamas when the doorbell rings at eight in the morning. Not that I was sleeping. Not even the Cooking Channel could soothe me last night. I spent the night cleaning up the disaster of my birthday party that never happened, trying not to cry and contemplating if I should even keep this job.

The answer is yes because I have to. I don't have any other options. Stumbling out of our room before the doorbell wakes Finn, I deactivate the alarm and answer the door. A huge metallic pink number one balloon hits me in the face.

"Delivery," a female voice says, but I can't see her through the sea of latex.

Moving the balloons aside, I find a smiling, middle-aged woman holding them with a wagon full of stuff behind her. "I'm sorry," I say. "You have the wrong house."

"Paige Hudson?" she asks, looking down at her clipboard.

"Yes, that's me, but the only baby here is a boy, and he's only six months."

Her head tilts. "This is for you, dear."

"For me?" I say. "Unless you have a number twenty balloon somewhere to add to that one, you're at the wrong house."

She hands me a folded notecard, and I see in Slade's handwriting: *For all the birthdays you missed.*

"You gonna tell me what's going on?" Catrine asks, hitting the balloons with her hands.

Every day for the past week, Slade has sent three deliveries—morning, afternoon, and evening. The first morning was an entire birthday party for a one-year-old little girl. Noon that day was a two-year-old party, then dinner was for a three-year-old. You get the picture.

All the birthdays I've missed. That's what he said.

He's kept his word, delivering to me every birthday I've ever missed.

The six-year-old party was puppy dog-themed. The ten-year-old party was a horse theme. Fifteen was for the popular boy band the year I turned that age. I have no idea how he found that one.

Other than his first note, there are no cards, but each birthday comes with a gift—a stuffed animal, a gift card, music. For my sixteenth, he sent me the title to the Mercedes.

I promptly sent each gift back, but he's relentless. Today, at least by his timing, I'm turning twenty-one, which is my actual age, so hopefully, this will finally end.

I haven't said a word to Catrine or anyone about what happened the night of my actual birthday. I don't have it in me to trash-talk him, although I secretly wonder if it would make me feel better. I haven't talked to Slade since then either. Clearly, he's waiting for me to make the next move, but he doesn't get it.

I'd be lying if I said his gesture didn't melt my heart a little. It's sweet. Most women would probably kill for a grand gesture like this, but not me. In my world, a man bearing gifts is a man who wants something.

I'm not the whore he thinks I am. No present or party will make me forgive him. That's not what I want. I refuse to allow myself to be treated like that by him or any man. I'm just going to do my job, keep my head down, and stockpile the money I make for school.

"Paige," Catrine says, "you've got to tell me what's going on. And you've got to eat some of this cake. Chewie and I are actually getting sick of cake."

"My birthday was a few days ago, and Slade ruined it," I say, pushing the latest cake aside.

"Happy Birthday!" she says. "I wish I would've known. What did he do?"

I just shake my head as the doorbell rings. "Would you mind getting it? I just can't see another clown or magician."

Sitting on the sofa, I lower my head to my hands, hoping the doorbell doesn't wake Finn. Perhaps I was blessed by never having birthday parties. Catrine walks over, sitting beside me. She places one single chocolate cupcake, a bottle of champagne, and an envelope in front of me. Cake is typical of Slade's speed birthdays. And the alcohol makes sense since I'm now legal age, but the envelope scares me.

"Do you want a minute alone?" Catrine asks.

Shaking my head, I reach for the envelope. It could be anything—airline tickets, a letter of apology, a letter of eviction, notice I've been fired. All I know is that it won't be good. Slowly, I pull it out, unfolding it.

My heart sinks. He's giving me something I really want. "Damn him."

"What is it?" Catrine asks.

Gently, I toss the paper in her lap. Her eyes widen, and she looks up at me. "Paige, you have to accept this."

"He can't buy my forgiveness."

"But this is him saying he's sorry in a big way."

"Please return it to him," I say.

"Paige, this is saying something more than he's sorry. He's paid off the next two years of your college tuition."

It's tempting. The most tempting thing he's tried to give me, but some things can't be bought. My heart is one of them. It's the one piece of me that hasn't been stolen or taken from me. I had to give up my education. I've had my body used and abused, but no one ever got to my heart. No one could take that from me, and I'm not about to sell it to him. It's not for sale. It has to be earned.

"All of this is," Catrine says, waving her arms in the air. "He obviously cares for you." When I don't respond, she grabs her purse. "But I'll take it with me."

As soon as she leaves, a slow rain begins to fall, marking the end of my birthdays. Any man would give up after this, and I'm not sure why my forgiveness means so much to him. He knew I was falling for him, and instead of just letting me know he's not interested, he chose to hurt me, to do something so crass that killing any feelings would be a guarantee. It worked, so why all the regret?

Maybe he's trying to force me to quit now. It's not that I haven't thought about it, but I have no other options, and nothing is worse than living the way we were before. My phone rings, Slade's name flashing. I should answer—he's the boss—but I doubt he's calling about work. So I just let it ring. A roll of thunder ripples through the house as it's really starting to pick up outside.

I hear Finn's cry even over the storm and rush to get him from his crib. Picking him up, Finn's baby chunk trembles in my arms. "It's okay," I say, cuddling him close.

He sticks his hand in his mouth as drool runs down his arm into the folds at his wrists. I thought crawling would thin him out, but no luck with that yet. He's still my little butterball. I try to place him in his high chair so I can prepare our dinner, but he's having none of it. I'm not sure if it's the rain or maybe that he's cutting a tooth, but he wants to be held.

He stays that way all afternoon and through dinner, so it takes me a little longer than usual to get him fed. Plus, Slade's been blowing up my phone. I know I'll have to talk to him eventually, but I need a clear head for that. I prefer not to have a cranky baby attached to my hip during that conversation either.

The lights flicker a little. I start opening cabinets to look for a flashlight but come up empty. Maybe in the garage? A huge bolt of lightning flashes through the window, immediately followed by a rumble of booming thunder. I remember as a kid counting the time between when the lightning flashes and the thunder hits. I'm not sure if it's true, but we used to say that every second between was one mile. This storm must only be about that distance from us. It's closing in.

I look out the window toward the horses, the stables, knowing they must be going nuts, but there's nothing I can do for them right now. The sky is dark except when lightning spreads across the sky. It looks like the gates of hell are about to open.

This time the lights flicker, then they turn off altogether. Finn starts crying even harder. Clutching him to my chest, I struggle to move around in the dark, waiting for flashes of lightning to guide my way. A loud alarm fills the room, my phone buzzing on the counter. I grab it, seeing a weather alert. More specifically, a tornado warning, and it looks like it's heading right for us. The last sentence says *take shelter immediately*. Another streak of lightning and crash of thunder hits right on top of each other.

Remembering this fancy new phone has a flashlight function, I use it to locate Finn's car seat carrier. I strap him in and head for the guest bathroom. It's in the most central part of the house and has no windows. Unfortunately, it's also the smallest room in the house. Finn is really freaking out at this point, no doubt picking up on my stress level. I tuck him into the corner of the room and give him my phone. The light fascinates him enough that he settles.

I need to conserve the battery life on my phone in case the power stays out for a while, so I need to find a candle or flashlight. Slade's not exactly the scented candle type, and I threw out all the little birthday candles in a fit of defiance, not that those would help me now. I have to get to the garage. I should also grab a couple of bottles for Finn, just in case. With a plan in place, I give Finn a little kiss, telling him I'll be right back.

Then I run, without any light, hitting my arms and legs on various pieces of furniture along the way. First, I grab the bottles from the refrigerator that were already made for the night, then I head toward the garage, ramming my leg hard against an end table. "Shit."

A huge flash of light startles me from my pain, and I look up at the huge two-story window in the front of the house. The wind is whipping, the lightning looks like a rave with its endless stream of flashes. It's dark, but I see it coming and duck down as a tree flies into the window. The loudest crash I've ever heard shakes the house.

I hear Finn's cry over the noise and start crawling across the floor toward the guest bathroom. When the lightning flashes again, I look back, seeing a crack in the window extending all the way to the ground. Dear God, don't let that break. Then I feel it, the water soaking my hands and legs. I know there's nothing I can do to stop it. The whole window caves in. Glass shatters everywhere, tiny shards ripping at my skin. The only thing I can do is get to Finn and pray.

Don't lose it. Don't lose it. You can't lose it. I'm not sure how many times I've repeated that in my head. It seems like we've been confined to this tiny room for hours. The storm is sitting right on top of us, pounding us over and over again. But the worst was when it went totally quiet and still. It was eerily quiet, not the peaceful kind. It was the breath the fighter takes before he slams you into the mat. The center of the hurricane before it engulfs you. The moment before you take your last breath. But it was long enough that Finn took his bottle and fell asleep. So it's just me alone in the dark, my phone battery having died already.

The wind howls so loudly it sounds like it's hollering my name, like death calling for me, unrelenting and unforgiving. I stick my fingers in my ears, closing my eyes tightly, willing it all to stop. It's gone on too long, and I'm losing it.

"Paige?" My name sounds through the wind, a tiny light coming in from under the door.

I look up as the door opens, his body filling up the entire doorframe. God, he looks rough, like he's been through a worse hell than us. His hair is crazy with bits of leaves in it. His hands are gripping the flashlight so tightly, it looks like it will break under the pressure, but it's his blue eyes that look the worst—black with despair.

"Slade?"

He glances at Finn, then back to me, falling to his knees. Somehow, I'm wrapped in his arms. I cling to the muscles of his back as he tightens his hold. I'm not sure anyone's ever held me like this before.

Every emotion in his body comes out in his embrace: the fear in his eyes; the worry in the tension of his biceps; the sorrow in the way his fingers caress my back; the relief in the rhythm of his breath; how much he wants me in the bulge of his pants.

His hand winds in my hair, pulling me to his lips, and for that moment, I forget I'm mad at him. I forget everything because my brain has no room for anything else, wanting to memorize every sensation—the soft feel of his lips, the strength of his hold, the explosion in my body as his tongue meets mine. There are no romantic candles. We aren't cuddling by the fireplace. The only light is from his flashlight, and I don't think anything else could be more romantic. He shifts, forcing my legs around him. He's hitting just the right spot, and I can't help the moan that escapes.

Clearly, he's forgotten about the tornado, the shattered window, and the baby sleeping just a few feet from us. Panting, I force myself to stop, resting my forehead on his. "The house," I whimper. "The glass. It shattered."

"I saw," he whispers. "It doesn't matter. None of it matters."

He pulls back slightly, his hands cupping my face and smoothing back my hair. Then he picks up the flashlight, shining it down on my bruised-up arms and legs. "We're alright," I say.

"Finn?" he asks, his voice with a worried edge I've never heard before.

"Not a scratch," I say. He glances back down at all my cuts and marks. "How'd you get here? The storm's so bad."

"Drove through it," he says like it's the simplest thing in the world. "You didn't answer your phone. Tornado warnings all over the state. All I could think about was getting to you."

A toe-curling crash fills the room, and I jump back into his arms. Finn starts to cry, and Slade reaches over, patting him gently, lulling him back to sleep all while holding me close. "I can't believe you drove through this."

"I had to," he says softly, his blue eyes lowering to the ground. "I'm sorry. So sorry. I don't care about any of it," he says. "All the reasons you're thinking that this can't happen. Your past, my father, the age difference. That was never my hesitation. I swear to God, it was never about you, Paige. I'm sorry I hurt you."

That was all I needed, not the gifts, the cakes, the gestures. Just the man—the real man. That's what I wanted. I lean up, pressing my lips to his. Both his hands grip my butt, and he settles himself back between my legs. His lips find my neck, kissing a path along my collarbone. No man has ever kissed me like this before. A kiss has never done this to me. My panties are soaking wet, and the ache between my legs is unrelenting.

"Slade," I whisper, looking over at Finn, "we have an audience."

Flashing me a smile, he takes Finn from his car seat and holds us both, and we ride out the rest of the storm just like that. He tells me that Catrine called him about the tuition and tries to persuade me to take the gift. I refuse. He won't tell me about his drive through the storm, and he tells me, once again, that nothing happened with his cake-ruining bimbo. I ask him why he wanted to hurt me, and he says he wanted to drive me away, but he won't tell me why. He just tells me over and over again that it's his shit, not mine. He describes how terrible his week has been without me, how he'll never intentionally hurt me again, and that he wants to give me all the things I've never had, which is why he gave me twenty-one birthdays. We talk until the storm passes and the morning light breaks.

And through it all, I'm wrapped in his embrace. I've finally found it.

The feeling.

Home is in his arms.

CHAPTER TWENTY

PAIGE

There's still no power at the house when we emerge from our self-imposed tornado shelter, but his cell service is back up. He's already called emergency services, concerned there might be live wires down. My cell is dead, and I have no means to charge it. Carrying Finn, I walk behind Slade. He holds one arm out behind him as if protecting us. Everything seems okay until we hit the threshold to the center of the house. The entire center window is out, a tree resting on the front porch. Glass and water cover the floor. Everything is soaking wet.

I reach up, patting his shoulder. "It's bad," I say, "but we'll get it all fixed. Soon, it will be just like new."

He turns to me, glancing down at Finn. "You were here alone with him," he chokes out. "I should've had a generator installed. I should've been here the whole time."

"We're fine," I say, cupping his face in my hands, unable to believe this is who we are now. We are emerging from the wreckage, from this storm, as a couple. How on earth did that happen? In my heart, I know I shouldn't let it happen. I should stop it. It's wrong and will only end badly. But it feels so right to be in his arms. Maybe that's what we are: the right side of wrong.

He glances down, saying, "You're barefoot."

Before I know it, he's scooped up both me and Finn and is walking us out of the house. The glass crunches underneath his feet as he carries us outside, the sun temporarily blinding me. Why does the weather always seem to turn beautiful after a storm? Is it supposed to give us hope or something? A new way to look at things? A new beginning?

Hearing a little cry, I turn and see Catrine and Jon rushing toward us. I hold up my hand. "Catrine, please stop running. Dear God, Chewie's liable to fall right out of you."

Jon and Slade both start laughing, but Catrine throws her arms around us, bawling. "I was scared to death," she says. "I saw it on the news, heading right for you. I tried to call over and over again."

"My phone was dead," I say, looking up at Slade. "We're fine."

She not-so-playfully smacks Slade in the shoulder repeatedly. "What were you thinking driving through that? You idiot."

He chuckles as Jon encourages his wife to stop. "I was thinking about Paige and Finn," Slade says. "Only them."

Her entire face blossoms into a smile. "It's about time," she says, taking Finn from me as Slade sets me on the ground.

Deliberately, he runs his fingers over me, examining the cuts and bruises on my skin. "Jon, can you make sure emergency services is sending an ambulance?"

Trying to get up, but for the first time feeling the soreness in my body, I say, "I don't need an ambulance."

"No offense, honey," Catrine says, "but you look like death warmed over."

Slade kneels in front of me. "I want both of you checked out."

"But I want to help clean up and check on the horses and . . ."

"And you're going to the hospital," Slade says. "Nothing is getting cleaned up today. And I'll make sure the horses are alright."

Slade wouldn't let Finn and me out of his sight all day. It's sweet and a bit over the top for a girl who's used to taking care of herself. I dodged a trip to the hospital after a head-to-toe examination by the paramedics, who agreed with me that a hospital trip was overkill.

Finally, I manage to slip away for a second, leaving Finn outside with Catrine. Walking through the house, seeing the damage, I realize how much this place had been home to me. Probably more of a home than I'd ever known before. My eyes fill with tears as I walk through the destruction. It could've been a lot worse, but it's still hard to see. Finn's little high chair is on the ground covered in water and debris, his playpen a tangled-up mess.

I walk to our room, pushing open the door. It's perfectly preserved, but the house is uninhabitable. I reach into my closet for a bag and start to pack a few things, forming a plan in my mind.

"I'll have Finn's crib moved to my place in the city," Slade says, leaning against the doorway.

That was not a part of my plan. "That's incredibly sweet, but there's a hotel not far from here. We should stay there. That way, I'll be close to the house when renovations start."

He smirks at me. "I thought you might suggest a family member, but not a hotel."

"There's no one," I say.

"There's me," he says.

"I'm not moving into your place in the city."

"Why not?" he asks. "We've stayed together plenty of nights here."

"That was before."

"Before this," he says, his lips softly landing on mine.

"Yes," I whisper, breathless.

"What if I said I won't take no for an answer?"

"I'd say that if you're going to be with me, you better learn to like the word *no*."

He laughs, and it's beautiful. "Then I'll rent the hotel room next door to yours."

And I know that's true. He would completely do something like that. "Slade, we've been . . ." I'm not sure what to call it—Dating? Together? Seeing each other?

"Paige, if you want a nice, normal relationship where the guy picks you up, and you kiss good night at the door, then you should know that's not me. I've been holding back with you for too long to live like that. I only know one way to be with you. And that's by giving you everything."

My breath catches in my throat. This is drive through the night, putting your life on the line for each other kind of stuff. Extreme, intense, and scary. "It feels too fast."

"It's the only speed I know," he says, flashing me a naughty smile. Then he reaches for my hand. "Just stay tonight. Give me one night. We should have more information on the repairs to the house tomorrow." He shakes my hand a little. "I'll be a good boy, and I'll eat green shit at every meal."

I look back at Finn in his car seat. He's still rear-facing, so all I can see are his little feet kicking. He seems unfazed by last night and by our new move.

Slade's holding my hand as he drives. It's a small thing, but it feels big. He spots me staring down at our intertwined fingers and gives my hand a little squeeze as the sights of Nashville pass by. This is lightyears away from where I used to live. Music row, Vanderbilt, and the Gulch are areas I always dreamed about.

Slade's penthouse condo is in one of the newer developments in downtown Nashville. It's sleek, modern, and doesn't look like one inch of this place is babyproofed. Slade uses a key card to access the private parking garage, pulling into his reserved spot. He takes Finn's carrier, guiding us through some doors to the immaculate lobby, with marble floors, a chandelier, and a front desk clerk on duty, who simply gives Slade a nod, obviously recognizing him.

"Do any kids live here?" I ask as he pushes the button on the elevator.

"Not that I know of," he says.

We step onto the elevator, rising all the way to the top floor. His is the only door on this floor. Slade opens the door, tossing his keys on a side table before taking my hand and leading me inside. The man likes his windows. There's a wide-open view of the skyline of Nashville through the windows in the den and a balcony with a hot tub. It's dark out now, so the lights of the city provide the backdrop.

He places Finn's carrier down, starting to unstrap him. "The office is through there," he says, pointing at an open doorway to the left. "Guest bathroom over there. And the kitchen is right through that doorway. No dining room. Bedrooms are all upstairs."

I poke my head in each door for a peek. The rooms are big but not nearly on the scale of those at the ranch. And the décor is all very clean and masculine—grays and deep blues. Finn fusses a little, reaching out to me. "I should get him to sleep. It's late, and he's been off his schedule today."

He takes my hand, leading me up the metal staircase. "I'll show you his room."

Finn's room?

I guess he's not planning on Finn and me bunking together anymore? He opens up a door, and Finn's crib is already set up inside. "Jon and Catrine brought your stuff over earlier," he says, then points at a doorway. "Bathroom's through there."

I look around. A bag of Finn's toys and clothes is on the dresser. There are diapers and wipes and even his baby monitor. But no bed for me. I place Finn down in the crib, patting his back and watching his big, beautiful eyes getting heavier and heavier.

"We'll have to get him new bottles and stuff," Slade whispers. "Anything that was in the kitchen I had tossed."

I nod, knowing I have enough to get us through tomorrow. "I've already started a list," I say, my voice sounding less nervous than I actually am.

Taking my hand again, he walks me down the hall a little, opens up a door, and says, "Our room."

The dark wood bed has a leather headboard, and the color scheme is the same as downstairs. Again, there are huge windows, but the curtains are drawn, and from what I can see from the doorway, the bathroom looks huge.

He takes a step, and I give his hand a little yank. "Finn might be scared being in a new place. I should probably stay with him. I can just sleep on the floor."

"You slept on the floor last night," he says, grinning at me. His head tilts. "What's wrong?"

"I've never actually shared a room with a man all night. Never slept next to one."

He inches me closer. "Crash course in sleeping with a guy. We sleep with our legs spread wide. Balls have to breathe, so don't expect a lot of room. Our dicks are rock hard in the morning and several times a night, so expect to be poked. I don't snore, and as long as you don't make me eat green shit, I won't have gas." I burst out laughing, and so does he.

"Sex," I whisper, briefly looking up at him. "I know you probably think that I'm easy or a guaranteed lay, but I don't want to rush into anything, and sharing a bed is going to make that harder."

His blue eyes turn a shade darker. "I don't think that way about you."

"You trying to tell me that part of this plan of me staying here isn't so you can fuck me?"

"No," he says, leaning into my neck. "The plan is to seduce you."

"There's a difference?" I ask, pushing away slightly.

"A big one," he says. "Fucking is just that. Straight to the point. And believe me, you'd like it, but you can walk away after. My plan is to make you want me so badly that you can't ever walk away. My plan is to make you crave me like I crave you. To need me like you need to breathe. My plan is to make your pleasure my sole purpose in life. The reason I get up in the morning is to make you come, watch your body explode, listen to you moan. So you don't ever have to worry about me just wanting to fuck you because I want much more than that."

I crash into him, kissing him hard. He picks me up, wrapping my legs around his waist, and carries me over to the bed. Pinning my hands over my head, he grinds against me, kissing my lips and neck. My body starts to tremble slightly as he hits the right spot over and over again.

His hand slips up the skin of my legs, sending tremors through my body. When he reaches my inner thigh, my legs fall open slightly, my body knowing what it wants. But my head has another plan. "I need to wait."

When the heat of his hand leaves my thigh, I almost whimper. A part of me hadn't expected him to accept my rejection. That's not been my experience in the past. He inhales deeply, like inflating his chest will deflate his penis.

"Okay," he says simply.

"Really?" I ask. "I thought your game was to seduce me."

He gently outlines my face with his fingers. "Has your life ever been about what you need?"

"No, not really," I admit.

"Well, it is now," he says. "And my life is about what you need. So if you tell me you need to wait, then we wait."

CHAPTER TWENTY-ONE

SLADE

Pushing her hair from her face, even in the darkness, I see her blue eyes ripple with tears. I wonder if anyone has ever put her needs before their own.

"I . . ." she starts but can't finish.

"Tell me," I say.

"I've never had sex for pleasure," she says.

I can see there's something else she wants to tell me, but she stops herself. "What about boyfriends?"

"Never had one," she whispers.

I'm trying to wrap my mind around that when she drops something else she's never had.

"Never had an orgasm either," she says, her voice so quiet I wonder if I misheard.

My eyes dart to hers, which she tries to avert in embarrassment. "You need me to remedy that, baby?"

She giggles, pulling me into a kiss. Her mouth parts, granting me access, and my tongue finds hers eager for me. Placing my hand back on her inner thigh, I don't go any higher.

"Whatever you need," I whisper, kissing her neck.

"Touch me," she pants.

I don't waste a second ripping off her shorts. Giving her thigh a little squeeze, I feel her legs fall open, inviting me. I take my time, toying with her, my finger sliding up and down her long, smooth legs, slowly sliding down her panties. I gently tug on her little triangle of hair. "I like this," I groan. "I can't wait to bury my face in it." Her eyes flash open, and I flash her a naughty little smile. "But only when you need it." I'm having entirely too much fun teasing her.

"Slade," she begs.

"Yes," I tease, my finger outlining her.

"Oh," she quivers under my fingertips. "Please," she begs.

"You trust me?" I ask. Her eyes find mine in the darkness. "You trust me to know what you need and give it to you?"

"Yes," she cries as my finger invades her, working her, stretching her open.

Christ, she's tight and wet and warm and so fucking beautiful. She's not naked. I can barely see her in the darkness, yet I can't take my eyes off her. The shadows of her body as her back arches, the sounds from her full pink lips, the feel of the bed moving as I give her what she needs. Her hand flies to my chest, grabbing my shirt. All I want is to bury myself deep inside her, give her everything, but I just promised her we'd wait. I can't push. As much as I want to, I won't. She's learned some shitty lessons about men in her life, and I need to undo those. Breaking my promise to her won't help that cause.

But that doesn't make this any easier. When she screams out my name, my cock throbs so hard it hurts.

Her back arches in a little stretch, and she yawns. Her blue eyes are half-open. I know she's exhausted between last night and what just happened, but she still reaches for me. Unfortunately, she is interrupted by Finn crying in the other room. Paige releases a deep breath, blowing her hair up out of her face.

"Your screaming woke him," I tease. Her hand flies over her mouth, realizing how loud she was. "I'll get him." Quickly, I kiss her forehead and adjust the aching bulge in my pants, then rush down the hallway and grab Finn from his crib.

Finn's got big crocodile tears covering his little face, his hand stuck in his mouth with a waterfall of drool running down. Walking back to my room, I find Paige fully dressed. "Look, there's Mommy," I say, soothing him.

"What's wrong with my boy?" she says, taking him and snuggling down on the bed. He lays his head down on her shoulder.

"Sleep," I say, placing a blanket over her legs.

How did my bed get so crowded? Leaning on my side, I watch Finn and Paige sleep. Seeing them side-by-side so still, it's the first time I've noticed they have the same little nose. Finn's almost totally bald, so it's hard to know if he'll have her brown hair. His little hand is holding a fistful of her hair, and she's completely out. Moving the blanket down slightly, I see her cuts and bruises look even worse today, a yellow color setting in. My plan to kiss those and make them better was interrupted last night. Clearly, I'm not going to be the only man in her life. And Finn is demanding for such a little guy, so I better up my baby game.

Finn squirms a little, his little mouth making a sucking motion. He's going to be hungry when he wakes up. I want Paige to sleep. I don't know the last good night's sleep she had.

How hard can giving a baby a bottle be? I've seen Paige do it a dozen times. Scooting out of bed, I stretch, hoping to get downstairs and have the bottle ready before he wakes up. Finn makes another noise, and I turn around, finding him about to crawl right on top of Paige.

Quickly, I scoop him up. Mistake. I must've scared him because he starts to cry. "Shh!" I say, holding him to my chest. "Don't want to wake Mommy. How about a bottle?"

Well, that gets his attention. Little dude might be on his way to alcoholism the way he loves his drink. We make it downstairs without incident, and I get the bottle Paige left in the refrigerator. Finn is wiggling around like a maniac. Do I just give it to him? Does she heat it up? Dammit, I can't remember. He seems to really want it, so I lower it to his mouth. He reaches up to hold it, but as soon as I let go, it falls to his chest, the baby pout following.

"Okay, I guess I hold it," I say, taking him into the den and sitting down with him. He reaches up with one hand, feeling the stubble on my face. His eyes study my face, so innocent, so trusting. "So here's the deal. You can't be such a momma's boy. You've got to give me a shot. I won't do it like your mommy, but we can have some fun." His little face scrunches up, forcing the bottle out of his mouth. "Don't be like that." I lift him up, and the biggest, most manly burp comes out of him. Then he giggles, a little regurgitated milk dripping from his chin. Even though I know the formula is not milk, it still smells like spoiled milk. He reaches for his bottle, and I stick it back into his mouth. "So we eat, then we burp. Easy enough."

Honestly, I never thought kids were in the picture for me. It's not that I don't like them. I do. It's that they come with a lifelong commitment to their mother, and up until this point, that was a nonstarter for me. All that has changed.

A few more gulps, another burp, and I'm in the zone. He finishes the bottle, still sucking on the empty nipple. Even I know that will give him more gas. No one wants that. I lift him up, and he giggles and burps at the same time. Drawing from my middle school days, I make myself burp right back at him. He squeals so loud, and I hear a little giggle behind us.

Turning to look, Paige is standing on the stairs, still in her clothes from yesterday. I should notice the highlights in her hair and her soft skin, but it's her smile that holds me hostage. Her eyes turn down, her skin turning a warm pink. "Good morning," she says shyly like she's waking up after a one-night stand.

Getting up, I meet her at the bottom of the stairs. She kisses Finn on top of his bald head while I kiss the side of hers, giving her ass a good squeeze. "Good morning."

"How long has Finn been awake?" she asks. "You didn't need to get up with him."

"Not long," I say. "We were just having some guy time."

"I heard," she says, taking him from me. "Did this happen to involve a diaper change?"

"Shit, I knew I forgot something."

She giggles a little, planting a soft kiss on my lips. "Thank you for the extra sleep."

"What time does he nap?" I ask.

"Usually around . . . Wait, why?"

"Because I need to take you back to bed," I say, capturing her in my arms.

She raises an eyebrow at me. "It's a workday, and my boss can be grumpy."

"I'm sure he understands that you get breaks."

The doorbell rings, and she starts for the door. "That's probably my co-worker now."

As soon as she opens the door, I know it's not Catrine or Jon. Her entire body stiffens. It's almost like her DNA changes at that moment, morphing her into someone else.

When he steps through the door, I know why. He fucks with everyone he meets.

"Son."

Lyle Turner, my father, but I don't call him that. I haven't called him that in years. Paige's eyes catch mine, and she looks like she just got thrust into a horror movie. She might as well have been. My made-for-TV life is just as bad. His blue eyes bore into me. Everyone says we have the same eyes. I hate to share anything with that man. But if he's focused on me, maybe he doesn't recognize Paige. She's not made up like she was the night of the party.

"Lyle," I say. "What are you doing here?"

"My son's home was destroyed in a tornado. I'm checking on him, and his . . ." He looks over at Paige and Finn. "Or should I say *my* lady friend."

Shit. I knew I couldn't hide her from him forever, but I hate that she's been blindsided, having no time to prepare for this. I motion for her to come to me, wanting to shield her from my father's wandering eyes.

"I knew you had Jon escort her out of the party," he says. "But I had no idea it was to your bed. Didn't think we had the same taste in women."

"We don't," I say, angling myself in front of Paige and Finn.

He shakes his head at me as only a father can. "You've gone and gotten attached."

"I work for your son," Paige says. "We're only here because the ranch suffered so much damage."

In some ways, she's so innocent. She's got no idea the man she's dealing with. "Similar work to what you did for me?" my father asks.

"I never did anything for you!" she barks, causing Finn to start crying.

Without looking back at her, I say, "Paige, please go upstairs and change Finn." Much to my surprise, she does what I ask. When she's out of earshot, I step toward my father. He's just as tall as I am, but I've got size and youth on my side. Still, there's a power a father holds over his son, no matter how terrible said father is. "I want you to forget you saw her here. Forget you ever met her."

"She's not a woman one forgets," he says with a chuckle.

My blood boils in my veins. I hate this man. Hate him with every cell in my body. But he holds my secrets, my shame, and he could wield that power at any moment. "You came to check on me. Well, you see I'm fine. You can go now."

"Relax," he says, slapping me on the back, "I can see you care for her. I think it's foolish, but I guess we all make that mistake once in our lives."

CHAPTER TWENTY-TWO

PAIGE

I can't stop trembling. I was calmer during the storm than I am now. Thank God, Finn is occupying himself with his toys and eating his various limbs. I hoped I could avoid this moment forever. It's never easy to face one's bad choices, but it's much worse to have to look them in the eye. Even though nothing happened with Lyle, he still represents all the reasons Slade and I couldn't ever be happy together. It's just very early in the morning to have to face that reminder.

I see Slade's feet in the doorway and can't bring myself to look up.

"He's gone," he says softly.

"I should go, too."

Quickly, he kneels in front of me. "I don't want you to go."

I look up at him, trying to steady my voice. "This can't work. We can't change how we met. It will always hang over us. And I doubt your father will ever let us forget, even if we tried."

"He won't tell anyone," he says.

"How do you know?" I ask.

"He's good at keeping secrets."

"His own, maybe."

"No, he's good at keeping mine, too."

"What secrets?" I ask.

"Sometimes secrets are best left buried."

I know that's true. I've got my own that need to stay hidden, so I don't press him. "And sometimes they stalk us."

He reaches out for my hand, saying, "You know you can tell me anything. I'm not going to judge you."

"You're not my priest. I don't need to confess my sins to you."

"How'd you meet my father?" he asks, refusing to give up.

"I was part of the cleaning crew that cleaned his office at night. He worked late a lot." Softly, I stroke the back of his hand. "He asked me out."

"Just a normal date?" he asks.

"Yes, but I wasn't interested for a lot of reasons. For one, he's old. I told him I didn't have time to date while raising Finn. That I worked every day and most nights. That's when he offered to pay me for my time." He tilts my chin up, forcing my eyes to his. "That night with your father—That was the first time I'd ever done anything like that."

I can't place the emotion I see on his face as he realizes I wasn't a call girl. It's not only relief but something else too.

"So no one ever paid you for sex?" he asks. "Any kind of sex?"

"No, and I've never stripped or anything either." I cup his face in my hands. "You saved me that night."

"No," he whispers. "I was such an asshole. Shit, for weeks, I was such a bastard." He looks up at me with those sapphire eyes of his. "Why didn't you just tell me? Why'd you let me think you were a . . ."

"Whore?" I say, finishing his sentence. "Because it didn't matter that I didn't do it. I would have. I'd already made the decision to."

"Paige," he says softly, wiping a few tears from my cheeks I didn't realize were there.

"My mom was a prostitute my whole life. She slept with all kinds of men for money, for drugs. I guess you live by example. In my heart, that's who I am. A whore, just like my mother."

"Don't talk like that."

"But it's true," I sob. "And I was a cheap one, at that. You said yourself I should've charged more."

"Stop it," he barks.

"I was willing to sell my body for five hundred bucks."

"No, you were willing to sell your body to save Finn," he says, capturing me by my arms.

I collapse into his chest. "I promised him," I say. "I promised that he'd have a better life than mine. I promised him I'd do whatever it took."

"I know," he whispers, stroking my hair. "You're a great mother. He's so lucky to have you. So many mothers say they'd give anything for their kids, and you proved you would." He pulls back, staring into my eyes. "You told me you never had sex for pleasure," Slade says.

"You thought that meant it was always paid," I say. "It wasn't." He knows what I'm telling him. His eyes close, his hands ball up in fists. "I always put up a fight," I say. "Sometimes, I lost."

"Who? How many have there been?" he asks, his voice in a controlled anger. "How old were you?"

Shaking my head, I say, "You don't need to know any of that."

"You mean you don't want to tell me."

"I mean, you don't need to know. You know I grew up poor, abused, and neglected. The details aren't important. Unfortunately, my story is the same as thousands of other girls. I don't know one single girl who grew up like I did that escaped without having someone touch, fondle, or force them into doing something they didn't want to."

"I hate this," he cries. "I hate thinking of you hungry or hurt or worse."

"Then don't think of me like that," I say, placing his hand on my cheek. His blue eyes soften. He's getting it. I don't want him to think of me that way, either.

"If there was something I needed to know, you'd tell me?" he asks.

"Yes."

"Finn's father?" he asks, holding my eyes. "If you never had sex for pleasure, and it wasn't work, then . . .?"

A rush of fear shoots through me, causing my whole body to tremble. How could I have screwed up so badly? My lies are getting harder and harder to keep up with. The truth wants out, but I can't tell him the truth. And I can't say what I really want to say—that he's more a father to Finn than anyone.

He pulls me into his arms. "Shh, baby. It's okay. We don't need to talk about it now."

"What about your father?" I ask, running my fingers through his hair.

"Let me tell you about my father and my childhood. I spent it cleaning up his messes. Literally, I would have to clean up empty bottles of alcohol from his drinking binges. Get a cab for the women the next morning when they'd wake up, and he'd be gone already. Listen to them cry, regretting what happened. Listen to them praying they weren't pregnant. When I saw you that night at the party, all I knew was that I couldn't let you end up like that. I just couldn't. I was a jerk and a dick, but it was only because I felt this need to protect you."

"I'm glad you did."

"Where the heck are my clothes?" I ask myself, dripping wet from the shower. I could've sworn I brought them into the bathroom with me. Slade's bathroom is like everything else about this man—big. The tub, the shower, the vanity, it all looks like it's made for a small village, not one man.

Drying off, I study myself in the mirror, the cuts and bruises making me look like I've been in battle. I'm used to my scars being hidden on the inside. My knees and legs got the worst of it, but it's my eyes that I can't stand to look at. I'm a liar.

Some people think it's never okay to lie. I say those people must've had a damn good life. They probably never had to lie about where their bruises came from or tell someone they weren't hungry when they hadn't had a meal in days. For some of us, lying equals surviving.

I came clean to Slade about a lot of things, but that's just the tip of the iceberg. I may not be a prostitute, but I'm a criminal just the same. There are things Slade doesn't know. Things he can never know.

My reasons don't matter, I still broke the law, and if I'm caught, Slade could get caught in the crossfire. I don't want that to happen; he's so good to Finn and to me. I don't want to let him go. He's one of the few good things in my life.

I run my fingers through my wet hair. It's midmorning already, and I need to get back to the ranch and see if anything can be salvaged. As soon as Finn gets up from his nap, we'll go. I'm not sure how I'm going to get anything done with him, but maybe Catrine can watch him. She shouldn't be in that mess either. Pushing open the door to Slade's bedroom, I see my bag resting on the bed and begin digging through it. I really must have been out of it yesterday. It's just a hodgepodge of items. I pull out the one bra and single pair of panties I packed.

"Paige," Slade says from the doorway.

"Hmm," I say, continuing to dig through my bag to pull together something that doesn't make me look like a hobo.

"You're standing in my bedroom in nothing but a towel."

I flash him a smile over my shoulder. "I'm all covered up."

"Not for long," he says, wrapping his arms around me and lowering me to the bed. Giggling, I hold the top of my towel up. His warm breath on my neck, he whispers, "Finn's napping. What do you need?"

Apparently, this is now our little code phrase for sex.

"To get to work," I say, pushing him back playfully.

He pulls me down on top of him in the bed. "I think you might need something else."

Tilting my head to the side like I'm thinking hard, I bite my bottom lip. "I need to take care of you."

"What did you have in mind?" he asks, grinning up at me.

"I thought we'd start with…" I lean over, letting my breath tickle his neck. "You eating a salad for lunch."

He smacks my ass hard. "Tease."

Planting a quick peck on his lips, I get to my feet. He stands up, gently running his fingers through my hair. "Any word from the contractor on how long to repair the damages?" I ask.

His head shakes. "I'm meeting him out there later."

"Then I should get out there and get the rest of our things. Salvage what can be saved."

"You should rest today," he says.

My eye roll lets him know that's not happening. "I'll go as soon as Finn gets up."

He releases a huge breath. The man hates not getting his way. "If you have to go, just go now. I'll bring Finn out with me when I come."

My mouth falls open. "You're kidding?"

Donning rubber boots and carrying a box of salvageable items, I walk through the house, willing a text, a phone call, something back from Slade. He hasn't been in touch at all, despite my dozen texts checking on him and Finn. What was I thinking leaving him alone with a baby? He's never changed a diaper. He only held a baby for the first time a few weeks ago.

I place the box outside next to a couple others that need to go to Slade's house in the city. The parts of the house that weren't affected by the storm are being sealed off, and the broken front window has already been boarded up, so the house is secure. The entire kitchen and den areas will be gutted due to wind and water damage. I've only got one more set of cabinets to look through before finishing up. All the electronic equipment was ruined. I managed to save a few books, but not much else.

A whole crew of people is here cleaning up and assessing the damage. Walking back into the house, I can't help but overhear how the beautiful floors need to be replaced, all the cabinetry, how they have to safeguard against mold.

"Some of the wiring is shot," one man says. "The whole security system, cameras. Everything needs to be replaced."

"Cameras?" I ask, turning to him.

"Security cameras," he says. "They cover basically the whole exterior and interior of the house, except the bedrooms and bathrooms."

He lied to me. That night when I asked how he knew I watched the Cooking Channel, he lied. I asked specifically about cameras, and he said there weren't any . . . no. Come to think of it, he never said there weren't. He simply dodged my question. Damn him!

He should've told me. Okay, so maybe that's not fair. It's his house. It's his right to have cameras. I know lots of people do—to watch their babysitter, their teenagers, or just monitor the comings and goings around their house. And I doubt any of those people inform the help that they're being watched. It's not like he saw me on the toilet or anything.

Still, I thought I was alone. He could've been watching me. What's the worst he saw? Me watching television? Crawling on the floor with Finn?

I could make a big deal out of this, and even though it hurts, he didn't fess up to it, so I'm not going to ruin what we just started by blowing this out of proportion.

Decision made. Time to get back to work.

I squat down, the floor still damp, and begin pulling out various items—ice bucket, throw blanket, an old VCR, and what I think is an original Nintendo—but they're all ruined.

Tilting my head to look inside, I notice something pushed back in the corner. I can see the edge is wet, but reach for it anyway. It's a canvas. The writing on the back says, *Mommy and Slade (Age 2)*.

I flip it over, and his sapphire eyes shoot right out at me like they are leaping off the canvas. Even at two years old, his eyes were captivating. His head is tilted to the side, resting on his mother's chest. One of her hands is in his hair and the other on his back as she looks down at him. I can tell from the photo she was beautiful with long dark hair, pale skin, and beautiful eyes, though not the same eyes as her little boy.

He looks completely loved and at peace in her arms. I wonder if he ever feels that way anymore. I carry it out into the sunlight. The edges are damaged, but the feeling in the photo is very much intact.

Slade is a big man. It's surreal to see him so tiny in his mother's arms. It makes me wonder what Finn will look like. Someday, he'll be taller than me, bigger than me, stronger than me. I'm raising a man and have no idea what I'm doing.

I hear a door slam and look up, seeing Slade pulling Finn out of his car seat. Rushing to them, I say, "Why didn't you call me? I've been worried sick."

"Call you? How was I supposed to call you? How do you get anything done with this kid other than holding him, feeding him, and playing with him? I haven't even pissed since you left," he says, laughing, but I know it's true.

"How'd it go?" I ask, taking Finn in my free arm and giving him some love.

"We're both alive," Slade jokes, kissing the side of my head. "It's a success. How are things here?"

I exhale, looking back at the house. "I've got a few things packed up to take back, but most everything from the kitchen and den is ruined," I say, holding up the canvas. "Except this. I found it in the cabinet in the den. It's a little wet, but I think it can be saved." He just stares at it blankly, his eyes a dark pit. "It's your mom and you, right?"

He takes it from me and walks a few feet away without a word.

"Slade," I say, touching his arm to stop him. "I'm sorry if the picture upsets you. I didn't mean to do that."

"You thought my dead mother would, what? Make me happy?"

"No, I just . . ."

"Not now," he barks.

I stand there for a second—stunned but not sure why. I've never been able to count on anyone, much less a man, so why did I expect Slade to be different? But I did.

"I'm sorry. I had no idea you'd react this way. I thought you'd be happy it wasn't ruined," I say. Walking away from him, I head to the stables to see the horses, to see for myself that Whiskey is alright.

I hold Finn a little tighter, wiping my face. Too much has happened in the past twenty-four hours. I need to give myself some space to think about things.

The stables held up well in the storm. It's a mess but sustained no real damage. The guys have been here all day getting things back into shape and working to calm the horses. I find my spot by Whiskey's door, leaning my head down. He walks right over, letting me pet him. Whoever came up with therapeutic horseback riding was really onto something. I feel my heart rate easing up with each stroke.

"Hey," Clay says, coming up beside me, stroking Finn's arm.

Finn reaches out to him. Finn is a very friendly baby, but maybe he's starved for male attention or something. He seems to love any attention from his fellow sex, so I go ahead and let Clay hold him.

"I tried to call you over and over again the night of the storm," Clay says. "I was so worried about you."

"My phone died," I say, not really looking at him.

"I'm a jerk. I shouldn't have ignored you," he says. "It's just, Slade's my boss, and I need this job."

"It's okay."

He elbows me slightly. "I should've told him to go to hell."

"Me, too," I say, smiling.

We stand there talking for a while, catching up. I'm not sure if I should, but I tell him that my relationship with Slade has changed. I don't give any other details, but he gets the idea. And he seems okay with it. He makes me promise that I'll let him give me my first riding lesson soon and tells me to call him if I need anything or want to hang out since I won't be around as much while repairs are being done. I tell him about a couple of classes I'm thinking of taking next semester, and he seems happy for me, just like a friend should be.

Clay looks over his shoulder, a worried crease in his brow as Slade appears in the opening of the stable. "Don't worry. I'll handle him," I say.

Clay laughs, handing Finn back to me. "See you later."

I walk toward Slade, who's holding his ground. Stubborn asshole refuses to walk over to me. Well, I'll show him. I walk right past him, seeing him smirk at me out of the corner of my eye. I hear him following me and turn around, halting him. I hate the amused look on his face. "Two words," I say. "I only want to hear two words come out of your mouth."

"Which two?" he asks, clearly thinking he's funny.

"Try again." Finn starts to squirm, wanting to get down and have some freedom. Slade takes him from me, kneeling so Finn's feet are touching the grass. He holds him there, like Finn's standing on his own. Finn's feet are moving all around as he giggles. I hope this isn't an indication that he's going to walk early.

Slade's blue eyes look up at me. "I'm sorry about earlier. I don't talk about my mom."

"You can just tell me that. You don't have to be an asshole."

"You're right," he says.

I flash him a smile. "Those are the two words every woman loves to hear."

CHAPTER TWENTY-THREE

SLADE

Sidestepping debris, I survey the house with Jon. The initial timeframe for repairs is four to six months. Apparently, the water damage is the real killer. Doesn't matter if you get one inch or a foot, still have to repair sheetrock, guard against mold, and redo floors and cabinetry. Since we're trying to maintain the building's original character, everything will have to be custom. It's going to be a major hassle, costly, and keep me in the city for most of the rest of the year.

"Contractor hopes to have you in for Christmas," Jon says, picking up one of Finn's toys that's now ruined and handing it to me, an *I told you so* look in his eyes.

Christmas? I look down at the broken toy in my hand, realizing I don't know Finn's birthday. Will he be one by Christmas? Will he like Santa? I haven't had a tree since I was a kid. I'll have to get one this year. A big one.

Without a word to Jon, I walk to the door, seeing Paige changing Finn's diaper in the back of my car. They never advertised that as a feature when I bought the Land Rover. I guess it can handle a diaper change. "Paige," I call out. Her head turns to me. "Will Finn be one at Christmas? When's his birthday?"

Her smile is priceless. "December first."

"Planning his party already," I say, giving her a little wink.

"You've had a lot of practice recently," she says, finishing up and walking toward me.

"Construction theme?" I say, shrugging.

She laughs, Finn following her lead, and I wrap my arm around her, stopping her from coming back into the house with Finn. Jon joins us outside. "I know Catrine was supposed to work until the baby comes, but if it's okay with you, I'd..."

"It's fine," I say. "I understand. This is a mess. The last thing I need is Catrine stepping on a nail or tripping. Tell her to enjoy her last few days of sleep."

"I will," Jon says, then looks at Paige. "Stay in touch with her?"

"I will," she says as Jon leaves.

"Why don't you and Finn go back, too?" I say to her. "Finn doesn't need to be out here, and you're still recovering. I'll just be an hour or so." She nods. "Jon's right. I'd rather you and Finn not be out here either," I say. "I know you want to oversee things, but..."

"My job is the house," she says firmly. "The stables."

"You can mail the guys their checks from Nashville. You don't need to be out here to do that."

"You mean from your place?" she asks.

"Four to six months, Paige," I say. "You can't live in a hotel that long."

"You pay me enough that I could rent something for a few months," she says. "That is, if I still have a job."

"Of course you have a job," I say.

"What's my job?" she asks. "Writing a few checks each week?"

"It's just temporary," I say, taking Finn from her. "You can take classes. You said you wanted to."

"I need to work," she says.

"No, you don't."

"So you want me to live with you?"

"Of course."

"Go to school?" she asks.

"Yes, if that's what you want."

"Which I'm assuming you want to pay for?"

"Absolutely," I say.

"And you're still going to pay me for a job I'm not doing anymore?"

"Think of it like a severance package," I say. "But yes."

"Isn't that basically what your father was offering me?"

Fuck, I stepped right into that one. How could she possibly think this is the same thing? I hate being compared to my father, but I don't want to fight with her. Blowing out a deep breath, I say, "You're the one thinking about it that way, not me."

She looks away, taking Finn's little hand in hers. "If I'm still going to be on your payroll, I need to feel like I deserve it," she says.

"Well, I'm not going to fire you," I say, tilting her chin up. "I suppose it would help me to have someone making sure shit gets done out here."

"I can do that," she says, her whole face brightening. "You've been on the receiving end of my airplane veggies. You know how tough I can be."

Shaking my head and smiling, I know I'm fighting a losing battle. "Okay, but I'm having a trailer put out here. You can use that as your office." Her smile gets bigger. "But at night . . ."

"Finn and I will stay with you," she says, giving me what I really wanted.

Their two laughs blend, filling the rooms in my penthouse like air. Following the sound, I find the door open to the master bathroom. "Paige?" I call out, not wanting to scare her.

"In here," she says.

Stepping into the bathroom, I find Paige and Finn in my bathtub, covered in bubbles. I guess she wasn't kidding when she said they sometimes bathe together. This is hardly the image I had in mind when I first saw Paige naked. Of course with all the bubbles, I can't really see anything anyway.

Her legs are propped up, and Finn's leaned back on them like she's a recliner. They both look over at me. "Are you eating his toes?" I ask.

She wiggles her head a little like a dog with a bone. "He thinks it's funny." Finn starts laughing so loudly his little belly shakes. "Besides, we're in the tub. He's clean," she teases.

"Umm," I say, pointing for her to look down, a trickle of pee currently filling the tub.

"Finn," she screeches, jerking up slightly, the bubbles cascading down her skin. "Boys!"

She reaches out in search of a towel, but there's not one close enough, so I grab one for her, then grab another. Reaching in and lifting Finn from her arms, I take care to wrap him up tight. Paige has stepped out of the tub and has the towel around herself by the time I've got him wrapped up. Dammit.

She tucks the towel into itself, making what looks like a strapless mini dress, only it's made of terry cloth. Grabbing her ass, I pull her to me, causing her to squeal a little. "When do I get to take a bath with you?"

"Next time." She laughs, taking Finn from me and walking into the bedroom. She lays him down on the bed next to a diaper and the clothes she has waiting there. I wouldn't have thought to have all that waiting. She keeps the towel covering most of his body, keeping him warm while she makes quick work of the diaper.

"Got to be quick," she says in a baby voice. "So we don't pee-pee on Slade's bed. I don't want to have to wash bed linens."

"You have a good mommy," I say to Finn, taking his little hand.

Paige flashes me a smile. I wonder if anyone's ever said that to her. She has to know. She's raised him all alone. And while they never had much, Finn has known an abundance of love. You can see it in how happy he is.

She grabs his little pajamas, the kind that are footed. These have little frogs all over them. "Getting a little tight," she says, zipping them up. "Time for some new ones. We better go shopping."

"We can go tomorrow," I say, leaving out that I intend to pay. I watch her pick him up, looking around for the bag of clothes she brought over last night. "Top drawer," I say, pointing at my dresser.

"Finn and I unpacked for you earlier."

"You unpacked my underwear?" she asks, raising an eyebrow at me.

"That's the funny thing," I say. "No underwear. Not a panty in sight." She shakes her head, rummaging through the drawer to double-check. "Guess you'll have to go without."

"You highjacked my panties," she says, coming over and playfully swatting me.

"No," I say, "you didn't pack any. Your subconscious must have . . ." She's laughing so loud I can't finish my thought. Pulling her and Finn into my lap, I say, "I'm really glad you're here." I give Finn a little kiss on top of his bald head. "Both of you."

"You kissed him," she whispers.

Suddenly, I wonder if that's not okay. When her eyes start to water, I know it was more than okay. "I know you're a package deal," I say, stroking her cheek. "I'm in. You and Finn don't scare me."

She nods, then quickly wipes her eyes. "I should get dressed."

They might not scare me, but it's clear that I scare Paige. She's fiercely independent and treats help like it's a trap, so I've got my work cut out for me. Good thing I've never been afraid of hard work. "I'll take Finn. Get dressed," I say, picking up Finn and getting to my feet. I head out of the room before she has time to argue with me.

CHAPTER TWENTY-FOUR

PAIGE
AGE 13

The mattress shifts under me, waking me. I don't want to open my eyes and find my mother slumped over my bed, doped up, needing my help again. Doesn't she know or care that I have school tomorrow?

I reach for my sheet, if you can even call it that. It's so thin it's basically see-through. Still, I want to cover up and roll over, giving her the message that I'm not available for her crap tonight. But my hand only finds the air. On instinct, my eyes open to search for it.

Two eyes stare back at me. Not my mother's eyes.

I dart up, knocking my head against the wall, but I don't cry out. He's just sitting there, staring at me. My mom's pimp was watching me sleep. Uncontrollably, my body starts trembling, but he just stares like he's waiting for something. I want to tell him to get out. I want to scream for my mom, but I'm frozen, staring back at him, waiting for whatever is coming.

Then, he gets to his feet without a word, picks up my sheet, lays it over me, and walks out.

My hand coils around the handle, my finger on the button. Most girls my age have stopped sleeping with their favorite teddy bear from childhood. I never had a teddy bear, but if I did, he'd have been replaced by my new security blanket—a switchblade knife.

No man will ever come in this room again uninvited. I'll be ready this time.

They say you should never bring your work home with you. My mom missed that memo. Sometimes she brings her work home with her. Sometimes her "work colleagues" have inquired if I'm part of the deal.

I stopped sleeping.

A man's voice nears my door, and I increase the pressure on the button that will pop out the blade. I've spent hours practicing how to open the blade and collapse it back down.

These men make a deal with my mother, not me. But that hasn't stopped them from making comments, undressing me with their eyes, or "accidentally" touching me. A knee to the groin or spitting in their face tends to let them know that I'm not for sale. But secretly, I wonder if my mother would allow it. I wonder if she'd even be sober enough to care.

Those men are gross, disgusting pieces of crap, but there's only one man who scares me. Her pimp.

Taking a deep breath, I hear the front door close. He's gone. I hope she is, too.

She takes me with her now, to the seedy bars, to the street corners. She dresses me up, making me look older. I'm the bait. Then we switch.

Now I have a switchblade.

I need to sleep. I never sleep.

My bedroom door doesn't have a lock. That will be my next purchase.

My stomach starts to knot. Hunger?

Probably not. My stomach grew accustomed to the pangs of hunger long ago.

Exhausted, I sit up, flicking on the lamp.

First, I feel it, then I see it. No! The bright red spot means one thing.

I'm a woman.

My period means one thing. The end of a childhood I never had—Period.

I stop at the receptionist's counter, and an elderly woman smiles at me. I've had my period for less than a day, but I know what I need to do. Or should I say what I don't need to do. Have a baby.

So while I have yet to figure the whole tampon thing out, I'm here for the birth control pill.

"Can I help you?" the receptionist with the friendly face asks.

Clearing my throat, I say, "I'm here for . . . the pill."

She looks up at me, her face now looking more judgy than friendly. "How old are you?"

"Thirteen," I say, cocking my chin up.

She can look at me like I'm trash all she wants. This is what responsible looks like. I don't expect her to understand.

"Since you are under the age of sixteen, you need to have a parent with you," she says.

My eyes start to well up. She stands up, reaching out to me, but I step back. "Why don't we get someone for you to talk to?"

"No," I snap, knowing that no one will understand. No one can help. "Please. I'm sixteen. I am."

She shakes her head. "I need proof of age."

Three years? Can my switchblade hold him off that long? As tears stream down my face, I run out the door. The receptionist cries for me to stop, but I just run—down the sidewalk, dodging people, not caring who yells at me. No one's ever cared about me before. Why care now? Because my fit doesn't suit them.

I run until my legs feel heavy, my chest is heaving, and my soul is screaming for me to stop. There's no escape, anyway.

CHAPTER TWENTY-FIVE

SLADE

"Where should I take your mommy?" I ask Finn, sitting on my lap in front of my computer.

Paige and I went from denying our feelings, our pent-up sexual tension, to her moving in with me in one swoop. I'm not complaining, but there are milestones you don't want to jump over—like the first date.

We've never had one. I'm not going to miss that, not going to let Paige miss that. So Finn and I are planning the perfect first date, and it's not going to be line dancing at one of the local honky-tonks on Broadway. We can ride horses anytime, so that's out. We cook together at home all the time. A romantic dinner? Is that out of style?

"What do you think, buddy?"

He starts banging on my desk. "Dadadadadada."

What did he just say? I'm not sure if I'm more shocked that he said something other than gibberish or what he said. Picking him up, I turn him around, sitting him on my desk so I can look at his face. "Finn?"

"Dadadadadada."

"Holy shit!"

Louder this time. "Dadadadadada."

"Shh!" I say, looking back over my shoulder at the doorway.

This time he fucking screams it. Clearly, this kid is mocking me.

"Mama," I say.

Blank stare.

"Ma Ma," I say again, making sure to stretch out the syllables.

Drool starts down his chin. Wiping it, I repeat, "Ma Ma."

There is no way in hell this kid's first word should be Dada. Plus, Paige missed it. The best course of action is deniability. "This never happened," I say to him. "Got it?"

"What never happened?" Paige asks from the doorway. "What are you boys up to?"

I give Finn a warning look before picking him up. "Just swearing him to secrecy about where I plan to take you for our first date."

The look in her eye tells me she doesn't totally buy that. Finn yawns, sticking his hand in his mouth, and rests his head on my shoulder. "Like dinner and a movie?" she asks.

"Well, I was thinking of something a little more . . ."

"I'd really love dinner and a movie," she says, wrapping her arms around me. "I can't remember the last time I saw a movie at the theater."

I should've known I was overthinking it. Paige appreciates simple things. "In that case, I'll get you the big bucket of popcorn."

Leaning up on her tiptoes, she presses her lips to mine softly. "That sounds really nice," she whispers. I love Finn, but I can't wait for him to go to sleep.

"Dadadadadada."

"Oh my God," Paige cries, leaping from my arms. "Finn talked. Did you hear that?"

This is the exact reason I didn't tell her before. I wanted her to have this moment. She's missed so much in her life. I didn't want her to realize she'd missed something else.

Finn starts clapping. "Dadadadadada."

It's not until this second time that it dawns on Paige what he's saying. Her eyes wide, she studies my face for a reaction. All she's going to get is a smile. "At this age, he doesn't really know what he's saying. It's not like he's identifying you as his father. Besides, D is one of the easier sounds to make," she says. "That's why babies always say Dada first. I read a whole article about it. It's in all the baby books. It doesn't mean anything."

She continues to give me a dissertation on the anatomy of the mouth, tongue position, the importance of teeth in developing language. Playfully, I whisper to Finn, "She's jealous you didn't say Mommy."

"No, I'm . . ." She takes his little hand and kisses it. "We don't need to encourage this," she says with quiet determination.

I hand him to her. "Do you not want him to call me Daddy?"

Her forehead wrinkles up. "Do you want him to?"

"What do kids usually call the man who loves their mother?" I ask.

One hand flies over her mouth, her head is shaking a little. If she wasn't holding Finn, I think she'd collapse. "You can't love me," she says, the disbelief in her voice as real as the floor under her feet. "No one loves me."

I've never seen her so shaken before. Not even during the tornado. "Finn loves you," I say, trying to calm her.

"I guess, but he doesn't say it."

I take a step back, reality hitting me hard. "No one's ever told you they loved you." It's not a question because I know the answer. Fuck me. Even my fucked-up father has said those words to me, and in his own screwed-up way, I know he does.

Taking Finn from her, I place him on the floor and hand him my keys and phone. There aren't any toys around. I take both of Paige's hands in mine and sit down on the sofa in my office. "Paige," I say, but she barely looks at me. It's as if I've shaken her to the core. Maybe that's what's happened. We each have core beliefs about the world and ourselves. Maybe one of hers is that she's unlovable. If you've spent your whole life with no one caring for you, showing you love, or saying those words to you, it's not hard to imagine that you'd start to believe something about you is inherently unlovable or undeserving of love.

Briefly, I glance at Finn, then back to Paige. "Look at me." She can't look in my eyes for more than a second, searching the ground like she's trying to steady herself. "I want Finn to call me Daddy." I hope she can hear how sure I am about this. I have no reservations about her or Finn. None.

That does it. Her eyes find mine. "I love you, Paige." She looks so confused, like I'm speaking Chinese to her. "I love you."

"I'm sure you've loved a lot of women," she says, letting go of my hands.

I grab them back. "I've never said those words to a woman except my mother," I say. "I love you. You are the only woman I've ever loved."

"But I'm so . . ."

"Beautiful," I say. "Yeah, I do love that about you."

"Slade," she says, cracking a smile.

"And sexy."

This time, she swats my shoulder. "I am not."

"Those knee socks you wear to bed drive me crazy." She starts laughing, and I capture her in my arms. "And stubborn. God, you are so strong-willed."

"You hate that about me," she says, looking up at me.

"You're wrong. It drives me fucking crazy, but I love how you aren't afraid of anything. How you take care of Finn, of me. Hell, of my damn horses. I love how strong you are." She looks into my eyes.

"I don't deserve your love," she sobs quietly. "There are things. Things you don't know."

"Tell me."

"I can't," she says, falling apart, and I pull her into my arms.

Of course, I want to know everything about her, but I also know what I feel. "It doesn't matter," I say. "Because nothing will change how I feel about you." She looks up at me, her face wet with tears. I can tell she doesn't believe that, but I can also tell that she wants to believe. Taking a deep breath, I know I'm about to risk it all. "Do you love me, Paige?" Her mouth opens, but I stop her. "Before you answer that. I need to tell you something."

"Okay," she says.

My chest suddenly feels tight, the secrets I've held bursting at the seams to get out. "Maybe you should put Finn to sleep first," I say. "He shouldn't hear this."

I know he's only six months old and can't comprehend what I'm about to tell Paige, but he can pick up on our emotions; therefore, it's best done out of his presence. For once, she doesn't argue, picking up Finn and taking him to his room.

As soon as she leaves, my mind begins creating scenarios of how to get out of this. I opened this bag of worms. I know Paige has her own secrets, and that's why she's never pressed me for mine. It's an unspoken agreement between us, but I just volunteered to tell her the worst of it. The worst thing I've ever done.

Opening a closet door, I reach for the portrait of my mother and me that Paige saved from the house. This picture hung in my room for as long as I can remember. On the day of her funeral, my father took it down and threw it in the garbage. I snuck out in the middle of the night to rescue it. It's been hidden in some part of every house I've lived in since then.

Hidden.

Holding my shame.

"You saved it?" Paige asks, stepping inside the office.

"*You* saved it," I say, not turning around to look at her.

"Your mom was beautiful," she says.

"My dad always used to say he had no idea how he got so lucky to be the man who got to walk into the room with her. Swore he married up." I turn and look at Paige. "He loved her. I wish you would've known him then. God, how much they loved each other. They used to embarrass me all the time. It wasn't even on purpose. I'd score a goal in soccer, and they'd kiss. They thought nothing of it."

"Sounds nice."

"It was," I say. "And my dad and I were close. We did all kinds of things together—sporting events, concerts, trips."

"What changed?"

"My mom died," I say. "She was the glue. He didn't know how to be that guy without her."

"How'd she die?" Paige asks.

"One night, my dad picked me up to go to a concert. I had just turned fifteen. We were running late. So I just ran out of the house and hopped in his car. He didn't even come inside. While we were gone, someone broke in. The police think it was a robbery attempt. They killed my mom."

I'm not lying to her, but I'm not telling her everything either. The truth is funny that way. It has many versions. But this is the only way I can tell her the truth, bit by bit. If I tried to tell the whole story all at once, I'd choke on the words, the guilt.

"Slade, I'm so sorry. I had no idea," Paige says, wrapping her arms around my waist. "Did they ever find the person?" she asks. "The one who broke in?"

"No," I say.

I give her hands a pat before unwinding myself from them. "After that, my dad lost it. He never got over her. Instead, he started bringing these women home. It got really bad. It's like he was trying to replace her, but no one was ever good enough. Eventually, he started keeping a woman set up in a condo for a while until he got sick of her or she disappointed him in some way, then he'd just find another. Loving my mom, then losing her, destroyed him. I never wanted to love someone so much it could destroy me like it did him. I didn't want that responsibility." I look into her deep blue eyes. "Now I do." She reaches her hand out to me, and I gently take it. "When you love someone, you're supposed to protect them."

"But you were just a teenager. You weren't even home, and you couldn't have saved your mom," she says.

"The alarm," I say softly.

She turns and looks toward the wall. "We'll arm it before we go to bed."

"No," I whisper. "I ran out of the house that night and didn't turn it on." I see the pieces clicking together in her mind—my reminders to her about the alarm, the detail in which I taught her how to use it.

"Oh, Slade, you have to know . . ."

"My dad used to remind me about it all the time. When I came in after being out with friends or something. He'd always remind me to arm it." A confession only works if you tell the whole truth. I look over at the picture of my mom and me, silently apologizing to her like I have so many times. "That night, my dad asked if I turned it on when I got in the car, and I lied and said yes."

Reaching up, she takes my face in her hands. "You don't know if having the alarm on would've made a difference or not."

She hasn't said it, but she must love me. This is how I know. When you love someone, you believe the best about them, not the worst. You give them a pass. You can always tell when a relationship is going south because you are all too happy to believe the worst about the other person. Clearly, Paige is in the *love is blind* stage.

Yanking my head back, I say, "The police said my mom probably surprised them. They panicked and killed her."

"Even they don't know that for sure," Paige says.

"My dad made it very clear that it was my fault," I say, leaving out the slap across the face that accompanied that verbal lashing.

"He said that? He actually said that your mother's death was your fault?"

A simple nod answers her question.

"I'm sure he didn't mean it. He was out of his mind with grief."

"That wasn't the only time he said it," I say. "And it doesn't matter how many times he said it or not. It was my fault. I knew to arm the alarm. I could've told my dad I forgot and gone back inside. Hell, I could've called my mom and told her I forgot to set it and asked her to do it. But I didn't do any of those things, and she's dead."

"I'm glad you told me."

"I've never told anyone that story, but I wanted you to know." She inches closer to me, holding my eyes to hers. "When we first met, you asked me why I cared. Why I got you away from my dad, gave you a job?"

"I remember."

"You remind me of her," I say, shaking my head, thinking how totally fucked up that sounds. "Not that you look alike or anything, but she was strong and didn't take shit from anyone. I don't know why exactly, but you just made me think of her, and I had this overwhelming need to protect you."

"And ultimately drive through a tornado to get to me," she says, shaking her head a little and smiling at the same time.

"I love you."

I watch my words sink into her skin like water into a sponge, taking them in, not squeezing them out, fighting.

"I wanted you to know exactly who I am. Why I fought this for so long. It wasn't about you. It was about me, my shit."

"You were scared," she whispers. "Scared to love someone so much."

I hate admitting that. I pride myself on not operating out of a place of fear, but the truth is, that's how I've operated in my personal life. Paige and I have that in common. "It's not perfect . . ."

"Nothing is perfect. Not even love," she says, a hint of a smile playing on her lips. "Ask me. Ask me again if I love you."

I already know the answer. A bigger question pops into my mind.

"Marry me?"

CHAPTER TWENTY-SIX

SLADE

"Are you insane?" she asks.

Not exactly the response I thought I'd get when proposing marriage. "For wanting to marry you?" I ask with a big ass grin.

"For wanting to marry me *now!*" she cries, lightly pushing on my shoulder. "I'm twenty-one."

"I'm thirty."

"I have a baby to raise," she says.

"I've met Finn."

"As you pointed out earlier, we haven't even gone on our first date."

"We'll have one before the wedding," I counter.

"I haven't even told you I love you."

"You do."

"Maybe I should rethink that," she says through a smile.

"Tell me why we shouldn't get married?" I ask.

"I have been," she says. "Have you not been listening to me?"

"Those were reasons?" I ask with a grin. "Any other so-called reasons?"

"I'm sure there are."

"Like?" I ask.

"Like we haven't known each other that long," she says.

"Long enough."

"We've barely just got together," she says.

"I've been committed since day one," I say.

"I seem to recall a cake-eating bimbo that indicates differently."

Not much I can say to that. "I'll never hurt you again, not on purpose."

"Slade," she says, her voice soft—an apology for bringing it all back up. She knows I never touched that woman. She knows I was just trying to push her away. She knows how sorry I am.

"Are you saying no?" I ask.

"I'm saying it's too fast. It's too soon. There are things you don't know about . . ."

"Like what?" I challenge her. I know she's keeping some shit from me and am more than curious if she'll tell me. No matter what it is, it wouldn't change my mind. When you know, you know. Why wait?

"Like. . ." She struggles for words, her arms flying around, searching for something to say. "Like how I am in bed. We haven't even slept together. What if we don't have chemistry?"

"We can figure that out right now. The bedroom's upstairs," I say. "Hell, there's a sofa. A desk. The floor would work." Her eyes roll as she laughs at me. "Seriously, that's not what you're really concerned about."

She wraps her arms around my waist. "You told me you'd give me what I need."

Crap, I hate it when my words come back to bite me in the ass.

"And I need us to go slow."

I can't deny her, and she knows it. Reluctantly, I say, "Okay."

"Promise you'll ask me again sometime," she says.

"I will, and I'll do the whole down on one knee, big diamond thing. The whole bit."

Laying her head on my shoulder, she whispers, "I love you."

CHAPTER TWENTY-SEVEN

PAIGE

Twelve ninety-nine times seven?

Quickly, I do the math in my head. That's going to be a hundred bucks with tax. My heart rate spikes. I should've said something when Slade suggested the mall to shop for Finn. I should've told him to go to a discount store or consignment shop—the places I normally shop. But for Slade, the mall is probably slumming it.

Looking down at the stack of baby boy pajamas in my hand, I have to admit they are cute, but Finn doesn't need seven pairs of pajamas. Of course, Slade's logic is with seven pairs, I won't have to do laundry as much. His other argument is that Finn is messy, and it's always good to have extra. That makes total sense, and honestly, I can't believe a man who was a committed bachelor up until a few days ago has eased into the whole family thing so well.

Marriage? He proposed marriage.

As if declaring his love for me wasn't enough, he upped the stakes and asked me to marry him. I knew he was a driven man, ambitious as the day is long. You don't have his kind of success at thirty without having those things. I didn't think drive and ambition had anything to do with love, but apparently, for Slade, they do. Like most men, he wants what he wants.

I've never even thought about getting married in any real way. I'm too young. My life was too chaotic until recently. My own mother was never even married. The concept is almost foreign to me, but the idea of it is nice. I don't believe it will ever happen, but that doesn't mean I don't like the idea of being his wife.

It's tempting to say yes and to jump headfirst, but when you're carrying what I'm carrying, you know if you jump, you'll sink and probably take those you love the most right down with you.

I look over at Slade across the store, pushing Finn in his stroller, stopping periodically to hold up some item of clothing to Finn, who apparently now has an opinion on his wardrobe. The current item under review is a baby leather bomber jacket. I really hope it's fake. I hate to think some poor animal died to make an overpriced baby jacket.

Slade holds it up so I can see. "Finn likes this one."

"Finn doesn't need a leather jacket."

"It's on sale," Slade says.

"It's on sale because no baby wears leather, and it's summer in Nashville."

Frowning, Slade hangs it back up. God, I love him. How did I let that happen? I shouldn't love him. My love will only get him hurt. As much as I know this is a bad idea, I can't stop it. It's as though Slade reached into my chest and took my heart. He didn't ask nicely. God knows he wasn't polite about it. He stole my heart before I even realized what was happening.

I doubt he'll give it back easily.

So when this goes south, and it will, I'll leave without my heart.

Slade flashes me a grin across the store, taking Finn from his stroller, picking up his little hand, and waving it at me. I wave back, giving my guys a smile. They walk toward me, Slade eyeing my arms. "That's all? I thought you needed those onesie things too?"

"This is good," I say, feeling stupid. Slade certainly pays me enough that I can shop at better places than the thrift shop, but some habits are hard to break. I learned early on that you should always save for a rainy day, always keep a little food stored behind for when there isn't any.

We trade the bundles in our arms. He gives me Finn, taking the clothes from my hand. "Think he needs to be changed," Slade says. "You need to teach me how to do that."

"You want to learn how to change dirty diapers?"

"I want to help you, so yeah."

There he goes stealing another piece of my heart. I don't think he even knows he's doing it. Grabbing the diaper bag, I head to the back of the store, toward the restroom. Finn starts crying, reaching his arms out in Slade's direction.

A boy needs his father.

And his mother.

"Shh!" I soothe Finn, wiping a few of his crocodile tears away. I swear, this boy's tears are just like his body, big and round and chubby. I wouldn't have him any other way. I love all his little rolls, and I know as soon as he starts walking, they will go away, so I'm going to enjoy them while they last.

I reach into the diaper bag and grab a wipe to clean off the changing table before laying Finn down. Better safe than sorry. Don't need him getting sick. "I'll change you quick, and we'll go right back out and see S . . ." I start to say Slade, then catch myself. Should I? I know it's what Slade wants. I can see that Finn loves him, but will this simply confuse him? I never called a man father or dad, but I promised Finn I'd give him better than what I had.

Taking a deep breath, I whisper, "Daddy."

Finn giggles, and that always makes me smile. My heart doesn't stand a chance against these two guys.

Quickly, I start to change him, thinking about how we must look to the outside world. We must look like a perfect little family. Something in my gut won't let me buy into that fairy tale, though. The secret I keep knows better.

Girls like me don't get those happy endings.

We might not get happy endings, but I can take a few good chapters, and this is a good chapter.

I snap Finn's onesie and walk back out to the store. Slade's checking out, and judging by the bags, he's added a few things. He pulls out his credit card, and I start to stop him when I see the sales lady lean over, her cleavage on full display and a smile on her face.

"Shopping for a little boy, I see," she says.

Slade nods, picking up a pair of socks next to the register, and tossing them down to buy, too. "My son."

My eyes fill up. He's the most incredible man. Why am I reluctant to let him be Finn's dad?

I was prepared to raise Finn alone. It never even occurred to me that there would be a man in the picture. Never has been before. Slade wasn't part of my plan.

Here's a little secret about being an abused or neglected child. You go one of two ways. Either you crave love, or it scares the piss out of you.

I fall in the latter category. I don't trust it.

That's the thing about the heart and soul. It remembers every hug you didn't get, every *I love you* that was never said, every smack, every hit, every bad name you've been called.

The memories of my heart are dark and lonely. My heart didn't learn the lessons of love. I'm playing catch-up with Slade, and it seems he has me on a crash course. Maybe my heart can make some new memories.

Slade's blue eyes find mine, and I head his way. He holds his hands up. "Before you get mad, there were just a few other things that . . ."

"I'm not mad," I say, kissing him softly.

Without another glance, the sales lady finishes up. We walk out of the store, Finn in his stroller and my hand in Slade's. "Thank you," I say.

He motions to the bags stuffed into the bottom of Finn's stroller. "No big deal."

"Not for the clothes," I say, then shake my head. "Of course for the clothes, but . . ." I stop, looking up at him. "For not flirting with that woman, not even glancing at her boobs, which she was shoving in your face." He starts laughing. "I also heard what you said."

"What?"

"About Finn being your son."

"It just came out."

"I know. That makes it so much more special. It's natural," I say. "Thank you for loving him."

Grabbing my ass in the middle of the mall, he says, "Now let's go buy you some panties."

A normal night for me used to involve working or worrying or a combination of both. Now things are totally different. Slade and I had dinner at home—takeout. He didn't want me to cook because, in his mind, I'm still recovering. The bruises from the storm are taking forever to go away, so they serve as a constant reminder to Slade. The only thing Slade knows how to make are big hunks of meat, so takeout was perfect.

We cleaned up, gave Finn a bath, and are now playing on the floor with him. Totally normal, totally boring, and completely perfect. I wonder how it compares to Slade's old life before Finn and me. "What were your nights like before us?" I ask, causing him to stop building his block tower for Finn to knock over.

"Are you asking me about other women?" he asks.

I wasn't. I was thinking more about parties, dinner with clients, drinks. "No."

"No?"

"I don't need to know about that," I say, though I can imagine. "I was just wondering if this feels weird to you. I doubt you were on the floor playing with toys two weeks ago."

"Toys can be fun," he says, raising an eyebrow at me.

"Is sexual innuendo your special talent?" I ask.

"One of them," he teases, and I start laughing. He's relentless. Pulling me into his arms, he says, "My nights were kind of boring. I worked late a lot and worked out. Sure, there were business things to go to. Parties, but mostly, I hate that stuff, which is why I spent most weekends at the ranch."

"I miss it," I say. "Even though I never learned to sleep out there. I miss walking to see Whiskey. The quiet."

"Me, too," he says as Finn kicks over the block tower with his foot. "When it's done, I think I'll live there permanently."

"Really?" I ask, unable to hide the happiness in my voice. "Most of your business is in the city."

"I can work remotely and commute to the office a few days a week."

"I've never seen your office," I say.

"I'll take you," he says, restacking the blocks.

"What about this place?" I ask.

"Probably sell it," he says. "There's not a lot of room for Finn to play. The ranch has more space. Kids need space."

"Kids?" I ask. "Did you say that like in the general sense, or in the you want more kids sense?"

"Um, the general sense," he says, eyeing me. "You don't want to have any more kids?"

"I haven't thought about it," I say.

"I didn't mind being an only child," he says. "Did you?"

I tell myself to lie, only the lie doesn't come fast enough. That's the thing any good liar learns first. The lie has to roll off your tongue seamlessly like the truth. Lies are like knots. They get tighter and tighter, choking you, stealing your breath. They get so tight that even Houdini couldn't escape.

"Paige?"

This is the hard part about loving someone. It makes lying harder. The second rule of any good liar: if you can't lie, dodge.

"I wouldn't rule out another baby down the road," I say, tossing him a smile. "Way down the road."

He tackles me to the ground, kissing me. "I was really hoping you'd say that."

"I know you were," I say.

Finn crawls over, tackling both of us, and Slade rolls on his back, bench pressing him in the air. "A little sister."

"Brother," I say. "No girls."

"Did your mommy not take biology? I control that," he says, continuing to lift Finn up and down.

All I can do is roll my eyes. Maybe a girl wouldn't be so bad since I'm already outnumbered. What am I thinking? If I've learned anything in my life, it's not to dream.

But Slade is a dangerous man. He makes me dream, want, wish for things that I know I can't have.

"What do you think?" he asks.

"Hmm?" I say, realizing he's continued the conversation without me.

"I asked how you'd feel about me legally adopting Finn," he says. "You know, later on, after you agree to marry me."

My heart sinks, knowing that won't ever happen. It can't. "I love the idea," I say. "But haven't we had enough serious conversations the past couple of days?"

"I guess we have," he says. "Right after you moved in, Jon told me that a baby ups the ante. He's right."

"He is," I say, "but maybe you should learn how to change Finn's diaper before you call your lawyer about adopting."

"Alright," he says, placing Finn on the ground. "Give me the crash course on diaper changing."

"Shouldn't I practice on a doll first?" Slade asks. "Jon told me in some baby class they took, they practiced putting diapers on dolls."

I'm trying so hard not to laugh. Even though I have everything lined up for him, he continues to ask me question after question. It's a diaper, not brain surgery. Still, it's sweet that he wants to get it right and do a good job.

"I don't have a doll," I say.

"One of Finn's stuffed animals?" he asks.

"Might be harder with tails," I say, a little giggle escaping.

"You find this funny?" he asks.

"A little," I say, giving him a quick peck. I want him to know he has nothing to prove to me. "This isn't a test, Slade."

"Don't pee on me," he says to Finn, starting to remove his dirty diaper.

He gets it off with no problem, then reaches for a baby wipe. "Make sure you clean everywhere," I remind him. My cell phone rings, and I reach for it.

"Don't answer that," Slade says. "I might need backup."

"You're doing great," I say, answering my phone. "Hey Catrine, anything happening on baby watch?"

She tells me she thought she felt a contraction earlier, but it turned out to just be gas. My poor friend is really starting to sound miserable. She's enormously pregnant, and summers in Tennessee can be brutal.

"Well, over here, Slade is changing his first diaper." She screeches so loud it probably wakes up Chewie, begging me to video him. "I'm not going to take a home movie," I say, causing Slade to turn around.

"Tell her she's fired!" he calls out.

"She says then Jon quits," I say, repeating Catrine's message from the other end.

Slade shakes his head, finishing up the diaper and holding up Finn for me to see. "Perfect," I mouth to him. He holds Finn's little hand up, giving him a high five.

"I promise I'll come see you soon," I tell Catrine before hanging up.

CHAPTER TWENTY-EIGHT

SLADE

I watch her put Finn to sleep. I'm supposed to be learning his routine, but I think I'm learning more about Paige than I am about Finn's bedtime ritual.

I listen to her read him a story. She doesn't choose a picture book or something with silly meaningless rhymes. She reads him the story of Paddington Bear, which isn't really about a bear at all. It's about what it's like to be without a home, the bumps and bruises life brings, and finally finding your family.

It might as well be the story of Paige the Bear.

I watch her hold him, kiss him, cuddle him, giving him all the love she wished she'd gotten. She doesn't rush the process and remains totally focused on Finn. Then her eyes close, her hand rests on his little chest, and I listen to her say a prayer—a prayer that Finn will be blessed and protected while he sleeps.

No one guarded Paige while she slept. That job is mine now.

Reaching out, I take her hand, encouraging her out Finn's bedroom door. She follows me, leaving the door cracked open. "It's my turn to put you to bed," I whisper, not caring at all that it's barely eight at night.

"You going to give me a bottle and change my diaper?" she teases.

"I was thinking more a glass of wine and . . ." I pin her to the wall with my hips. "Trust me, you'll need your panties changed when I'm through with you."

The way she's grinding into me, I'd bet her panties are already soaked. Locking eyes with her, I know this isn't it. She hasn't said a word. Her body is giving all the right signals, but the message in her eyes is very clear. Tonight is not the night.

My job as the man is not to try to convince her. My job is to respect her decision. I know how my dad treated my mom, and I know how he treated the other women. I want what he and my mom had. "What do you want?" she asks.

She's been taught it's a man's world. What the man wants, he gets, especially in the bedroom. It's past time for her to learn how a real man treats a woman. So this is her first lesson. "I want to kiss every inch of you," I whisper, leaning into her neck. "Would you like that?" She gives me a moan. "Say it," I say, my voice making it sound more like an order than I'd like.

"Kiss me," she says, her breath ragged.

I take a step back from her, my hands on the bottom of her shirt. Slowly, I lift it, the smooth skin of her flat stomach coming into view. Getting on my knees, I plant a light kiss over her belly button. She lifts the shirt over her head, finishing the job for me, her perfect, full tits before me. She gives me a coy smile at her lack of bra. Suddenly, I can't wait to find out if she's without panties as well, slipping my hands under the waistband of her shorts and yanking them down.

She stands naked before me.

"Jesus Christ, you're beautiful," I say, falling back on my heels and looking up at her. She's absolutely perfect. Her body blushes a soft pink. "Turn around."

"Slade!" she says, using my name as her protest.

Women are funny creatures. I'm about to eat her pussy, but letting me see her naked ass is an issue. "Turn," I say with a grin, motioning with my finger.

Slowly, she starts to turn, taking the opportunity to step all the way out of her shorts as she does. I grab her hips, holding her still, and gently bite the milky skin of her tight little ass.

"Ooh," she gasps, looking back over her shoulder at me.

Lightly, I give her booty a little smack. She jumps a little, turning all the way back around. I get to my feet, capturing her in my arms. She steps away from me, and for a second, I think she's about to slap me. Instead, she reaches for the bottom of my shirt, saying, "You need to catch up."

She doesn't have to ask me twice. Helping her, I remove my shirt, then toss it aside and pick her up. She laughs, wrapping her legs around me. Her tits press against my chest, and my dick throbs. As I take her down to the bed, she reaches for my cheek. "Only what you need," I whisper, reminding myself that I need to let her be in charge. "Only what you want."

Smiling, she says, "A get-to-know-you session."

"Exactly," I say, kissing her neck. "I'm going to find every spot that makes you tremble."

Her body quivers underneath my tongue. I know she wants me to hurry, but I'm going to take my time. Her body is uncharted territory that needs to be claimed. Using one hand, I pin her wrists over her head, kissing along her collarbone. Her back arches up slightly, her nipples hard and begging for me. Looking down at her naked and writhing beneath me, I know just how lucky I am.

Releasing her wrists, I lower my head to suck on her tits, gently pulling her nipple between my teeth.

"Oh!" she groans long and deep.

My planned trip farther south is temporarily halted by her moan. I certainly don't mind hanging out here for a while. Using my tongue, I circle her nipple, softly at first, working her over—kissing, biting, sucking her until she's grabbing the bedsheets, begging me to finish her.

She reaches for my hand, pushing it lower. It's not like I don't know what she wants, but I'm greedy. I pin her wrists to the bed again. "Slade," she begs, my name the only weapon she needs.

I'll give her whatever she wants.

With a growl, I give her clit one little slap, sending her flying over the edge. Her back arches, her legs kick out, and she's biting her lip so hard to keep from making a sound that I fear she'll draw blood.

Smoothing her hair, I lightly kiss her lips. Her eyes flutter open. "I didn't wake Finn that time."

"I want to hear you," I say. "We're going to have to find someone to watch Finn for a night or two."

She places her finger over my lips. "Now, I want to hear you."

Grinning, I say, "But it's still your turn."

She laughs, rolling over and playfully pinning me to the bed. It doesn't take much for me to break free, taking hold of her hips. Flat on my back, I look up at her, naked, straddling me. Her brown hair cascades down over her tits as her eyes roam down my body, her hands outlining the muscles of my chest and arms.

Sliding down my body, she slips her finger under the waistband of my pants. My body tightens at the slight touch and the promise of more. I reach for the zipper of my pants, but she beats me to it, tugging at my pants leg. I can't help but smile. There really is no sexy way to remove a man's pants while he's lying down, but Paige looks adorable trying.

Unfortunately, unlike Paige, I do have on underwear. The hint of a smile on her lips lets me know she's thinking the same thing. Sitting up, I take her in my arms, pulling her onto my lap so her legs are wrapped around me. I can feel her warmth calling me, begging me, and my resolve weakens. "Are you on the pill?"

She shifts slightly and doesn't answer, slipping her hand over my bulge. She's not even touching my skin, the fabric of my underwear between us, but my toes curl just the same. Lowering her lips to my neck, she whispers, "Just getting to know you, remember?"

Fuck. I knew that. She's not ready. Hand jobs, blow jobs, dry humping—all great. But there is something about being buried balls deep in a woman that can't be explained. Maybe it's primitive, wanting to spread our seed or something. Maybe it has to do with our desire to be in charge and take control. Whatever the reason, I want to know what it will be like to slip my dick inside her, watch her eyes close, her mouth drop open, and hear her come as I pound into her. It's not even about my own orgasm. It's about hers.

If I can't bury my dick in her, my tongue will have to do. Taking her to her back, I give her one long, slow lick. "Oh God," she moans.

"Shh," I say, blowing a little air between her legs, knowing that will only make her more crazy. Her hands fly to my hair. Hoisting her thighs onto my shoulders, I settle in, not wanting to ever leave this spot. "You taste incredible."

Lots of guys use oral sex as a warm-up. They don't actually make their women come this way. Whether that's lack of talent or sheer laziness, they don't know what they're missing. I plan on making Paige come like this every day of my fucking life.

One of the most incredible things about a woman is her ability to come multiple times. I can make her orgasm like this, and she'll still be able to come again through sex. If you give a guy head, and he gets off, he'll need a little recovery time. Hell, some guys would be out for the count.

"Slade," she moans, letting me know how good it feels.

Fuck right it does, but there's an art to this. If you're too soft, it's more like a tickle. If you're too hard, you'll hurt her. You can't just focus on her clit either. The lips are just as sensitive. And a little massage of her inner thighs never hurts.

Her muscles start to clench over and over again, a sure sign she's getting close. All I can think is no. As much as she's ready to come, I don't want this to end.

"Please don't stop doing that," she begs.

No way I can slow down now. Pushing her thighs open wider, I devour her. If this is going to be over quick, I'm going to get my fill. Her hand flies up, grabbing a pillow and biting down on it, her muffled scream the most satisfying sound on the planet.

I suck down on her, determined to take every last ounce of her pleasure. Her body writhes on the bed, her legs kick out, but I don't stop until she stops quivering beneath my mouth.

Her body falls limp, her legs collapse open. Using her inner thigh as a pillow, I stay right where I am, planting feather-light kisses around her folds, hoping for another spark.

She looks down at me with a fully satisfied smile on her pink lips. "Don't make me leave this spot," I beg in a whisper.

Arching her back in a little stretch, she moans quietly, "Okay."

And we start all over again.

"Just one more," I plead, knowing she's tired but wanting to watch her come for me one more time.

She laughs, shaking her head at me and cuddling into my side, a clear sign she's spent. We basically spent the night trading orgasms. Sex can be a lot of things—romantic, robotic, angry, slow, fast, hard, soft.

Tonight was pure fun.

Even though technically we never had sex, it was still the best night I've ever spent in bed with a woman.

"I think I can get used to this eight o'clock bedtime thing," I say, squeezing her tighter and listening to her drift off to sleep.

CHAPTER TWENTY-NINE

SLADE

I wake up to the smell of bacon. A satisfied Paige equals bacon for breakfast. That's good to know. Throwing on some sweatpants, I walk downstairs, finding Paige at the stove and Finn on a blanket on the floor. Definitely need to get him a new high chair.

"Morning," I say, kissing Paige on the cheek, then picking up Finn. "I must've done something right if I'm getting bacon for breakfast."

She flashes me a look over her shoulder. "Several somethings right," she teases as she walks over and puts two plates down, one for each of us. I don't want her to think she has to cook for me. "Looks good. Tomorrow, breakfast is on me."

"I like cooking," she says, smiling at me.

Adjusting Finn so he can't reach my plate, I take a bite of toast. It's just a simple meal of toast, bacon, and eggs, but Paige is a good cook. Paige reaches for her orange juice, and our brief conversation from last night flashes in my head. "You never answered my question last night."

"What question?" she asks.

"The pill? Are you on it?" No man likes to wear condoms even though I always do, so I'm really hoping I won't have to with Paige. "I figured with Finn and all, you'd be extra careful."

"I am," she says quietly, getting up from her chair even though she's barely had two bites.

For some reason unknown to me, I've struck a chord with her. I know birth control can be a tricky topic sometimes, but this is more than that.

"I should get Finn his applesauce," she says.

"He's fine," I say. "You've never told me much of anything about his birth or your pregnancy. How you found out?"

"Slade." She says my name like a warning, like I'm about to step on a landmine.

"I thought most women like to talk about that stuff. God knows, Catrine has told me about everything from her hemorrhoids to accidentally peeing on herself."

She sits back down, taking Finn from me. "He was actually born almost three weeks early."

"Catrine says first babies are usually late," I say.

"Not Finn," she says.

"Were you scared? Alone?" I ask, more than curious about his father since Paige hasn't uttered one word about him.

"Finn was a home birth," she says.

"You didn't go to the fucking hospital?" I bark, not meaning to sound as pissed as I am. She or Finn could've needed a doctor.

Her head shakes. "No hospital."

"Anyone with you?" I ask, my fishing expedition in full force.

"My mom," she says, looking down at her hands.

"I thought you said . . ."

"Slade," she says, getting to her feet. "Please don't make me lie to you."

Asking Paige a question should not back her into a corner so far that she feels like she has to lie to me.

I'm in a tough spot here. I know if I push, I run the risk of losing her. But I'm not a pushover, and I hate the idea of her keeping things from me. I told her things that I've never told anyone. Shouldn't she want to do the same? I want her to trust me enough to be able to tell me anything. I know trust is earned and takes time, and things between us have moved quickly, but my gut tells me something else is going on with her.

She comes downstairs dressed and ready to go to the ranch. I'm supposed to be staying in the city, going to my office. This is supposed to be our mutual introduction to our new schedule, but we need to get a few things straight first.

Without so much as a glance my way, she starts to buckle Finn in his car seat. "I don't want to talk about it."

"Paige!" Her name comes out harsh. "I'm not asking you to name his father. Even though I wish you'd trust me enough to tell me."

"Why do you think you have the right to know anything about Finn or me?" she snaps back.

They say some people wear their heart on their sleeve. Well, Paige wears hers on her sleeve under a coat of armor, some barbed wire, and a few explosive devices. Clearly, I've stepped on one of her trip wires. The thing is, I don't always see them or know where they are. Paige is not an easy woman to figure out. With her upbringing, I know she's kept herself guarded. I get it. But I want her to understand that she doesn't need to be that way with me.

"Because I love you both."

"So you think love gives you certain rights?" she asks, grabbing her purse and diaper bag, preparing to flee.

"Yes."

"You're unbelievable!" she barks, trying to head for the door. I block her path. Staring me down, she asks, "We haven't been together that long. You're telling me I know every detail about you? There's nothing that you're hiding, leaving out?"

Fuck, she's stubborn. I'm sure she's used to wearing people out with her defensiveness, but she's met her match with me. I'm as stubborn as they come. "I'm sure you don't know everything about me, but there's nothing I'm intentionally not telling you."

"No lies?" she asks, leaning back slightly as though she knows I'm caught.

I haven't lied to her. Oh shit, I forgot about that one little white lie. I'm completely fucked here.

My answer takes too long because she says, "That's what I thought." She opens the door, walking away then turns back. "I know about the cameras."

CHAPTER THIRTY

PAIGE
AGE 15

"Please," I hear my mom beg. "Please just give me a little."

Her bedroom door opens, her "boss" stomps toward me, my mom clinging to his shoulder. What I wouldn't give for a pair of noise-canceling headphones to block out a whole slew of noises.

"Washed-up whore," he sneers, pushing her off him.

He should know. He created her, paying her with drugs, using and abusing her. And me.

Attempting to ignore them, I stare down at my books. Honors Chemistry is not going to learn itself. These books are my way out, my path to a different life.

She tugs at his belt, saying, "Suck you off, right here."

I can feel the heat of his stare on me. "Paige, what do you think?" I don't look up. "Should I let your mom suck my cock for a few Oxy?"

My eyes land on my mother, so thin and small. She looks like she needs those pills more than she needs to breathe. And she probably does need them. To do the things she does, they are probably essential.

"Let her study," my mom whispers, and for the slightest second, I see something in her eyes. A glimmer of the woman she could've been. A speck of the mother I could've had.

"No," I say, getting out of my chair and walking over to the only parent I've ever known. Wrapping my arms around her, I say, "Mom, I can get a job on the weekends and after school. I'm old enough to help. We can get you help."

He grabs me by the elbow. "You're right. You're old enough to work." I try to yank away, but he's too strong. "For me."

"Never!" I scream, trying to tear myself away, but he punches me in the gut.

I double over, all the air in the room gone. I'm coughing and choking on my own tears. Looking up at my mom, she just stands there. His fingers stroke my face. "Pretty girl like you. Your mother, she's all washed up, but you . . . That sweet pussy of yours could make me a rich man."

"Mom," I cry.

He holds a pill out to her. Reaching for it, she looks at me and says, "Nothing less than five hundred."

My mouth falls open. "Mom, please," I beg, but he's dragging me toward my bedroom.

I scream and start to kick and hit, my arms flailing around like a wild animal. He lands a hard backhand to the side of my face, then another and another. I fall to the floor, and he kicks my back, his boot sinking deeper and deeper with each contact.

He leans down, pulling me up into his arms. "I can be rough if you want."

"Don't, please." Tears run down my face. "Please."

He exhales, and for half a second, I think maybe he has one decent bone in his body, but then he takes hold of my shoulders and tosses me down on the bed like a rag doll.

My head starts to spin. His body is over mine. His fingers go through my hair, and my body shudders. "Open your mouth." I shake my head, pursing my lips closed. He chuckles, holding up a pill. "This will help you relax."

Suddenly, I realize I'm about to become my mother. I don't know how she became the woman she is, but it could have easily been just like this.

"No," I whisper, slipping my hand under my pillow.

With one hand, he grabs my wrists, pinning me down. His other hand reaches under my shirt. I feel myself starting to slip away, drifting up out of my body, like I'm watching a horrible movie, like I'm not the star of this tragedy.

He pulls me to his mouth, his tongue invading my mouth, rough and hard. I'm not going to win a fight. I can't overpower him. But if there's one thing my mother has taught me, it's how to manipulate a man.

Closing my eyes tightly, I move my tongue with his. Am I doing this right? He moans. Guess I am.

He grinds into me, the length of him between my legs. My instinct is to fight, but instead, I moan, my hand slipping back under my pillow.

"Horny little bitch, aren't you?" he asks, smiling down at me.

In one smooth motion, I push the button on the blade and hold it against his dick, that one little pierce causing it to deflate.

His eyes flare, but he holds his hands up. We both know he could probably get this knife from me, but he's not going to risk his balls over it.

CHAPTER THIRTY-ONE

PAIGE

I take Finn's little finger, tracing the raindrops rolling down the window of the trailer. Of all the crappy places I lived as a child, I never lived in a trailer park. Sometimes, I wish we did, envying those double-wides. They can be very nice.

I used to love this game as a child. Never having many toys, I always loved it when it rained. Rain meant mud puddles, splashing, and hopefully, rainbows. I never did any sports teams, not that we could've afforded it, plus I was more of a loner, preferring the library to the baseball field. Now the rain means I'm stuck inside with Finn, who's not yet old enough to play outside in the rain. So I share my favorite rainy-day indoor activity with him.

Raindrop chase.

Basically, you just trace the path of the raindrop as it twists and turns down the window. You can get really creative and use two fingers, racing to see which raindrop makes it to the bottom faster.

Finn smiles up at me, and I kiss his little finger. My new office stinks. Basically, it's a trailer with a desk, a chair, some file cabinets, and a playpen and play area for Finn. There's a little bathroom, but that's it. I shouldn't complain because it's actually not that bad. I'm just in a bad mood.

My argument with Slade this morning set the tone for the whole day. He's obviously still pissed, too, because I haven't heard from him all day—not one email, text, or phone call. That's not like him. Well, actually, it is kind of like him, but I thought boyfriend Slade would be different.

It's not him I'm even mad at. I'm mad at myself. I'm not even mad about the cameras in the house, yet I used that as ammunition against him, making him out to be a liar, scapegoating him to take the heat off myself. Deflection is one of my strengths. Some would call it a character flaw, but I call it a means of survival.

I'm the real liar here. We both know it. How long before he gets sick of it and starts demanding answers?

The thing is, I have answers. They differ from the truth, but I still have them prepared. Any good liar has to have a story, something plausible, believable, something you say with a smile to shut people up, to diminish suspicion. I have my story. I have the story of Finn's birth, his father, my pregnancy. I have the whole thing, but when push came to shove, I didn't want to look into Slade's blue eyes and lie.

I begged him not to make me.

But he couldn't let it go.

The truth is not an option. I wish he could understand that.

"Come on, Finn, let's go home," I say. No work is getting done on the house in this weather, no deliveries are being made. I can't even walk to see the horses, so there's no use in staying except to use the trailer as a hideout, and I've already been doing that most of the day.

Gathering my stuff, I wait a few minutes for a break in the rain. I don't even have an umbrella to shield us, so we just have to face the storm. Sometimes life is poetic like that. I fear the time is coming when I'm going to have to face my own personal storm, and this one is going to make the tornado look like a cakewalk.

I open the door of the trailer, finding Jon pulling up in Slade's SUV. Forgetting about the rain, I rush out to meet him. "Is Catrine alright?" I ask right as he opens his door.

"She's fine," he says, motioning with his hand. "Get in. Get in."

Finn and I rush into the back seat, where a new car seat has been installed. My heart immediately melts. Slade bought his own car seat for his car. I've been transferring mine whenever we needed to. God, that man is the best. I don't deserve him. And for the life of me, I can't figure out why he keeps putting up with me. No one ever has before.

"Slade sent me to pick you up," Jon says, starting the car. "He was worried about you driving in the rain."

Of course he was.

He doesn't call me all day but sends a chaperone for me. Was he worried I wouldn't come home if he didn't? "What about my car?" I ask.

"He'll send someone to come get it."

"He shouldn't have sent you," I say. "What if Catrine goes into labor?"

"She practically kicked me out of the house when he called. I think I'm getting on her nerves."

Laughing, I say, "I'll come see her soon." He smiles at me in the rearview mirror. "Pull over, please. I want to hop in the front seat. I hate sitting back here. Feels like you're my chauffeur or something."

He pulls to the side, and I quickly make the transfer to the front seat, shivering from the rain. He points at a button for me to turn on the heated seats, and we start moving again.

"Don't you get sick of Slade making you do this kind of thing?" I ask. "What's your job title, anyway?"

Jon looks over at me, grinning. I can't believe I ever thought of him as a goon. He's more like a teddy bear. "Vice president."

"You're VP of Slade's company, but you drive me around?"

"Yep," he says. "There are certain things that Slade only trusts me to handle. Those things include you and Finn." Lightly, he touches my arm. "You think he'd trust anyone to drive you? Could you imagine his reaction if he ever saw you in a taxi? The man would lose his shit. I'm the same way about Catrine. Slade and I understand each other."

"But Slade could do those things himself. He could've come and gotten me today."

Jon raises an eyebrow. "Would you have gotten in the car with him as easily as you did with me, or would you have argued with him about it?"

My smile is all the answer he needs. I look back over my shoulder, seeing Finn's little head resting to the side, a sign he's fallen asleep. "How long have you and Slade known each other?" I ask, realizing it's my chance to pick Jon's brain. Catrine said Jon is the only person who really knows Slade.

"Since we were teenagers. He's like my brother."

I angle my legs to the side, facing him in the car.

"Oh no!" he says. "I recognize that posture. That's the girl talk pose. You're settling in for a long talk."

I just raise my eyebrows at him, and in a sing-song voice, I say, "So tell me. How'd you meet?"

He chuckles. "It's a long story."

"It's a long drive." It's actually not that long, about an hour from the ranch to the city, but long enough to pry.

He glances out the side window of the car like he's traveling back in time to that moment. "Did Catrine ever tell you about my baby brother?"

"No."

He looks back at Finn through the rearview mirror. "He died when he was six."

"Jon," I say, instinctively reaching for his hand. He squeezes mine, not letting go. "I'm sorry. We don't have to talk about this."

"You asked how I met Slade," he says. "Do you know the Natchez Trace Parkway Bridge?

"Isn't that out toward Franklin?" I ask. I actually heard about the bridge on the news a few months back. It's long been known for suicides, so much so that they've recently installed two emergency phones there that are linked to 911 and the crisis hotline.

"Kind of," he says. "When I was sixteen, I was babysitting my little brother. My mom and dad were at some parents' night for my high school. We were watching movies and eating trash Mom wouldn't normally let us eat. Typical brother stuff."

"Sweet."

He tightens his hold on my hand. "We were laughing, and I don't know what happened. He just started choking. One minute, he was fine, and the next, he couldn't breathe."

"Oh God." I know that fear well. Anyone who lives with a small child knows it.

"I tried to help him. Call 911, but it was too late."

"Jon, that was a horrible accident. I'm sure you did everything you could."

"I'm okay," he says, patting my hand. "It's taken a long time and a lot of love from my parents, Catrine, and Slade."

"Slade?"

He glances over at me, holding my eyes. "I met Slade at the top of that bridge."

He doesn't say it, but I know why he was there.

"What was Slade doing there?" I ask, although I already know. I can't imagine Slade on that bridge. He's such a big guy, strong, stubborn, and fills up a room like no man I've ever met. I know what drove him there. We might have grown up in different worlds, but we both had crappy childhoods. I don't know if he was serious about his intentions that night. But I know his pain.

"Good question," he says, giving me a sad smile. "He never told me why he was there that night. We've never discussed it. I'm sure if I asked, he'd tell me he was just passing by and saw me."

I look down. I'd just assumed Jon knew about Slade's mother. I'm the only person Slade's ever talked to about all that, and I'm keeping so much from him.

"How'd he convince you not to do it?" I ask quietly.

Grinning, he shakes his head. "You have to remember, we were teenage boys."

"So what did he say?"

"It's what he didn't say," Jon says. "He didn't ask why I was there. He didn't ask what was wrong. He didn't tell me it couldn't be that bad or how much I'd be missed. All the things you think you'd say. Slade didn't do any of that. Instead, he walked up, like seeing me on the ledge was absolutely normal, and asked me for directions."

"You're kidding?" I say with a half chuckle.

Jon laughs. "Nope. That was his big ice breaker."

"What did you say?" I ask.

"I don't even remember," he says. "But we spent the rest of the night sitting in the middle of that bridge, just talking about my brother, about nothing, about everything." He looks over at me. "I owe him my life—literally," he says.

"He's a good man," I say.

"The best," he says. "Saved my life that night. Became my best friend. Ultimately, became my boss. Hell, he's even the one who introduced me to Catrine. Everything I have is because of Slade and what he did that night. So if he needs me to escort some woman out of a party or drive you somewhere, then I do it. No questions asked."

"I'm glad he was there that night," I say, knowing Jon's presence there that night probably saved Slade too.

Jon releases my hand, looking over at me. "If you let him, he'll pull you down off that ledge too."

CHAPTER THIRTY-TWO

SLADE

Paige Hudson, Nashville is typed into my search engine.

Nothing on my Paige.

Paige Hudson, Tennessee.

More empty results.

Paige Hudson, Facebook.

Same results.

The more I try, the more I realize how little I actually know about her. I don't know where she went to high school or where she briefly attended college. Her name and birthdate are the only two pieces of substantial information I have on her, other than her address, which is the same as mine.

I have her former home address, and I'm sure I have her social security number on the employment and insurance forms I made her fill out, but nothing that tells me who she really is.

Pushing my chair back from my desk, I stare out my office window, the lights of Nashville turning on for the evening. My offices sit on the thirtieth floor. From this chair, I can see the Cumberland River snaking its way along downtown Nashville with Nissan Stadium in the background. Not far from here, the bars and honky-tonks of Broadway are filled with college students from Vanderbilt, locals, and tourists ready for a good time. And the smell of Tennessee barbecue fills the streets. Somewhere on those streets below, people are hooking up, breaking up, and falling in love. I wonder how many of them have Googled their partners?

You don't own your own business these days without having the ability to run a background check on your employees. It's a pretty common practice, although I never did one on Paige. Considering what I thought was her profession when we met, I probably should have. But seeing her with Finn, how much she loved him, and the conditions they were living in, I knew she was a good person.

One email to the right person, and I could have all the information on her I want. It's tempting, but I won't do it. Searching for someone on social media is far different than doing a full-scale background check. I know Paige would never forgive me for something like that.

Even if Paige never found out, I don't want to learn things about her that way. I want her to tell me. I'll be damned if my imagination isn't getting the better of me. I keep thinking Finn's father abused her or raped her, and she's on the run from him.

I just don't know why she wouldn't trust me enough to tell me that. I could help her.

"Something interesting out there?" Paige says from behind me.

Swiveling around in my chair, I see her leaning against my doorway, her hair a little messy from the rain, her jeans and T-shirt slightly wet. God, she's beautiful. What could be so terrible that she can't tell me? She let me think she was a "working girl." She let me think she was with my dad. She told me about how she grew up. What is worse than all that?

"Jon gave me his key card to get in," she says softly. "I hope that is okay."

"Where's Finn?" I ask, standing up but not going to her.

"He fell asleep on the car ride back from the ranch. Jon's circling the block with him. I wanted to see you."

I toss my phone down on my desk. "I have a security app on my phone. You can check it. You'll see I've logged in twice since I've known you. The first night I hired you and . . ."

"I don't need to check some app," she says, stepping closer. "I'm sorry."

I take a deep breath, almost wishing I could be mad at her. Turning my laptop toward her, I say, "And just so you know, I was Googling you."

"Don't think I have much of a footprint in cyberspace," she says.

"That by design?" I ask.

All I get is a shrug.

"You have to tell me something. Let me in. At least a little bit," I say.

"I have," she says.

"You have to give me something more, Paige."

"I'm giving you my love," she says, stepping closer to me, her eyes welling up. "My body, Finn. Can that be enough?"

If anyone knows how hard it is to let someone love you after you've been through hell, it's me, but I'm greedy when it comes to Paige. I want all of her—now.

She clears her throat, sucking back in all her emotions. Her posture straightens, and she looks me right in the eye, asking, "Do you want me to go?"

What the hell kind of question is that? She honestly doesn't seem to know what it means to have someone love you. Love sticks, and it doesn't go away the first time the person pisses you off. I know that better than anyone. No matter the terrible things my father did, I've always loved him, despite himself and despite the fact that I don't want to.

"Don't ever ask me that question again," I say, taking her hand. "The answer will always be the same."

Looking down at our joined hands, she says, "I wasn't mad about the security cameras."

"Could have fooled me," I tease, pushing her hair off her face.

She takes a huge breath. "Even though I was taken from my mom when I was a teenager, I still snuck out and visited her, took her food or money if I had any. She wasn't a great mom, but she still was my mom. She was the only family I had. No matter how terrible things were." She looks up at me. "Does that make sense?"

Love sticks.

Even if it shouldn't, love sticks. Even if the person neglected or abused you, love is hard to walk away from, especially between a mother and her child. Nodding, I say, "So you stayed in touch even after she lost custody of you?"

"On and off. I'd try to stay away, but something would always pull me back."

"Like Finn," I say. She nods. Even though there's a shit ton more I want to know, I realize this is how I'm going to have to get to know Paige—in bits and pieces, like a trail of breadcrumbs that hopefully leads me to the whole story.

These are the broken, beautiful bits and pieces that make up the woman I love.

"Did you ever talk to anyone? Get counseling? You went through hell."

"When I was in college, they had free services, so I went. It helped. But there's a bond between a mother and child that's hard to break."

I know that better than anyone. "Anything else?" I ask, hoping to gather another piece of her.

"Eloise," she says, cracking a smile. "My middle name is Eloise."

Paige is out like a light. For someone who struggled with insomnia at the ranch, she sure is making up for it now. I wish the same was true for Finn. I've heard him over the monitor twice already tonight, and it's only one in the morning. It's not like him to be so fussy. Paige got up with him the first time, so I guess it's my turn. She didn't say that, but it only seems fair.

Stumbling through the darkness, I push open the door to his room. He's sitting up, wailing. "What's wrong, buddy?" As soon as I reach for him, I feel it. I can feel the heat radiating off him before I even touch him. He's burning up. "Paige!" I yell. I've gotten good at feeding Finn, playing, even changing diapers isn't a big deal, but a sick baby is out of the realm of my wheelhouse. "Paige!" I yell again, rushing down the hallway with Finn in my arms.

Paige is already out of bed and on her feet. "What is it?"

Handing her to him, I say, "He cried, so I went to get him, and he's really hot."

She rests her cheek on his forehead. "I don't have a thermometer here. I forgot to pack it. It's still at the ranch."

"Can you give him some medicine?" I ask. "Do you have anything?"

"I do, but . . ." She feels his forehead again, this time with the inside of her wrist. "I think we need to go to the emergency room."

Paige grabs the diaper bag, not even bothering to get herself dressed. She just throws on some shoes. We're out the door in under two minutes flat. It's like I go on autopilot, driving toward the local children's hospital. How the hell I even knew where the children's hospital is, I have no idea.

Finn is screaming his lungs out in the back seat while Paige holds him tight, trying to soothe him. It's killing me that he's not in his car seat. Paige isn't even buckled up, but I know better than to say anything to her right now. She's in full-on momma mode.

I drive like a bat out of hell to the emergency room, pulling my car right up to the door, like my Land Rover is suddenly an ambulance. Sirens or not, this is an emergency. They can tow me. I'll pay the ticket. I don't care.

Hurrying around to the side, I help Paige and Finn out of the back seat. We hustle to the front desk, and I swear to God, every kid in Nashville is sick tonight. The place is mobbed. I'm not going to have Finn wait for medical care. I get a nurse's attention, and she comes out from behind the desk, quickly looking at Finn and listening to his chest. "He's really hot," Paige says, looking at me.

The nurse smiles at her. "I see that. Let's get you checked in, and a doctor will be with you as soon as we can."

"How long?" Paige asks. "Finn isn't a crier. Something's not right."

"Poor little guy isn't feeling well," the nurse says, motioning toward the desk to check in. "We're busy tonight, but we'll see him as soon as we can."

One look from Paige, and I can tell she's about to lose her shit on this woman. I beat her to it, though. "Now," I bark. "I want him seen now."

The whole room stops. No one moves. No one speaks. Hell, I'm not sure if anyone is even breathing. "Sir, I know you're worried, but he's crying. His airway is open. His heart and lungs sound clear. He..."

"He's in pain!" I snap. "Is that not high enough on your list of priorities?"

Paige touches my arm, her eyes flying to a security guard, whose eyes are now glued on us. The nurse raises her eyebrows at us as if to ask if we're all good, and Paige gives her a little nod. The nurse steps away while we are left with a screaming baby to wait in line.

"Fuck this," I say, pulling out my phone. "I have to know someone who works at this damn hospital and can pull some strings." My mind is racing, trying to come up with something. Between Jon and I, we know a lot of people, lawyers, police officers, congressmen, singers, but not one pediatric doctor comes to mind.

Finn lets out another deafening scream. "Slade?" Paige pleads.

A woman in front of us turns around—her child covered in vomit. "First kid?" she asks.

"Yes," Paige says.

"First is always the hardest." She leans a little closer and peeks at Finn. "He's adorable. I've got five. All boys. I'm here every other week. I've seen it all. Odds are, it's nothing serious."

"Thank you," Paige says, forcing a smile.

"These things always seem to happen in the middle of the night," the kind stranger says.

"I'll be right back," I say to Paige and step a few feet away. Close enough that I can still see her if she needs me, but far enough away that she won't know what I'm about to do. I look over at Paige, still chatting with the vomit-covered kid's mom. Somehow, she now looks calmer. This woman is an angel.

I can't remember the last time I dialed this number. The last time I asked him for anything. He answers almost immediately. For a second, I hesitate, but one more look at Paige and Finn, and the choice is clear. There really isn't a choice.

"Dad?"

I also don't remember the last time I called him that. I can hear the worried edge in his voice. "Slade? What is it?"

As quick as I can, I explain the situation. I think the whole phone call is under two minutes. Sure enough, my dad knows the head of some department here. I knew if I didn't know someone, he would. I thank him, and that's that.

Stepping back over to Paige, I rub both her and Finn's backs. A phone rings behind the desk, and the nurse's eyes fly to me. Checkmate!

Paige catches the look, too. "What did you do?" she whispers.

I just shake my head. I'll tell her later. The nurse comes over with a clipboard. "We have a room for you."

Paige's eyes fly to me. "Thank you."

"Good luck," the lady in front of us says.

"Her, too," I tell the nurse, nodding my head toward the stranger in front of us. "I'm sure you have a room for her, too."

I don't feel the least bit guilty about skipping the line and jumping ahead. Everyone else in that waiting room would've done the same thing for their own kid if they could. If it were me, I would've happily waited, but when it comes to the people I love, I don't give a damn who I cut in front of in line.

Finn lays in Paige's arms, quietly whimpering. "An ear infection," she says, shaking her head. "I can't believe it's just an ear infection." She kisses Finn's head. "I feel so stupid. The lady was right. First-timers, all the way. I totally overreacted. I've just never heard him cry like that."

"It's good we brought him," I say, rubbing the heart-covered bandage that covers the spot where they drew blood. That wasn't fun, but Paige wanted to be absolutely sure nothing else was wrong. My mom had the same tendency to worry, so I get it. The doctor appeased her, as well, pointing out that her medical degree doesn't hold a candle to a mother's intuition.

"And you?" she says, grinning. "Took the overprotective thing to a whole new level." Her smile lets me know she appreciates it, no matter how over the top I was. She reaches out for my hand, and I lean down, giving her a soft kiss. "Thank you," she says. "But how'd you pull it off? Who'd you call?"

"My dad," I say, sitting down beside them.

She sits up straighter. "You called your dad?"

"I couldn't think of anyone I knew who worked here. I knew he'd know someone who could help."

"I know that couldn't have been easy for you," she says.

"I'd do anything for you," I say, looking down at Finn. "And him."

She leans over, kissing me slowly, her soft lips parting. Her tongue meets mine, and the stress of the night falls away. Something about the way she's kissing me tells me if we weren't in an emergency room, she'd be on her back. And her rule of going slowly would be out the window. "I love you," she moans between kisses.

"Uh-hum." The nurse clears her throat as she enters the room, forcing us apart. "The doctor says you can go. Just need you to fill out the paperwork that didn't initially get filled out," she says, tossing me a look.

I take Finn as the nurse hands Paige the papers and gives her discharge instructions for Finn's medication. He's still uncomfortable, but his fever has come down some. They gave him a dose of an antibiotic and something for his fever, so hopefully, we all can get some rest when we get home.

"License and insurance card?" the nurse asks. Paige reaches into her purse, handing them to the nurse, who goes to make copies while Paige finally fills out the forms.

"Make sure to add me as an emergency contact," I say, looking down at Finn in my arms. Since I've known Paige, I've been scared out of my mind twice. First the tornado, and now this. Is love usually this damn frightening? I heard someone say once being married increases one's life expectancy—I'd need to see more research on that.

For the first time, I think about what my dad lost when he lost my mom. It would be like if I lost Paige. I can't imagine it. I can't imagine I'd respond like he did, but grief is a funny thing. I don't even want to think about what my life would look like without her and Finn in it. Not that long ago, I was happy living the single life, but now I wouldn't go back to that for anything. Even nights like this are better than the best night as a bachelor.

In some weird way, I have my dad to thank for this, for them. If it wasn't for him, I wouldn't have Paige and Finn in my life. Shit, life is strange sometimes.

The nurse comes back in, and Paige hands her the clipboard of paperwork. She hands Paige back her license and insurance card, then scans the paperwork. She holds it back out in front of Paige, pointing at a spot on the first page. "I need the baby's social security number."

Paige freezes for a second, taking Finn from me. "I don't have it with me."

"You should really keep it with you at all times," the nurse scolds. "Keep it in your contacts or something."

I get to my feet, clearly done with this woman. I know she's just doing her job, but she could do it a little more nicely. "If there's any problem filing with the insurance," I say, "you can call us for it." She gives me a half-hearted nod and leaves. Grabbing our stuff, I head toward the door. "You'd think someone who works in pediatrics would be a little nicer."

"Let's just go," Paige says, following me.

CHAPTER THIRTY-THREE

PAIGE

Finn sleeps peacefully between Slade and me. He used to sleep in bed with me a lot when he was first born, but gradually, I moved him to a crib, so we don't do this very often anymore. But this is the second time in just a few days, he's been in bed with Slade and me. The baby books debate co-sleeping, whether it's good or not. I think each baby is different. Each situation is unique. For me, there was no way my sick little guy was going to sleep anywhere else last night. I know Slade felt the same way.

Slade reaches out, caressing my cheek. "He's fine. You can sleep," he whispers.

I repeat the motion and his words back at him. "He's fine. You can sleep."

His blue eyes sparkle even though I know he's dog tired. We were up all night, and when we got home, neither one of us could sleep, keeping watch over Finn all night.

"Think I'll call in sick today," I say. "Think my boss will understand?"

Slade yawns a little. "Yeah. Your boss not only understands, but he may take a sick day, as well."

"You know you don't have to stay and watch over us," I say. "We'll be fine."

"Maybe I'll go in later for a few hours," he says, inching closer to wrap his arm around me. "But for now, I'm staying right here."

Smiling, I say, "Did I thank you for last night? You were so great. With me. With Finn. With that god-awful nurse."

"My pleasure," he says. "I love you." I can't help it, but my eyes close. "Paige, please look at me when I tell you I love you."

"I am," I lie, briefly making eye contact with him. I think most people are probably ready for love when it finds them. They've probably been searching for it. That's not me. I love Slade. I know I do. I'm ready for that, but I'm not ready for him to love me back. I want to be, but love means to trust and let the other person in. You can't be scared. You have to be brave to let someone love you. I've always considered myself brave, a fighter. I had to be, but when it comes to love—I'm a coward. I'm not ready for love.

"I love you," he says again, and I know I look away. "Why do you do that?"

"I don't want to get used to your love," I say. "I can't let myself get used to feeling like this."

"Why not?" he asks.

"Because then I'll start to rely on your love."

Leaning over, he tilts my chin up, directing my eyes to his. "Rely on my love," he says. "It's yours. Forever."

A worried Slade is adorable. I'm not sure why he bothered to go to work. He's texted and called me constantly, making sure we don't need anything. Seeing if I want him to pick up dinner. Asking if he can bring home anything special for Finn. Making me promise I'll call if Finn gets worse.

I gently remind him that it's just an ear infection and babies get them all the time. His response is that it's a first for Finn, a first for me, and a first for him, so apparently, that makes it a big deal. Clearly, I overreacted last night and freaked the man out.

Still, I can't shake this worried feeling. Finn's still cranky and clingy, but his fever is down some. I'm hoping we're on the road to recovery, but a gut feeling tells me something bad is coming.

As a kid, I got really good at anticipating bad news. My body would tense, knowing I'd need to react. I feel that way again. Maybe it's Finn, but more than likely, it's that I'm a big ole liar. Either way, I can't shake the feeling that shit is about to hit the fan.

Babies get sick. This is just a part of it, but Finn being sick must be big news because Catrine called to check on him. I guess Slade told Jon and Jon told Catrine, and our little trip to the emergency room became big news.

I don't want Catrine to worry or stress. She's about to pop any day now, and she needs to be focused on that—on happy things. I plan on going to see her tomorrow. I know Finn's not contagious, but we were in the hospital filled with germs, so no telling what he has now. I swear, if you're not sick going in, you're sick coming out. The last thing Catrine needs is to get sick, so I'm going to be extra careful.

Laying Finn down in his crib, I grab the monitor. It's a little late in the day for a nap, but I'm a firm believer that rest is the best medicine there is. So schedule or not, he's tired, and he should sleep.

I should probably take a nap myself, but I'm not the best sleeper at night. I'm an even worse napper. Walking downstairs, I collapse on the sofa, needing to catch up on a few things, but I can't help my mind from wandering to more pleasant things.

Slade's question about birth control tells me he's more than ready to take the next step. Who am I kidding? The man's been ready. But I think I finally am, too. I should've been more prepared for his question about birth control. The last thing I wanted was to bring a baby into my old life. Ironic, because now I have Finn. But I got him out. We aren't in that shitty life anymore.

I'm keeping my promise to him. And it's not that we are living in this fancy place, or can now shop at the mall. Those things do make life nice, but . . . The doorbell rings, disturbing my thoughts. Rushing to answer before it rings again and wakes Finn, I open the door without looking to see who it is.

His blue eyes look around me. "My son home?"

A visit from Slade's dad was not on my agenda today. "He went to the office for a couple of hours."

"I called him there, but they said he wasn't in." Lyle raises an eyebrow. Obviously, Slade made his secretary relay that lie. "I thought he was probably home with you and Finn."

"He's not here," I say, opening the door a little wider for him to see I'm telling the truth.

"How is Finn?" he asks. "Slade never updated me."

Sometimes, I think I'm too soft because that just made my heart hurt a tiny bit. Slade called his dad for help, then doesn't update him or let him know what's going on. He simply used him for his connections. That's cold, but I have to remember the history between them.

"It turns out, it was just an ear infection," I say. "He's asleep."

His eyes glance at the stairs. "I remember Slade's mother and I rushed him to the emergency room when he was only about a year old. He was just learning to walk. You know, unsteady. The dog ran past him and knocked him over. He got quite a bump on his head. Scared the hell out of us. Turns out, he has a really hard head," he says with a knowing smile.

Smiling back slightly, I say, "Finn's not walking yet. I'm not looking forward to it."

"When your child takes his first steps, it's this strange mix of pride and fear. I remember thinking those were his first steps away from me."

Dial another dose of sympathy right up. His blue eyes cast down. He and Slade are a lot alike. To the outside world, they both look like men not to be messed with. They carry an air of power, control, but those of us who know them, know the softer side of them—the side that's been hurt and broken. I'm much the same. I open the door wider. "Would you like to come in?"

He walks inside, but I don't close the door behind him. He looks back over his shoulder, noticing I've left it open. If he's offended, I don't care. Being in a locked room with a man I barely know isn't going to happen, Slade's father or not.

"Thank you for helping last night," I say, not taking a seat. It's strange to be in the same room with him, given how we started. Awkward doesn't begin to describe it, but I want to move past it, and he seems to want to as well.

Lyle sits down on the sofa. "It was nothing. Besides, if this thing between you and my son goes where I think it's going, Finn will be my grandchild."

Why that never occurred to me, I don't know.

He chuckles to himself. "Never thought that would happen."

"Why not?" I ask, stepping a little closer.

"Have you met my son?" he says with a grin. "He doesn't let people in. Ever since his mother died, he's been very hard to reach."

"Maybe that's because you blamed him for her death," I say with attitude.

He looks up at me. "He told you about that, huh?"

"He told me everything."

"You know, I've tried over the years to make amends with him. I've apologized to him countless times. It's no excuse, but I was out of my mind with grief. Slade won't hear any of it."

"I thought he told me everything," I say, sinking down into a chair. "But he never told me that."

"Slade's real problem isn't needing me to forgive him. It's him needing to forgive himself," Lyle says. "It was my job as his father to help him do that. I didn't do a very good job."

"He told me you two used to be close."

He clasps his hands in front of him, looking over at me. Something is different about the way he looks at me now. I can't pinpoint it. "After my wife passed. . ." Even after all this time, his voice gives when talking about her. "I was a real bastard. The things Slade saw me do. The things I said to him." He shakes his head at himself. "Eventually, I moved that out of the house, but the damage was done."

More than a little curious, I ask, "And now?"

"I like my life," he says. "My relationships are simple. I gave my heart to one woman a long time ago, and she still has it. The rest of my life is just passing the time."

I've heard and seen a lot of sad things in my life, but what he just said broke my heart. Even though his wife has been gone for years, I can feel his pain like it happened yesterday. I'm new to love, but I'm no stranger to pain. Perhaps, that's our common ground. I haven't been a fan of Lyle Turner, but maybe I need to think again. "I just realized I don't know her name. Slade's mother?"

"Juliet," he says.

"That's a beautiful name."

"She'd be so disappointed in what Slade and I have become."

I want to tell him there's still time to fix it, but I know better than anyone that things can't always be fixed. I don't think this is one of those times, though.

"You're a mother. You understand?"

"Dad?" Slade says from the doorway. I was right to keep the door open. "What are you doing here?" Slade's eyes go to me as if to ask if I'm alright.

I give him a little nod. "Your dad just stopped by to check on Finn."

"I should go," his dad says, getting to his feet. "I'm glad little Finn is feeling better."

"Thank you again for helping last night," I say.

He looks back at me, and this time I place the look in his eyes. Now he looks at me like a father looks at a daughter. Growing up, I never had that. It's slightly uncomfortable to have it now, especially considering this man once had his hand on my ass. If my relationship with Slade is going to last, we need to fix this family stuff. A relationship doesn't happen in a bubble. It includes the people around them, their family.

"Maybe next time, Finn can thank you himself," I say as Slade's head whips around. "He's pretty good at blowing kisses."

"I'd like that," he says, smiling at me before looking at Slade. "She reminds me of your mother."

Slade glances at me. He'd told me the same thing. With a mischievous grin on his face, he says, "She makes me eat my vegetables just like Mom used to, too."

His dad chuckles, and I wonder when the last time they talked about Juliet was. "God bless her, your mother was a terrible cook. For Finn's and your sake, I hope Paige isn't like her in that way."

"I'm a good cook," I say, moving to Slade's side. "Maybe you could see for yourself sometime. Come over for dinner."

Both of them look at me like I've grown an extra head. Perhaps it's stupid of me to try to help mend this relationship. But I see potential here, potential I'll never have in my own life. I don't even know who my father is, so I hate to see others throw away what so many of us would kill to have.

"She backed us into a corner with that one. Didn't she?" his dad says, looking at him.

"She has a tendency to do that," Slade says.

"I do not," I protest, but neither one of them is paying attention, each waiting for the other one to make the first move.

"You let me know if or when you ever want that to happen," Lyle says to his son. "And I'll be there."

Slade gives him a nod, the ball fully in his court. I have a feeling it's been there for a long time, but he's just never picked it up. Lyle reaches out, giving my hand a brief squeeze. "Thanks for inviting me in," he says, and I know he's talking about more than me inviting him into the house. He's referring to my invitation to include him in our lives.

When the door closes behind him, I make a break for the upstairs, suspecting Slade is not going to be happy I let his father in. Slade stops my escape, taking hold of my waist. "What the hell was that? You and my dad are best friends now? Did you forget how you met?"

Pulling away, I say, "No, I didn't forget. Not that you'd let me."

"Am I just supposed to forget about the fact that my father wanted to bang the woman I'm with?"

"If he and I can move past that, then you should, too. He obviously doesn't think about me that way anymore."

"You sure about that?"

"Yes, I am." We stand there staring at each other for a few moments, neither one of us willing to give an inch. "Both of us know this isn't about me," I say, breaking the standoff.

"He can't just make a phone call to help Finn one time and . . ."

"You're right," I say. "That doesn't make up for years of shit."

"You're crazy if you think he's going to be some sort of grandfather to Finn. Can you really see that man on the floor playing trucks with Finn?"

I shrug. "Yeah, I kind of can."

"I know you grew up without much of a family and are probably starving for some sort of fairy tale family life, but . . ."

"How can you say something like that to me?" I say, stepping away from him. "This doesn't have anything to do with me. Maybe I overstepped with the dinner invitation, but I wanted you to know that I don't want to be the reason you two don't work things out. That's all."

He hangs his head, making him look so young. He reaches out for me. "I'm sorry, baby. That was a terrible thing for me to say."

Moving toward him, I lightly touch his cheek, knowing he's tired from last night, and dealing with his father is never easy on him. It brings up a lot of bad crap. "He seems lonely." Slade leans his forehead on mine. "Think about the way he lives his life. How lonely that must be? And not to have any relationship with his son on top of that."

He pulls back slightly, looking into my eyes. "That would be like if, in thirty years, Finn doesn't want anything to do with me."

I nod, but all I can think about is how I hope Slade's still talking to me in thirty years, how I hope we're all still a family.

CHAPTER THIRTY-FOUR

SLADE

Finn in his stroller, I push him through the streets of Nashville. It's hot as hell today. I hope Clay and the rest of the stable crew are keeping the horses hydrated. It's a miracle the stable stood up to that storm. The horses were spooked for a few days, but I've been told they've settled down nicely. Construction has already started on the house, and I only hope we can be in before Finn's birthday.

Since it's technically a workday, I should still be at the office, but I'm the boss, so I do what I want. Besides, with the golf course opening behind me, things have settled down a little. Of course, there are always other projects, but I've worked hard to build my business, so I can afford days like this. And it's going to be a big day.

I used to be the master of my own universe, but now the master is this little guy and his mommy. It's amazing how quickly life changes. My life used to be ruled by work, women, and whatever the hell else I wanted. Now it's ruled by nap schedules, diaper changes, and whatever the hell Paige wants. And I wouldn't have it any other way.

Since Paige is occupied for the afternoon, I decide to take advantage of her absence. Babysitting so she could visit Catrine was the perfect cover. Finn and I have a special outing planned. I know Paige said it was too soon, but I'm not a man who takes no easily. The next time I pop the question, I'm going to be ready, and that means I'm coming armed with a ring.

It can't just be any ring either. It has to be special and one of a kind, so I'm taking Finn to a local jewelry designer. She only works by appointment. And you better know someone if you want an appointment. You can't just walk in.

Two armed guards wait at the entrance. Once I give my name, I'm allowed to enter. I push Finn inside. The place isn't large. The lights are turned down low except for the spotlights on the jewelry cases that line the walls.

A table in the center is covered in black velvet and has a seat on each side. That's it. The diamonds and gemstones are the focus of this place. Each wall is lined with cases, set against black velvet again, and the light makes everything glisten. Some bigger pieces rotate on a pedestal while others are set in their own private cases.

"Mr. Turner." A voice greets me, coming through a door in the corner I hadn't noticed. "Josephine," she says, extending her hand. She's a slight woman, very petite with dark features, and probably in her late forties.

I shake her hand, and she bends down to shake Finn's, too. "This is Finn. We're shopping for his mother, Paige," I say.

"Engagement ring," she says, and I remember telling them that when I made the appointment.

Taking Finn from his stroller, I hold him on my hip. He immediately starts playing with the stubble on my face.

"What do you have in mind?" she asks, leading me over to a case on the wall. "Size, shape, color?"

"I don't know," I say, my eyes scanning the sea of jewels. "I just thought I'd know it when I saw it. Kind of like the woman. I knew she was special the instant I saw her."

"Take your time," she says. "Think of Paige."

That's easy to do. She's a constant in my mind, my heart, my soul. All the space that used to be filled up by work or other things has become occupied by Paige. She's taken up permanent residence in my heart. Whispering to Finn, I say, "What would Mommy like?"

He reaches out for the glass case, his hands covered in drool, and I try to snatch him back before he leaves his fingerprints all over everything, but I'm not fast enough.

She laughs. "Please don't worry about it. Would you like me to take him while you look?"

I shake my head. "No, thanks. This is something he and I need to do together." Right as the words come out of my mouth, I see it. My breath stops just like it did the first moment I laid eyes on her.

That's the ring I'm going to slip on her finger when she becomes my wife.

Josephine follows my gaze. "You have excellent taste."

That's code for this is going to cost me. Paige is worth every penny.

CHAPTER THIRTY-FIVE

PAIGE

My hands full with Mexican takeout, I ring the doorbell of Catrine and Jon's house. I've never been here before. The house is in a gated subdivision just outside Nashville. It's one of those picture-perfect neighborhoods where the kids still play outside, neighbors barbecue, and every lawn is meticulously manicured. It's the fairy tale—at least from the outside.

Behind closed doors, it's the same crap that happens in every neighborhood. In one of these houses, some man beats his wife or is cheating on her. In another, they struggle to pay their bills, living paycheck to paycheck. And in countless others, drug and alcohol abuse. The only difference is here those things are wrapped up in prettier packages.

Catrine opens the door. She looks fabulous, as always. Even carrying another human being in her belly, she can put any woman to shame. Her arms open wide, I think she's pulling me into a hug, but she's really grabbing the food. "You're a lifesaver! Did you get the extra peppers?"

Laughing, I follow her inside through the foyer. "Got 'em."

She puts the food down on the kitchen island. The kitchen opens into a great room with a fireplace and a view of the backyard. "Jon won't let me eat anything spicy. He thinks it will make the baby come before he's ready." She opens one of the cartons. "I told him that's the point. He also won't let me exercise, and you don't even want to know the last time we had sex."

"No, I don't," I say, laughing.

"Speaking of," she says, digging into some guacamole with a chip. "How are things going with you two? I have to tell you, I almost died when I saw him carrying you out of the house after the tornado. It would take a forklift for Jon to carry me now."

"It would not," I say. "You look amazing."

"The other day, some woman at the store told me I looked pregnant in the face!" Catrine throws her hands up. "Seriously? Why does everyone think they can say things like that and touch your belly when you're pregnant? Did you get that when you were pregnant with Finn?"

"I think everyone gets that," I say. "Did you and Jon decide on a name yet? Or is he permanently Chewie?"

She rolls her eyes, pushing the bag of food over to me so I can grab something. "At this point, I think we're going to have to meet him."

"Good plan," I say. "I need to see his nursery."

"Oh, it's a circus theme," she says, leaping to her feet. "I'll show you. It's upstairs next door to . . ."

Suddenly, a gush of water hits the floor, stopping her in her tracks. Her eyes wide, she looks up at me. "Tell me you just peed on yourself?" I say.

Her head slowly shakes. For all her excitement and readiness for the baby to come, she's frozen still. "What do I do?" she asks.

"I don't know," I say, holding my arms out like she could fall over any second.

"What do you mean you don't know? You've been through this?" she cries.

"My water never broke."

"They had to strip your membranes?" she asks.

"What? I had a home birth," I say. "You should sit down."

"I'm soaking wet," she says.

"Okay, um . . . you should take a shower then?"

"I read in the baby books, you aren't supposed to do that if your water breaks. Something about bacteria."

"Right. Sorry," I say. "It's been a while."

"Call Jon," she says, giving me her best eye roll.

"Right, right," I say, looking for my purse. She points toward the counter, another look flying my way. Reaching in my purse, I feel around for my phone. Why is it you can never find your phone when you need it? "It's got to be in here somewhere."

"Hey, babe," I hear Catrine say. I look up, finding the phone to her ear. "My water just broke. I'm fine. Paige is here. She's freaking out, but she's here. I'll have her grab my bag and bring me to the hospital. Meet me there!" She smiles. "Love you, too."

CHAPTER THIRTY-SIX

SLADE

"How long does this usually take?" I ask, looking over at Paige, who's biting her thumb nail. She hasn't calmed down at all since she walked in with Catrine eight hours ago.

Paige simply shrugs her shoulders at me. Thank God, Finn is relaxed and sleeping happily in his car seat. It's not easy to wait and even harder with a baby. We really need to find a sitter for times like this.

Jon called me as soon as he got the call from Catrine, telling me Paige was driving her, so I rushed over to meet them, figuring Jon could use the support. He's texted a few updates now and then, even told us to go home, but I want to be there for them. It's Finn's bedtime, though, and we've missed dinner.

Taking Paige's hand, I say, "Why don't you take Finn home? I'll stay until the baby's born, then I'll meet you there."

"I really want to see Catrine," she says.

"We'll come visit her and the baby tomorrow. Who knows how long this will take? We probably won't get to see them tonight anyway," I say, tilting her chin to me. "What's wrong? You seem off."

"I'm fine," she says, giving me a small smile. "You're right. I'm tired. It's been a long day."

I don't know that I've ever seen Jon so happy in his life. Well, maybe the day he married Catrine, but this was close. Their son was born not long after Paige left. Theo is perfectly healthy and beautiful, according to Jon.

Since it was late, I didn't go in to see them. I texted Paige the news, but she hasn't responded. I wonder if she's asleep. No way will I be able to sleep tonight. Too much is going through my head.

Jon's been through some shit in his life, so that makes this moment even sweeter. I was there on that bridge with him all those years ago, and I was there tonight when his child was born. I've seen him at his lowest and at his highest. If anyone deserves this happiness, it's Jon.

I hope Theo and Finn will be friends. It's nice to imagine Jon's son and mine growing up together, playing at the ranch, riding horses. I can imagine us taking them to football games. Hell, maybe one day, they will even take over the company. And while Finn isn't mine biologically, I feel the same way about him that Jon does about his son. It's immediate. It's the most natural thing in the world to love him.

When I open the door to the penthouse, Paige meets me, wearing one of my T-shirts and those damn knee socks. Her hair is down and loose, and her lips are on mine before I can even say hello. "Finn?" I ask.

"Asleep," she says with a naughty smile.

With my hands on her ass, I hoist her up, wrapping her legs around my waist. I'm not sure what's gotten into her, but I'm not going to ask. Carrying her, I walk over to the sofa, sitting down with her straddling me. Pushing her hair back from her face, I plant a soft kiss on her pink lips. Her eyes roam my face, her hand runs through my hair. "You know I love you, right?" she asks in barely a whisper.

"You better," I say. Yanking her forward, I hit just the right spot to make her moan a little.

"I need you," she whispers, ripping her T-shirt off.

This is her way of giving me the go-ahead. She's finally ready. She's in my lap, her hair falling over her tits, wearing nothing but a pair of panties and those damn knee socks. Pushing her hair over her shoulders, I look into her blue eyes. I'm a lucky son of a bitch, and not because I'm about to finally have her, but because looking at her, I know I'm looking at the rest of my life.

I'm not sure how I manage it, but I ask one last time, "You sure?"

"I've never been more sure of anything," she whispers, sliding down my body to her knees. I kick off my shoes. Looking up at me, she unfastens the button on my pants. I lift my shirt over my head, feeling her slide my zipper down. She leans up a little, kissing me, slipping her hands under my waistband. I lift my hips to help her, and she slides my pants off, taking my underwear with her.

Paige has the best lips, especially when they're slipping my dick between them. She knows I'm complete putty in her hands, giving one long, slow lick, circling my tip. "Holy fuck!" I moan through gritted teeth.

The little smile playing on her lips lets me know she's pleased with herself—pleased she can render me so powerless. A lot of women don't like to be on their knees. Giving a man a blow job is the last thing some women want to do, but not Paige. She gets off on this, I can tell. She likes having power over me. That's what some women fail to realize. If a man loves you, then you have power. Love is the single most powerful weapon there is.

You can get someone to do just about anything in the name of love. Real love is choosing not to yield that power but instead to guard and protect it.

I watch her slide my cock between her lips until I'm hitting the back of her throat. She doesn't hold back, taking as much of me as she possibly can, sliding me in and out slowly. She's not using her hands at all. This isn't to bring me to the finish line. She's simply warming me up. Silly woman, one look at her is all the warming up I'll ever need, but I won't tell her that because I'm enjoying myself too much.

She moans a little, sending vibrations through my cock, making me grow even harder in her mouth. I hold her hair back, and her eyes lock on mine as she takes me deeper. As much as I like her mouth on me, the promise of her pussy has my full attention tonight. "Take off your panties," I order softly.

Slowly, my dick slips out of her mouth, heavy and hard. She gets to her feet in front of me, sliding her panties down her long smooth legs. I cup her in my hand, feeling her warmth, her wetness. "Sucking my cock makes you wet," I say with a smirk. "I like that."

She blushes, and I pull her forward, hiking one of her legs over my shoulder so I can bury my tongue deep in her pussy. "Slade!" she cries out.

"Shh!" I whisper against her, causing her to tremor.

She runs her fingers through my hair. "I want you," she whispers. "I want to feel you."

She doesn't need to ask me twice. Taking her down to the sofa, I run my fingers down the curves of her body until I reach her socks, slowly sliding them down. I don't want one ounce of clothing between any part of her skin and mine. I want to show her how great sex can be. She grew up with sex being used as a commodity or a weapon. From this point on, it's only about love. I want to wipe all that from her mind.

Leaning over her, she looks up at me with so much trust. More trust than I thought she was capable of. With my cock resting between her legs, she whispers, "Pleasure."

I take hold of myself, gently outlining her folds with the tip of my cock. She bites her bottom lip, and I feel her stretching open, inviting me in. I give her a little slap with my dick, and she cries out, so I do it again. "You like that?" I ask.

"Harder," she says, her hands gripping my shoulders. This time, I use my hand, slapping her pussy a little harder. The truth is—love is too messy for the sex to be clean.

"Oh God," she moans. "More."

Only this time, I don't give her more and simply use my dick to outline her folds again. "You ready to get fucked?" I ask.

"Yes!" she cries out.

Pinning her arms over her head, I slowly slip just my tip inside. Her muscles clench around me, wanting more. Fuck, she's strong. Her body quivers under mine, and she takes me the rest of the way in. For half a second, I don't move, unable to believe where I am. She whispers my name, and I look down at her, our bodies joined together.

"I love you," I say, starting to move. I start slow, building her up, stretching her open, making her crazy. Orgasm is always the goal, but the fun is getting there. She matches me thrust for thrust, her hands on my ass letting me know she can take everything I can give her. There's not a second of awkwardness. We find our rhythm as though we've done this a thousand times. The harder I go, the harder she wants it. The faster I go, the faster she wants it. But I slow down, not wanting this to go quickly.

Leaning over, I run my tongue around her nipple. With each pass, the muscles between her legs clench together. Slowly, I slip my dick out of her, and she whimpers at the loss of me. "Sit up," I say, helping her up on the sofa. Guiding her hands to her thighs, I say, "Spread your pussy for me." She looks at me with surprise in her eyes. "Christ, you look incredible," I say, seeing her spread out before me, glistening. On my knees, I rest my cock at her entrance, feeling her trembling for me. "This is going to be deep," I warn, gliding myself inside her.

She cries out a little, and I reach down, spreading her folds even farther apart. "Oh God," she moans. "Please make me come. Please."

This time, I don't start slowly and pound into her. My balls slap against her, feeding that little bit of roughness she so clearly likes. "Oh yes," she groans, her whole body coiling around me. I hold her close, feeling her quiver. It's not the first orgasm I've ever given her, but it feels like the most important, and God, do I want to give her more. Her muscles are so tight, she almost pulls my orgasm right out of me, but I manage to hold off.

She falls limp in my arms, enjoying the last tremors of her orgasm. Lightly, I kiss her neck as she moans softly. My plan at this point is to take her to her back and slowly make love to her until she comes at least one more time, and then follow along behind her, so I'm completely taken by surprise when she slips me out of her and straddles me on the sofa. If I didn't love her before, I've definitely fallen in love with her now.

She lifts up slightly, taking hold of my dick and sliding me deep inside her. There is nothing quite like having a woman on top of you. Her tits rise and fall, her hair moves with her body. With my hands on her hips, I help lift her up and down, bouncing on top of me, riding me. She keeps her eyes locked on mine the whole time. I hope she sees all my love for her—how beautiful I think she is—how I never want to spend a day without her.

I feel my body start to tighten and pull her into a kiss as I release inside her.

"I think orgasms are addictive," she says, giggling. "The more you have, the more you want."

"Oh really?" I say, letting my hand roam between her legs. We've been naked all night. Sometime in the early morning hours, we moved upstairs to bed, but we've been laughing, talking, and fooling around for hours.

She captures my hand, and I frown at her. "All those times I told you I wasn't easy and look," she says, tossing her hands up in a laugh. "It turns out I am."

Flipping her over, I pin her to the bed. "Thank fuck for that."

She laughs again. "I don't want this night to end."

"We have tomorrow night," I say. "And the night after that, and the night after that."

"Promise?" she asks, a serious tone falling over her voice.

"That's the easiest promise I'll ever make," I say.

CHAPTER THIRTY-SEVEN

PAIGE

Things with Slade and I are like a dream. It's nothing I ever hoped I'd have—love, support, passion. It's only missing one thing—honesty—but I only have myself to blame for that. I guess no one can have it all.

Finn and I go out to the ranch most days. Slade hates Finn and me commuting out to the ranch to oversee repairs. He calls me almost every morning, making sure we got there okay. He'd much rather be the one making that drive. I actually don't mind it. It's a pretty drive, and Finn loves the car, so he's usually happy.

Progress is slow, but I can see the ranch starting to take shape again. The front window has been repaired, and the new flooring and cabinetry should arrive any day. As far as remodels go, Slade assures me this one has been pretty smooth. Slade works from the city. He already has his hooks into a few other projects at work, so I know he's happy that Jon is back in the office full-time now.

And when work is done, we're all just together—having family dinners, playing on the floor with Finn, strolling with him through one of the many parks of Nashville. It's the family life I always dreamed of. The kind that I didn't think anyone really ever had. And it's mine.

Finn has become quite the crawler. You'd think it would make him nap more, but Finn's crawling has made Slade and I more tired than Finn. But it's fun, too, chasing him around, playing peekaboo, and hearing him squeal. I actually came home a couple of weeks ago and found gates on both the top and bottom of the staircase, as well as covers on all the outlets. Slade hired a whole childproofing crew to anticipate any possible thing Finn could get into. Of all the things he does, that kind of thing melts my heart.

After Finn goes to bed, Slade and I get to just be a couple. Which always means we end up naked at some point. I can't complain about that. Slade's begging me to find someone to watch Finn from time to time, so he and I can actually have some time together out of the house, but I haven't done it yet.

Tonight, someone is joining our quiet family dinner. This could be an amazing night or the worst idea in the history of family dinners.

I'm standing at the stove making dinner when Slade walks in from work, slipping his arms around me, kissing me sweetly, and eyeing what I'm making. I can tell he's happy it's roast and not eggplant. The condo doesn't have the expansive kitchen of the ranch, but I love cooking for us. I'm a freak, I know.

"Jon had a whole slideshow on his phone of the baby," Slade says, looking through the kitchen door at Finn playing in his playpen in the next room. "You'd think the kid was more than a month old by the number of photos."

"It's got to be hard for him to be back at work full-time," I say.

I haven't seen Catrine since the day after the baby was born. The name Chewie was replaced by Theo. I know I should go see her, but I slipped up, and I don't know how much she picked up on. So I've been keeping my distance. But it's eating at me.

She's planning on being a stay-at-home mom now. Slade suggested I stop by to visit, but I've resisted. A new mom adjusting to a baby has been the perfect excuse. Add in feeding schedules and nap times, and visits are virtually impossible. At least that's what I've been telling Slade. I have tried to call her a few times, and she either doesn't pick up or keeps it short. "Maybe you should go see her since Jon's back at work now?"

"Maybe," I say, suddenly feeling sick to my stomach.

"Jon asked me to be godfather to Theo," he says.

I kiss him softly. "That's great."

"You okay?" Slade asks, giving my arms a little rub.

"I'm fine," I say, shaking it off.

"We can cancel tonight," he says.

I throw him a look over his shoulder. He's not getting out of this one.

He finally invited his dad over for that dinner I promised. It surprised me that he did. I guess seeing Jon as a dad, feeling like he's a dad to Finn, made him think about his own dad. Whatever the reason, Slade reached out, and Lyle accepted. My part is to make dinner, and Slade made me promise there wouldn't be anything green. But he never said anything about the color orange, so I made sure to have carrots with the roast.

"Dada!" Finn laughs out.

Slade looks through the door, waving at him. When Finn first said, "Dada," I wasn't quite sure he knew what he was saying, that he was identifying Slade as his father, but it's clear now that's exactly what's happening. It makes me happy and scared at the same time. I want Finn to have everything—all the things I didn't. That includes a father, and Slade is the best father any child could ever have. But it also scares me that he's getting so attached. When this . . . No, if this ever goes south, Finn will be devastated. He won't be the only one.

Slade walks closer to me, his eyes studying me. Gently, he places his hand on my forehead. Giving him my best smile, I plant a light kiss on his lips. He's right that I don't feel the best, but I'm sure it's my nerves getting the better of me.

The doorbell rings, and Slade looks back at me, inhaling a deep breath. "Maybe just scream 'Dada' at him. That seems to make you happy," I suggest.

"Very funny," he says, smacking my butt.

Washing my hands off, I watch him pick Finn up, carrying him to the door. Finn's his buffer, I guess. When I suddenly hear the loudest screech I've ever heard Finn make, I rush from the kitchen to the den, a bit panicked, not sure what to expect.

The largest stuffed polar bear I've ever seen comes through the door, carried by Slade's father. Finn is going nuts in Slade's arms, shrieking, his arms flailing and his legs kicking.

"You didn't need to bring him anything," I say, walking over to them.

He looks over at Slade, putting the bear on the floor. "Polar bears were Slade's favorite when he was little."

Slade kneels, letting Finn hug the bear. "Must run in the family," Slade says.

His dad looks up at me, and I'm not sure if he's surprised to hear his son talk like that or proud that he did. Either way, it makes my day. I kneel beside them, taking hold of Finn. "Say thank you." It's not that I actually expect him to utter those words, but it's never too early to start instilling good manners.

"Dinner will be ready in a few minutes," I say, heading back toward the kitchen.

"Paige?" Slade says, his eyes begging me to stay, but I'm not going to be his buffer. The man has multiple houses, cars, business ventures, and makes million-dollar deals, so he can handle dinner with his father. "Five minutes tops."

I might stretch the five minutes to ten just to give the ice a chance to thaw, but we'll see. I get Finn's food together, setting it on his high chair and sneaking a peek at the three of them in the den. Slade's on the floor with Finn, holding him up while he moves his legs like he's trying to walk. Finn's making too much noise for me to really hear what they are saying, but at least they're talking, and it doesn't appear to be angry. That's an improvement.

Taking the roast out of the oven, I call the guys in for dinner. The condo doesn't have a dining room. The only place to eat is the table in the kitchen, so dinner will be pretty casual, which is best, less pressure.

They each file in, and Slade puts Finn in his high chair. I've positioned Finn between us tonight. It's best to have a two-man offense to combat his spills with company over.

"Smells good," Lyle says, taking his seat.

I smile but think he must be lying. I've got no appetite. I'm not sure if it's the pressure of having Slade's father over, the fact that I'm lying to the man I love, or a combination of both. Nothing smells good to me, but I have to muster through this dinner for the sake of Slade and our family relationship. It's too important. Slade starts filling our plates, and I notice he's not putting any carrots on his. It would serve him right if I called him out on that in front of his father, but Lyle beats me to it and spoons a few on his son's plate. "Need to set a good example for Finn."

I can't help but burst out laughing and reach out, holding my hand up for his dad to give me a high five. "I'm not eating those," Slade says, grinning at me.

"Did you ever make him sit at the table until he ate his vegetables as a kid?" I ask Lyle.

"Only once," he says, looking at his son. "You remember."

"Brussels sprouts," they both say in unison, a disgusted tone in each of their voices.

Lyle looks over at me. "We found him asleep at the table at breakfast the next morning. Stubborn kid sat there all night."

"Did you ever eat them?" I ask, moving the food around on my plate but not able to take a bite.

Slade eyes my plate then looks at his dad, something sweet in his eyes. "Mom packed them in my lunch box that day. She called the school and asked them not to let me throw them away."

"My Juliet," his dad says.

"When I brought my lunch box home, and she saw they were still there, she put them on my plate for dinner."

"I like her," I say.

"Slade figured they'd eventually get old, and he'd get out of eating them," Lyle says.

Slade rolls his eyes. "She just made me new ones."

"How long did this last?" I ask.

"A month," Lyle says.

"You're kidding?" I say. "Who finally won?"

Lyle looks at his son. "I ate the damn Brussels sprouts, okay? Happy?" Slade says.

"What made you eat them?" I ask.

He looks at his dad, grinning. "Dad came home from work late one night, and I was sitting at the table with those damn sprouts. He didn't say a word. He just reached into his briefcase and pulled out a bottle of that spray cheese."

"That stuff is disgusting," I say, my stomach churning at the thought.

"Yeah, but all kids love it," Slade says. "He covered those Brussels sprouts in that cheese."

"We just smiled at each other, and he ate them," Lyle says.

"Did you ever tell Mom that?" Slade asks.

"I told your mother everything," he says. "You can't be in a relationship and have secrets. Even small ones."

My stomach clenches.

"Besides," Lyle says, "it was your mother's idea."

CHAPTER THIRTY-EIGHT

SLADE

I peek in on Finn, fast asleep in his crib. He stayed up later than usual, having taken to my dad. It was a good night. Leaning against the doorway, I listen to him breathe and watch his little chest rise and fall. Paige has given me so much more than I ever expected or even knew I wanted.

Which is kind of ironic since she didn't have a penny to her name when I met her, living in that run-down apartment in the worst neighborhood in Nashville. On the other hand, I was the one who seemingly had it all—career, money, houses, yet she's the one who's given me everything. Without her, I wouldn't have Finn. Without her, I wouldn't be speaking to my dad again. Without her, I wouldn't be remembering my mom or talking about her. I haven't done any of that in years. All of that I owe to Paige.

It's not that I think things with my dad are fixed by any stretch of the imagination, but we seem to have found some common ground again. We both loved my mom. If for no other reason, we can get along to honor her memory. She would want peace. She would want us to get along. And surprisingly, my dad seems to really enjoy being around Finn.

It was surreal to see him holding Finn at the dinner table, feeding him mashed-up carrots. Watching him with Finn, it's like watching him with me when I was little. I'd almost forgotten about that. The bad was so bad that it overshadowed the good we had together. As I said, I haven't forgotten all the things he said to me, the women he brought into my mother's house. I won't ever forget, but somehow, it seemed a little easier tonight to remember the good things.

Stepping away from Finn's door, I walk to my bedroom, finding Paige all curled up under the covers with her eyes closed. She's still, but I don't think she's asleep already. We usually end up under the covers when Finn goes to sleep, but we're usually together and naked. We've come a long way since I first found her asleep in my bed at the ranch.

"Paige," I say, walking over and taking a seat beside her on the bed. Her eyes flutter, and she looks up at me, and it's obvious that she's sick. She didn't look herself before dinner, and during dinner, I noticed she didn't eat much, simply moving the food around on her plate. "What's wrong?"

"I don't know," she says. "I just don't feel right."

"You didn't eat much earlier," I say. "Maybe you need to eat something."

Her nose wrinkles up. "Nothing even sounds good. Besides, my stomach is kind of cramping and . . ."

As soon as she says the word cramps, the light bulb goes off. "Period?" I ask.

She shakes her head, and I touch her forehead. She doesn't feel hot, not that I'm an expert, but clearly, something is going on. "What can I get you?"

"Nothing," she says. "I'm too nauseous to eat anything."

A year ago, that wouldn't bring up any red flags, but I've spent the past nine months with Catrine, and I wasn't kidding when I said she told me every symptom she had. My heart misses a few beats. "Could you be pregnant?"

"No," she says, her blue eyes wide with fear, and her voice not sounding very sure. "I told you I'm on the pill."

Isn't the pill like ninety-something percent effective? It couldn't have failed her twice—Finn and now? Then again, I never asked if she was on it before Finn.

She looks scared shitless. I don't know what happened when she told Finn's dad she was pregnant, but from the look on her face right now, I'd say it wasn't good.

"Hey," I say, taking her hand and pulling her into my lap on the bed. "It would be happy news if you were."

She looks up at me. "Would it?"

Lightly, I place my hand on her flat stomach. "Very happy news."

She starts giggling. "You're insane. I'm not pregnant."

"You could be," I say.

"Stop saying that," she says. "Finn isn't even a year old."

"I know you've been through this before," I say, and she gives me a sad smile. "And if you are, I'll be there with you the whole way. You won't be alone this time."

The tears start flowing.

"But no home births. Your sexy ass will be in a hospital where God intended babies to be born."

That makes her laugh, and the tears seem to slow down a bit. She says, "Lots of babies are born at home and . . ." I kiss her hard on the lips to shut her up and feel her smile underneath my kiss. "What am I saying?" she says. "I'm not. I can't be."

"Only one way to find out," I say.

"Slade," she whispers, her blue eyes begging me to drop this.

These days, you can have pretty much anything delivered to your home with just a few pushes of a button—takeout food, groceries, dry cleaning, or in this case, pregnancy tests. Paige was freaking out. I wasn't about to leave her for one second, not even to run to the store.

I don't even want to know what the delivery person thought when they got the order for multiple pregnancy tests, all different brands. I didn't know which one was best, so I got a variety.

Five pregnancy test sticks line the back of my toilet. The fact that these things come in packs of two is a clear indicator that no one takes just one. We're almost a half dozen in, and even though they all indicate the same result, we still can't seem to believe it.

"The line on that one doesn't look very clear," she says, pointing at number three.

"The box said any line is a positive result," I tell her.

"The positive sign on that one looks more like an X. And an X would not be positive."

She's really starting to confuse me now. I point at the last one she did. "This one actually says 'pregnant.'"

"I'm pregnant," she says to herself as if she's trying it on for size.

"Looks like," I say, although I've been convinced she was pregnant since she told me she was nauseated. I didn't need her to pee on a stick to confirm it, but apparently, that is what she needed. I hold up one more package. "Still have one more left. Want to make it an even half dozen?"

Her head shakes, and she repeats, "I'm pregnant."

I keep waiting to hear some excitement in her declaration, but she just sounds confused. "I would've thought you'd have some idea. You've been through this before. Do you not feel the same way as you did with Finn?"

Her head shakes again.

"Paige," I say, taking her hands. "Everything will be . . ."

"I had wine with dinner," she says, squeezing my hands.

"I'm sure one glass this early on is . . ."

"I've been taking birth control pills."

"We'll get you a doctor's appointment, but I'm sure that happens all the time and won't hurt anything."

"I didn't eat anything green today," she says, shaking her head at me.

This time, I can't help but chuckle. "Well, that does it. Our baby will be born with three heads."

Her lips purse together, trying to hold in a laugh. "I'm being crazy."

"A little," I say, hugging her.

"Slade," she says softly. "Could we not tell anyone for a few weeks? I want to see the doctor first, get through the first trimester."

"Sure," I say. "Whatever you want."

CHAPTER THIRTY-NINE

PAIGE

"You are definitely pregnant," the doctor says, washing his hands. He's a pretty old guy, tall with a lanky build. It's my first time seeing him. In the past, I've just gone to clinics, never had a regular doctor. He's the doctor who delivered Theo, so I figured he was reputable, and I was relieved to be able to get an appointment with him so quickly.

I just smile. What else can I do? "We can do an ultrasound today or in a couple of days if you'd like to wait on the baby's father or . . ."

"He's out of town working," I lie. Now I even lie to my OB/GYN. Slade's not out of town. He's at the ranch with Finn. He doesn't even know I'm here. He thinks my appointment is tomorrow. I truly am a terrible person for keeping him from this moment. I know he's going to have to meet my doctor at some point, and I can't ask my doctor to lie. My lies are catching up with me.

At least I was honest on my medical history forms. That's something.

This past week, Slade has been so excited that we found out I'm pregnant. A part of me is, too. I love the idea of carrying his child, but I don't love the idea of him finding out the truth about me.

My phone rings in my purse. "That's probably him now," the doctor says.

Picking up the phone, the doctor gives me a little wave as he leaves. "Just let the nurse know about the ultrasound."

I answer the phone. "You're never going to believe what Finn just said," Slade says.

"What?" I ask.

"Where are you?" he asks. "The connection is bad."

"The doctor's office," I say, feeling my stomach lurch. "They called me with a last-minute opening, so I took it."

"But that's supposed to be tomorrow," he says.

"They asked if I wanted to come today, so I . . ."

"I'm on my way," he says. And my heart breaks. He's at least an hour away. There's no way he'd make it, but he'd try like hell to get to me, just like he did the night of the tornado.

"Slade, it's fine," I say, feeling like the shittiest person on the planet, now wanting to flog myself for this. "I'm just about done."

"I missed it?" he asks, his voice confused.

"They didn't do much," I say, a few tears rolling down my cheeks. "Have to come back for blood work and . . ."

"Why didn't you call me?" he asks, and I can hear the anger rising in his voice.

"I knew you were busy."

"Did they do an ultrasound?" he asks.

My eyes close. "I was just about to schedule it."

"I'll see you at home later," he says, hanging up.

To say he's cold when I get home is an understatement, and he has every right to be. I did a horrible thing. I didn't do it to hurt him. I did it to protect myself, my secrets, everything we are trying to build now. But that doesn't make it any better.

Finn is down for the night, and Slade's in his office, avoiding me. It's been this way for a few hours, and I can't stand it any longer. I need to apologize to him. Lightly, I knock on his office door. When he doesn't bother to respond, I open it up slightly. He doesn't even look up at me. I walk over.

"I'm really sorry."

"I'm trying really hard to understand why you wouldn't call and tell me about the appointment change," he says, his voice with an angry edge that I've never heard from him before. Sure, he can be an asshole, but it's never been like this.

"It was last minute. You were busy, and they weren't doing anything important. Just basically confirming the pregnancy. I'm sorry."

He still won't look at me, and he doesn't even bother to reply. I don't want to cry in front of him, so I head for the door.

"Did you hear the heartbeat?" he asks.

Turning back, I say, "No, it's too early. But we'll be able to see it on the ultrasound."

"You going to tell me when *that* appointment is?" he snaps.

With tears rushing down my cheeks, I quickly turn, heading toward the staircase. I deserve for him to be mad at me, but I don't have to like it. I hear him mumble a curse word behind me. I don't make it to the stairs before his arms slide around my waist.

His mouth lowers to my ear, his warm breath giving me goose bumps. "You aren't alone this time," he growls. "Stop acting like you are."

"But . . ."

"This is when you rely on me, on my love for you," he says, lowering his hands to my stomach. "On my love for our child."

Placing my hands on top of his, I whisper, "You won't miss another appointment because of me." But I have no idea how I'm going to keep that promise.

I watch Slade holding baby Theo. I've seen him hold Finn lots of times, but never when Finn was that small. Slade's a big man, and seeing him with such a tiny little person makes me excited to see him holding our newborn.

I'm carrying Slade's child. A tear rolls down my cheek. Of course, I'm happy, but this complicates things even more. I'm in a mess, a mess of my own making, and if I'm not careful, I could drag Slade down with me. I don't see a way out, and I can't just leave, not now, not while I'm carrying his child. I would never do that to him. He looks over at me, giving me a little wink as someone takes a picture of him with his godson.

The christening service was pretty small with just family and some close friends, but it was absolutely lovely. It was held in a small church not far from where Jon and Catrine live. They were beaming the whole time, and little Theo didn't cry once, not even when the priest drizzled the water on his head. Slade looked incredibly handsome holding Theo on the altar, promising to guide him and be there for him. I sat toward the back in case I needed to make a quick escape with Finn. He obviously doesn't understand the significance of the moment or that he needed to be quiet through it. I held him the whole time, trying to keep him occupied.

We're back at their house now for a little party. Finn's about had his fill, though, anxious to be able to crawl around, sick of being confined in our arms. "Jon?" I ask. "Is there someplace I can put Finn down to play?"

"Go up to Theo's room," he says, nodding toward the stairs.

Carrying Finn, I walk up and open the door to the nursery. Catrine's at the changing table with little Theo. "Oh, sorry," I say. "Jon said I could bring Finn up here to play."

"It's fine," she says, giving me a small smile. "Finn's gotten so big."

"Theo, too," I say, smiling back. "I'd like us to get together once you get settled, get a routine."

"Maybe," she says, finishing up the diaper, not making eye contact with me. She's not the same with me. Maybe it's hormones, or maybe she's suspicious. I need to smooth this over.

"Sorry I freaked out so much when you went into labor. It's just different when it's your friend."

With a tight-lipped smile on her face, she gives me a little nod. "I need to get back to the party."

"Catrine, are we okay?" I ask.

She exhales. "Paige, is there anything going on?"

"What would be going on?" I ask, my heart starting to pound.

She shakes her head. "I'm sorry. I'm just having all these crazy thoughts."

"Like what?" I ask.

"I'm embarrassed to even say," she says. "I think mommy brain has struck. Poor Jon, he must think I'm crazy."

I wonder what she's shared with her husband. They seem the type of couple who would talk about everything. My stomach twists. I want to be like that with Slade, but I can't. It's what's best for him. Still, I wonder if Catrine said anything crazy about me? I give her a little side hug, but she still seems stiff. "I'm here if you want to talk or anything. I understand the stresses of having a newborn."

"If you say so," she says, walking out of the room. I call after her, but she ignores me. Clearly, she's got some suspicions about me. I hope they're the wrong ones. Quickly, I pick up Finn, my head growing dizzy for a second. When I get to the staircase, I pause for a moment, waiting for the room to stop spinning.

When it doesn't, I sit down, making sure to hold Finn tightly as if my life and his depend on it. "Paige?"

I hear Slade's voice and look up, finding him rushing up the stairs toward me, noticing something's wrong.

"I'm fine," I say, handing him Finn. "Just got up too fast and got a little dizzy."

Before I know it, Jon and Catrine are there, too. "She alright?" Jon asks.

Catrine looks me right in the eye and asks, "Anything you need to come clean about?"

My head starts to spin again. Slade's eyes fly to me, and he says, "Guess we have to tell them?"

Jon looks over at his wife then to Slade. "Tell us what?" Jon asks.

"Paige is pregnant," Slade says with a beaming smile.

I look over at Catrine, and her mouth is on the floor. I'm not happy about Slade blabbering our news, especially when I asked him not to. But I'll forgive him because it seems to have shut down Catrine's suspicions.

"That's great news," Jon says, patting Slade on the back. "I remember Catrine used to get dizzy early on. Juice usually helped."

"I'll take her to the kitchen to get some juice," Catrine says, handing the baby to her husband. Slade uses his free hand to help me up, guiding me down the stairs where Catrine takes over, leading me into the kitchen.

She opens the refrigerator door. "Last time I was in here, your water broke," I say.

She pours me some juice, placing it in front of me, clearly in no mood for a trip down memory lane. "Did you do this on purpose?" she asks.

"Do what? Almost faint?"

"No," she says. "Did you get pregnant on purpose to trap him?"

That's the last straw. I get to my feet, my head still cloudy. "I thought we were friends."

She draws a deep breath. "I don't want to think these things about you," she says. "But you have to tell me what's going on. Because something is off with you."

"I don't have to tell you a damn thing," I say, thinking I should tell Slade what she said about me getting pregnant on purpose. That would discredit her forever in his eyes, but I can't do it. It would destroy his relationship with Jon, threaten their business, and I don't want to hurt Slade. I'm doing my best not to.

CHAPTER FORTY

SLADE

I hold up the strip of black and white pictures. Paige is only about six weeks pregnant, but we still saw the flutter of a little heartbeat. Not much else, but the lump in my throat tells a different story. This little gray kidney bean will change my life. I don't know that I've ever believed in miracles until this moment. This little blob in the ultrasound picture is going to grow up to be an adult. How can anyone not believe in miracles when you are in fact a miracle yourself?

Glancing down at Finn in his car seat, it's hard to believe that he started out like this, too. I wish I'd been there for him and for Paige.

A hand slaps my shoulder, the doctor taking a seat behind his desk. He's an older guy, looks like he's been doing this a long time. That puts my heart at ease. I only want the best care for Paige and our child. "Paige is just doing some initial blood work and leaving a urine sample. She'll be right in."

"Great," I say.

"I like to make sure I meet with my first-time moms. They tend to have a lot of questions," he says.

"This isn't her first pregnancy," I say, taking Finn from his car seat. "This is Finn."

"Right, oh, I'm sorry," he says, looking at her chart. "She's a relatively new patient for me. I've just seen her a couple of times. I didn't deliver this little guy," he says, shaking Finn's hand.

"He was a home birth," I say.

His brow wrinkles up, continuing to look at her chart. "Must be some mistake. Her medical history shows no prior pregnancies, no live births, no miscarriages."

"Must have the wrong chart," I say.

A nurse sticks her head in, and he gets to his feet. "Excuse me for a few moments."

I might be committing a felony, but as soon as he walks out, I swipe the chart from his desk. Her name is in bold letters. It's her chart. Her first ultrasound, examination, notes on her office visits, everything looks normal until I get to her medical history form. Plain as day, in her own handwriting, where it asks about prior pregnancies, she checked none.

My hand goes through my hair. I look down at Finn in my lap. This can't be right. I pull out my phone, my lock screen set to a photo of Paige holding Finn. There is definitely a resemblance between them, the same nose. I still have no idea who his biological father is. Apparently, there's a lot I don't know.

"What's going on?" I ask Finn, but he just smiles up at me. Love this kid.

This has to just be some oversight. I mean, when you go to the doctor, they give you dozens of forms to fill out, and perhaps she just overlooked it and checked the wrong box. But wouldn't her doctor be able to tell if she'd been pregnant before when he did an examination? Wouldn't he have asked her a bunch of questions himself, and noticed the mistake and corrected it?

Quickly, I search online whether a doctor can tell if a woman has ever been pregnant. Leave it to Google to have the answer. Apparently, I'm not the only one who's ever asked this question. Much to my disgust, there are actual pictures of how a doctor can tell. I'll leave out the gory details. Let's just say the cervix of a woman who's given birth looks different than a woman who hasn't.

"Slade," I hear Paige say softly. Quickly, I hold up the ultrasound pictures and toss the file aside. She glances at me, looking scared to death, but there is something else in her eyes—a resolve. I've seen this look from her before, several times, beginning with the night we met. A thick silence fills the space between us, and if one of us doesn't say something soon, I fear it will push her away from me.

When someone's caught in a lie, they tend to do one of two things. Either they fess up, or they fight like hell to get out of the corner they're blocked in. I've seen this happen with employees countless times. From the look in her eyes, I know if I confront her now, I'm in for a fight. Better to let her think I'm still in the dark.

CHAPTER FORTY-ONE

SLADE

I need some answers, and clearly, I'm not going to get any from Paige.

"Hey," Jon says, walking into my office with his briefcase. "What's up?"

"I need you to do something for me. This can go no further than you. Understand?"

"Sure," he says. "What is it?"

"Paige," I say, feeling like I'm breaking a vow to her. "I think she's hiding something. I don't know what, and she won't tell me."

He holds his hand up, putting me out of my misery, then he takes a seat across from me, pulling an envelope out of his briefcase, Paige's name at the top. "Ran a background check on her the morning after your dad's party."

My eyes dart up. Anger boils in my chest. What the fuck? "I never asked you to do that."

"No, you didn't," he says, tossing the file down on my desk. "But I've always got your back, whether you want me to or not."

I hold the envelope, conflicted. I debated doing a background check on Paige myself but didn't want to invade her privacy. I wanted to give her the chance to tell me herself. Things have changed. She's left me no choice. If she gets pissed, I'll blame Jon. "And?"

"And nothing," he says. "From what I can tell, she's telling the truth. Grew up in and out of the system. Rough childhood. Her mom died a couple of months back from an overdose. Paige's test scores are off the chart. She's smart as hell. Dropped out of college about eight months ago, which corresponds with Finn's birth."

"So you found nothing," I say.

"Initially," he says. "That's why I never said anything when you moved her into your house. But then the night of the baptism after you left, Catrine told me she thought something was off about Paige. So I did a little more digging."

"Your wife is your excuse for everything."

He shrugs, reaching back into his briefcase and pulling out another envelope. "I ran a check on Finn."

"He's a baby. What did you expect to find?"

"That's just it," Jon says. "I didn't find anything. No social security number. No birth certificate. Nothing. There's no record anywhere that he was ever born."

"Paige said she gave birth at home."

"You still have to apply for a birth certificate and a social security card," he says.

Our emergency room visit pops in my mind. She didn't know Finn's social security number. How did she sign up for health insurance through my company without giving the number? Did she leave the spot blank? Did no one ever notice that? "Maybe it's under a different name. Hudson is Paige's last name. Maybe Finn's birth certificate is under his father's last name."

Jon says, "I ran a check for any boy named Finn born on December first of last year in the whole state of Tennessee. There were two, and neither one of their mothers was named Paige."

"Maybe she wasn't in Tennessee. I never asked her. Or maybe she just never filed the paperwork or . . ."

He pulls out another piece of paper, this one with information on Paige's mother—arrest record, various addresses. He points at her last arrest. The charges were dropped, but there's another piece of information that has my attention. "Maybe," Jon says. "Or maybe it's something else."

Paige darts out of bed, one hand over her mouth, the other over her stomach. The bathroom door slams behind her, and I hear the unmistakable sound of her vomiting.

Hurrying out of bed, I call out her name, "Paige?"

"Oh God," she groans as I hear more come up, followed by Finn crying.

"Get Finn!" she yells out to me.

What a way to wake up. Not that I got much sleep last night anyway, going over and over again in my mind what Jon dug up about Paige's mom. I'm not sure what to think, but I know I can't lose Paige. Under no circumstance will I let that happen.

Pushing open the door to Finn's room, I find him sitting up in his crib, and as soon as he sees me, a big smile covers his little face. Everyone should be greeted by a smile like that.

Picking him up, I give him some love and quickly change his diaper. When we make it back to my bedroom, Paige is emerging from the bathroom, looking like something the cat dragged in. But she smiles at me just the same.

Her life has taught her how to do that—smile through shit.

"Morning sickness?" I ask, encouraging her back to bed.

"Guess so," she says, snuggling under the covers.

I sit down beside her, Finn on my lap, and she kisses his little hand. "Did you have a lot of morning sickness with him?"

"Each pregnancy is different," Paige says. "Old wives' tale is that you throw up more with girls."

"A girl," I whisper, realizing she dodged my question. "Maybe we should wait to find out. Let it be a surprise."

"Isn't this pregnancy enough of a surprise?" she teases.

"Did you know Finn was a boy?" I ask.

Her blue eyes glance away for a second. "Not until he was born. The little stinker was a couple of weeks early."

"Were you ready? I mean, since it was a home birth."

"I don't think you're ever totally ready to have a baby."

"Was he born in Nashville?" I ask.

"No, we moved here shortly after he was born," she says, throwing me a look.

"But he was born in Tennessee?"

"Yes," she says, sitting up slightly. "What's with all the questions?"

"Am I asking a lot of questions?" I ask with a grin. Her head tilts to the side like she's annoyed, and I'm sure she is. She just threw up, and I'm hounding her for information. "I have one more question."

"Slade."

"And I need you to give me the right answer," I say. Her mouth starts to open, no doubt ready to give me some sassy response. "I'm taking Finn to the ranch. Meet us out there when you're ready to answer."

"Wait! What's the question?" she asks.

Holding Finn, I head for the door. "The ranch."

CHAPTER FORTY-TWO

PAIGE

He knows. No, he can't know.

He wants the truth. That's his question.

Truth?

My mind is telling me to run. I've done that before, and I can do it again. I hate to run, to uproot Finn from everything he's known for the past few months. In that respect, it was easier when he was an infant. Now it seems we are leaving so much more behind. I can't think about it, though. This isn't about me. This is about Finn. It's always been about Finn and protecting him.

My hand goes over my belly. Slade's baby. I can't do that to Slade. I won't.

Tears stream down my face. I'm trapped, and there's only one way out.

There's only been one way out this whole time.

I start to drive. It wasn't that long ago that Jon was driving me out to the ranch for the first time. Here I am again, watching the buildings of Nashville turn into the rolling hills of the countryside, the noise of the city fading away to the quiet that used to keep me up at night.

For a few short months, I had it—everything—the fairy tale. The poor girl who falls in love with the rich prince. That was me.

I knew it couldn't last, but I hoped it would be longer than this. That's what really hurts. I started to hope, to believe.

To rely on his love. He promised I could.

I bought into it all when I knew better.

I'm a felon, a criminal. It doesn't matter why I did it. I still did it.

Slade doesn't deserve to feel the kind of pain that's coming. He simply fell in love with the wrong woman. That's his only crime. Loving me.

I know he suspects something, but I don't know how much he really knows. If he knew everything, he could very well have the police waiting for me. I don't want him to have to make that decision. I turn down the road that leads to the ranch. On my first trip out here, I remember searching for a sign, the name of the ranch. I never spotted one.

Until today.

I pass under a wood and metal archway, and engraved at the top in simple lettering, it reads:

Paige's Home

I cover my mouth to try to contain my cry. The house comes into view. I know the inside is a mess, broken.

I know that feeling. I am that house.

Only the house can be repaired. What I've done can't be.

Getting out of the car, I remember the story Jon told me about being on that bridge. I'm on the ledge, and I've got to get off or jump. I can't keep walking the line.

When I turn the knob on the front door, it still feels like home, just like his sign reads. Slade has Finn on his hip, both of them waiting for me. Both of them smile at me. My heart cracks. I don't deserve for Slade to look at me like that, to love me.

He holds Finn out, letting me know he's mine to take. I hold my arms out to Finn, whose chunky arms and legs are flailing around, clearly happy to see me. Holding Slade's gaze, I take Finn in my arms and whisper my promise. "I'll do whatever I have to."

That includes walking away from the man I love.

I've lied to him enough. It's time I tell him the truth.

"I know you have questions," I say.

"Just one," he says, and I brace myself to hear the question I've been dreading for almost eight months.

He looks at me with those stunning blue eyes of his, then drops to one knee. "Marry me?" All the air in my chest comes out in a swift breath, and my knees wobble. "You shouldn't be so shocked. I've asked you before."

Tears start flowing down my cheeks, and I drop to my knees beside him. "I can't marry you. I can't."

"Because of whatever you're hiding?" he asks.

"Yes," I sob.

"I don't care what it is," he says. "I want you to be my wife."

"But . . ."

"I need you to listen." He tilts my chin up to look in my eyes, rubbing his finger down Finn's arm. Finn's little hand wraps around Slade's finger. "You are my son," he whispers.

I close my eyes tightly. "Dada," Finn says happily.

"Forever," Slade says, kissing the top of his head before turning his eyes to me.

"Slade?"

"I need you to hear me." I nod, knowing he's sucking me in. I knew he'd put up a fight, but I didn't know it would be this hard. "This will always be your home."

Softly, I kiss his lips. "No matter where I am, *you* will always be my home."

"Mamamamama," Finn babbles out.

Tears stream down my face. I try to stop them, but I can't. I know Finn probably doesn't know what he's saying, but this should be a happy moment. Unfortunately, it's wrapped up in too many lies. I've been lying to everyone for months, and my lies have run out.

"No, Finn," I say. "Not Mama."

CHAPTER FORTY-THREE
LAST YEAR
DECEMBER 1ST

PAIGE

Leaving my dorm, I take two buses across the city of Memphis to reach the run-down public housing where my mom lives. If the kids at school who whine about having roommates and using community showers spent a night or two here, they'd never complain again.

Holding my purse tight across my chest, I walk the mile from the bus stop to my mom's place. Anyone who grew up here knows there's a certain way to walk. You can't show fear. You have to walk with confidence, an attitude that you aren't to be messed with, but it's a fine line. You don't want to look cocky, like you're daring someone to start something or looking for trouble because you will find it.

I don't fit in here anymore. I can still walk the walk, but my clothes, my hair, everything else screams college girl. Of course, I don't really fit in on my college campus either. My clothes aren't designer, my hair isn't highlighted, and my shoes are for comfort instead of style. So basically, I don't fit in there, but I don't fit in here.

You won't hear me complain, though. I have a full college scholarship and a small stipend for incidentals. I work on campus, too, and that's enough to afford me clothes from discount stores and any other thing I might need.

I'm lucky. When you age out of the system, you typically get nothing. You are no longer the state's responsibility. You aren't your foster parents' responsibility. Basically, you're the walking dead. I'm one of the lucky few.

Some guy from an above balcony yells something obscene at me. My instinct is to flip him the bird, but I don't want to invite trouble.

I really thought I was done with this neighborhood, this life. I hadn't heard from my mom in close to a year when she sent me a letter six months ago. No matter how many times I've moved around, I always let her know where I am. The first few years, I stayed in touch a lot more, but as I got older, I realized I couldn't save her, so I vowed to stay away. That is, until I got her letter.

Her ground-floor apartment door is splintered and chipped. No woman should ever live on the ground floor, that's self-defense 101, but my mom thinks it's the best for her "work" and easy access when she's flying high.

I've done my best to try to keep her clean these past few months, but I can't watch her all the time. I bring her what little money I can scrape together. I'm sure I'm breaking all kinds of student aid laws doing that, but my mom has made it clear she can't work in her condition. Who'd want to pay to have sex with a pregnant woman?

Actually, I'm sure some perverts would be into that, but if her ever-growing belly is the excuse she needs to stop turning tricks, then I'm not going to fight her on it.

"Mom!" I call out as I open her door, which she hadn't even bothered to lock. The place is basically three rooms. You walk into the small den, which is attached to the even smaller kitchen. One small corner of the den houses baby items I've been collecting over the past few months. The rest of the apartment is my mom's room and one bathroom. The whole thing is a mess. Papers scattered about, old food and dishes litter the counter and the coffee table. She doesn't have nice furniture or anything, but I've always thought it would be a lot nicer if she at least kept it clean.

A small groan comes from her bedroom. Pushing open the door, I find her on the bed wearing only a long T-shirt, her arm in a tourniquet as she attempts to stick a needle in her vein. Instinctively, I hit her hand, knocking it to the wall.

"Stupid bitch," she yells at me. "I need that. The baby's coming."

"What?" I cry, putting down my purse and hustling beside her. "You said you had three more weeks."

She just shrugs and says, "I need that for the pain."

For the past six months, I've come over two to three times a week, making the one-hour trip by bus to bring her food, money, vitamins. I didn't do it for my mom. I did it for my little baby brother or sister. My mom doesn't deserve my help, but that little baby does. To my knowledge, she's had very little prenatal care. She says she's gone once or twice to some free clinic, but who knows what's true and what's not. Honestly, I'm not sure why she even kept this baby. I know she's had abortions before. How many? I can't tell you. Maybe she didn't realize she was pregnant until it was too late? Maybe she thought this baby would heal her? I have no idea.

She cries out in pain, and I look at my watch to try to time the contractions. I know that much from my nursing classes. I thought I had a little longer. I'd planned to read up on labor and delivery when my final exams for the semester were over. I'm not prepared for this.

I don't know what contractions only two minutes apart even means. "Let's get you to the hospital," I say, trying to help lift her.

"No hospitals," she says, moaning and groaning in bed, trying to find some position that may be comfortable.

Nothing with my mom is ever easy unless you're a paying customer. That's not very nice of me, but it's true. Looking at my mom, anyone can see that she was beautiful once upon a time—long dark hair, dark eyes, model thin. Perhaps she would still be considered beautiful if she wasn't so messed up.

"We have to go," I say, trying to pull her up. I'm a college student. I can't deliver a baby. Yes, I've had some basic nursing classes, but nothing that would qualify me to do this. Nothing beyond what I've read in a book.

"Paigey Poo," she says, pulling out her little pet name for me that she only uses when she wants something. "Don't make me go. They'll take the baby from me just like they took you."

That makes me hesitate.

"You know how the system is. You want that?" she says. "You want to never see your baby brother or sister again?"

"Mom?" I beg.

"I'm barely using now," she says. "You know I'm better."

I look over at the needle on the floor. I don't even want to think about how she got that. Did she use the money I gave her for food? Did she trade her body for it? Neither would surprise me. I've seen it all before. Better? I know she's trying, but she has a long way to go, and I don't know that she'll ever get there.

"Ugh!" she screams out in pain. "I have to push."

"No, don't push," I say. She's never listened before, and she doesn't now, bearing down, her teeth gnashing together.

"Shit," I cry, moving between her legs. As much as I want to call 911, I know my mom is right. Social services would take the baby. I may never see my baby brother or sister again, and I know firsthand that foster situations aren't always better.

"Get it out!" my mom screams.

I look down. God, I don't want to see this. I don't even have gloves. There's blood and various other liquids, and all my mom's private parts are on full display. She's never been a shy woman and now is no different, spread eagle on the bed. My heart rate is through the roof. My mom has put me through some shit in my life, but this might take the cake.

She starts to bear down again, and I see the tiniest glimpse of the top of the baby's head. "Oh my God," I cry. "I can see the head."

At that moment, my body settles. I know what I have to do. Get the baby out. I can't focus on my mother's screams, her drug use, none of it. My sole focus is on the baby.

I don't know how long or how short of an amount of time it takes. It could've been two hours, or it could've been two minutes, but either way, it was the longest experience of my life. I just kept telling myself that women have given birth in worse conditions, in worse shape. Heck, I've even heard stories of a woman giving birth in fields, then attaching the baby to their back, and continuing to work. If they can do that, then I can do this.

Finn Albert Hudson entered the world at three thirty-three. I like to think that was good luck or something. My mom picked the name. I have no idea why or for whom. I didn't ask. She'd told me she didn't know who his father was, so perhaps she just liked the name.

I missed school the next two days to stay with them. My mom refused to nurse him. I don't know if she was worried about drugs passing into his system, or she just didn't want to be bothered. I'd been stockpiling formula and diapers for a couple of months but hoped she'd change her mind for monetary reasons. Breastfeeding is cheaper than formula, but she didn't care.

Finn slept in my arms the first two nights of his life. Amazingly, he seemed *totally healthy and normal. My mom wouldn't let me take him to a doctor to be checked out. She wanted me to wait a week. She didn't say it, but I know that was to make sure any drugs in his system were gone. Keeping her ass out of trouble was more important to her than her son's life.*

As I held him and stared down at him, I fell in love. I never love easily, but with him, it was immediate. He is my family. I always wanted to know what that would feel like. Taking care of him, I knew what love was for the first time in my life.

Those first few days, my mom mostly slept. She was just as indifferent to him as she was to me. By day three, I had to go back to school. Finals week. I needed to study, and I needed to take my tests. Even more than before, it was vital for me to do well and graduate to help take care of Finn.

Before I could leave, I wrote down his feeding schedule for her, reminded her to put the diaper cream on so he wouldn't get a rash, and promised I'd be back as soon as I took my last exam.

Then it was time for me to go—past time, really. Placing Finn in my mother's arms, I immediately felt sick, a huge pit forming in my stomach. It didn't feel right. My mom could barely take care of herself, but I couldn't stay forever, so I ignored the little voice in my head, warning me of trouble.

Those few days back on campus were the longest days of my life. I tried to study but couldn't concentrate. I would try to call my mom between study groups and taking practice tests, but my mom never answered her phone the whole time. By the morning of the third day, I was so consumed with worry and fear I skipped my final and made the hour-long bus ride across town. I couldn't get Finn's little face out of my head.

If I didn't already know that something was wrong, it was confirmed when I approached my mom's apartment complex and saw her in the alley on her knees, some strange dirty man tossing one dollar bills on the ground as she sucked him off.

I don't have any idea if she ever saw me, but I took off like a bullet into her apartment. All I could think about was Finn. Where was he? It was quiet. I was more scared than I've ever been. It was not a peaceful quiet, but quiet like when death comes. Somehow, the apartment looked even worse than it did before, a nasty smell now filling the place.

I found Finn on my mom's bed. His lips were dry, the soft spot on his head was sunken in, and he was just lying there, almost lifeless. His eyes were open, and his face was scrunched—almost like he wanted to cry, but no tears or sound could come out.

I scooped him up, made a bottle, and stuck it in his mouth, praying he'd have enough energy to eat. His lips didn't move. "Come on, Finn," I begged, tears streaming down my face. This can't be happening. He can't . . . I wouldn't even allow myself to think the word. "Eat," I cried, running the nipple across his lips, wetting them. "I'll never leave you again."

His lips twitched a little, and I stuck the bottle in his mouth, continuing to move it around a little. I saw his cheeks pinch in one little sucking motion. Just one! Wiggling the bottle again, he did the same thing. He let out the smallest little cry, and it was the most beautiful sound I'd ever heard. Leaning over, I kissed him and whispered, "I love you."

Before I knew it, he finished the whole bottle.

I sat there holding him for hours, waiting for my mother to come back, wanting to scream at her, yell at her. She must have moved on from the guy in the alley to some other, or perhaps she was strung out somewhere. Whatever she was doing, the hours passed, and she never came back. Finn would've died there alone if I hadn't come—and stayed.

That's when I decided. That's when I promised him that I'd do anything to give him a better life.

I packed a bag with what little my mom had in clothes, formula, and diapers, and walked out the front door with him, keeping my promise.

CHAPTER FORTY-FOUR

PAIGE

I look at Slade, who'd just learned the truth. I kidnapped my baby brother, stole him from our worthless mother. The house around us is still a mess, a fitting environment for the shit I just laid on him.

"Finn is my baby brother," I say. "Not my son."

"I'm so sorry, Paige," he says, reaching to caress my cheek.

Holding my hand up, I stop him, unable to handle his kindness or sympathy right now. It's always been easier for me to be kind to others than to let someone be kind to me. When you grow up like I did, you feel like you don't deserve it. And you don't trust it. "I withdrew from school, took what little money I had, and caught a bus to Nashville. It was too risky to stay in Memphis. I obviously hadn't been pregnant, so I skipped town."

"You didn't know anyone here?" he asks.

"Not a soul," I say. "The first thing I did was take Finn to a pediatrician to get him checked out. That took a big chunk of my money." He tries to wrap his arms around Finn and me, but I resist. "Slade, don't you understand? I stole him. I don't want you messed up in that. I can't have that on me. I've hurt you so much already."

"You haven't hurt me," he says.

"I lied to you," I say, wiping my eyes.

"You did what you thought was right."

"I couldn't watch another child grow up like I did. I couldn't leave him to that."

"I know," he says. "And you didn't trust the system."

Shaking my head, I say, "I thought about reporting her, but I didn't think they'd give me custody of Finn. I was barely twenty with no real job, no income, no place of my own."

"So you took him."

I nod, rubbing my belly. "I made a promise to him that he'd have a better life, a home." I look up into Slade's blue eyes. "I kept that promise. He has you." His lips softly land on mine, his fingers grazing my belly. For an instant, I let myself fall into his kiss, memorizing what it feels like to have him love me. "I'm going to turn myself in."

To his credit, he doesn't look surprised. "Then you should know I plan on stopping you," he says with a little grin.

"I have to . . ."

"No, you don't," he says.

Finn reaches up, playing with the tears quietly falling from my eyes. Goodbyes used to be so easy for me. I was always saying them. To my mother. To foster families. To neighbors. I've always been good at them—they always came naturally, like breathing—but my body is fighting this one, my voice refusing to utter the words.

I don't want Finn to be as good at goodbyes as I used to be. I get to my feet, finally ready to face the truth. "And I want you to keep Finn for me."

"No, Paige," he says, taking hold of me. "I'm not going to let you do this."

"I have to. It's the only way to protect you, him. And our baby."

"No," he says, catching me by the arm. "You're not the only one who'll do whatever it takes."

"What does that mean?"

"Catrine said something to Jon, and he did some digging."

"On me?" I ask heatedly. "So you knew all this already?"

He holds his hands up in peace. "I found out that your mom was picked up for solicitation in the early stages of her pregnancy. No charges were filed that time, but it was noted that she was pregnant."

"That's what made her get in touch with me," I say. "How long have you known this?"

"Not long," Slade says. "Things starting clicking into place. Your reluctance to talk about Finn's father, your pregnancy, why you didn't have his social security number, why you lied about your first doctor's appointment."

Looking down, I say, "I felt like I had to be honest on my medical forms. I didn't want to lie and possibly affect anything with our baby."

"I know." His lips land on mine. "Paige, there's something else."

"What?"

He turns over a box for me to sit on, wrapping his arm around my shoulder, and I brace for whatever news he's preparing to deliver. "Your mother. She died four months ago. Overdose."

No tears come. There's nothing. Nothing for the woman who gave birth to me, to Finn. I have nothing left to give her. She took my childhood. She took my innocence. I won't cry for her. I won't.

I look up at Slade, confessing another sin to him. "What if that's my fault? What if she overdosed because I took Finn, and she was so distraught?"

"She didn't even know you were there that night," he says.

"Still, I stole her baby. She had to be grief-stricken and . . ."

"And it was just another excuse for her to stick a needle in her arm," he says coldly. "Finn would have died without you. I will not let you blame yourself for her death. The only thing you get credit for here is saving Finn's life."

I lean into his body slightly. It's hard to explain how much I love this man, and I'll never know why he loves me.

"Sometimes I wonder if the reason Finn eats so much now is because he was starved the first few days of his life," I say, guilt hanging over me like a dark shadow. "I'll never forgive myself for leaving him those few days."

He runs his hand across Finn's head, mussing the few strands of hair he has. "I know what it's like to blame yourself for something," he says, looking at me with the most understanding blue eyes.

"We're quite a pair," I say with a hint of a smile.

"As long as we're a pair," he says.

"Slade, no matter the reason, what I did was illegal, and if anyone finds out . . ."

"Your mother is gone. No one can prove you took Finn." He looks down at me. "One more lie?" he asks. "One more lie and then we never lie again."

Sometimes you have to lie to keep a promise. This is one of those times.

Slade sits down beside me in the lawyer's office. All the lies, all the secrets, they've all just been the warm-up, the rehearsal for this moment. The lie to save me from all the others. The lie that makes Finn mine and Slade's. The lie that lets me keep my promise.

I tell the lawyer the same story I told Slade. The best lies are mostly truths. That's what makes them effective. The only detail that changes is that when I returned, my mom asked me to take Finn, knowing she couldn't take care of and provide for him. Finn will grow up knowing our mother was troubled, but she made the best decision for him. Our lie will give him that little bit of comfort.

At her request, I took Finn, moved to Nashville, and haven't heard from her since. I just recently found out she was dead, which is true, and realized I didn't have any documentation giving me custody of Finn. He never even received a birth certificate or social security number.

Of course, I had to prove that I was indeed a blood relative, his half sister. A simple blood test took care of that. We were also required by law to prove we tried in good faith to find his birth father. We took out ads in various personal columns of local Memphis papers, even sent a private investigator to ask neighbors who lived in my mom's apartment complex. All of this took time, but of course, nothing turned up.

Slade intertwines our hands, the massive blue diamond on my

engagement ring a stark contrast to the simple platinum wedding band he wears. We got married in a simple ceremony at the ranch just a few days after I told him everything. Not only did I vow to love him in sickness and in health, for richer or poorer, but I also vowed to love him when he's an asshole. That got the crowd laughing. Not sure how the pastor felt about that one, but it had to be said.

That was a couple of months ago now. His father, Clay, some other ranch hands, Jon, and Catrine attended. They got the same story we just told the lawyer. I'm sure Jon suspects it's not the total truth.

"This shouldn't be a problem," the lawyer says. "This kind of thing happens all the time. An aunt or grandmother, or in this case, a sister, takes custody of a minor while the parents get themselves clean or find work. That kind of thing. No paperwork is ever filed in those situations. Now, of course, your mother is deceased. The fact that your mother never filed for a birth certificate or social security number makes this a little more challenging, but we've established that you're his last known blood relative. You have the means to provide for him. Now that I have the necessary evidence, this should be a pretty straightforward case."

"Thank you," I say, reaching out to shake his hand to end the meeting, but Slade stops me.

"There's one other issue," Slade says. "Once this is all settled, I'd like to start the process of adopting Finn."

He looks over at me and smiles. Just when I think I can't love him any more, he does something like this. I lean over, kissing him on the cheek, and whisper my thank you. I have so much to thank him for. For having Jon escort me away from his father, for giving me a job, for looking past everything I threw at him, for stepping up to the plate with Finn, and for loving me. I don't know that we do that enough—thank the people who love us. We should all do that each night before going to bed. Turn to the one we love and say:

Thank you for loving me.

Slade had mentioned adopting Finn a while back, but I had no idea he was going to bring it up today. As usual, Slade is full of surprises and full steam ahead. When he makes his mind up he wants something, he charges at it. Since Finn is so young, I plan on him calling us Mom and Dad. As he gets older, I will tell him the truth about who we are, but I think it would be too confusing for him to call us anything else right now.

Still, when I think about it, if Slade does actually adopt Finn, then I will be married to the father of my brother. That sounds very wrong, but I've learned that sometimes a wrong does make a right.

EPILOGUE

SLADE

"Happy Birthday, buddy," I whisper in Finn's ear. He looks up at me and smiles, not having any clue what to do with the cake before him.

My dad, Catrine, Jon, baby Theo, Clay, and some other ranch hands are all here to celebrate Finn's first birthday. Paige has been planning this day for weeks and weeks. The theme is the number one. The number one is on everything from the plates and napkins to the balloons and cups. Even the cake is in the shape of a huge number one.

We moved back into the ranch two days ago, barely making it in time for his birthday. I knew Paige really wanted his first party to be here, at our home. I made sure to make that happen by paying the construction guys overtime and hiring additional workers, doing whatever I had to do to give her this.

The day Finn was born, and the few that followed weren't exactly picture-perfect, so I will make sure that his birth is a day to celebrate for the rest of my life. My son deserves that.

Yes, he's officially my son. Since there wasn't anyone contesting the adoption, the process went smoothly, and yesterday it became final.

Finn Turner.

And his little brother is due in late spring, just before the oppressive Tennessee heat kicks in. Initially, we wanted the sex of the baby to be a surprise, but the little guy had other plans when he had his legs spread eagle during the ultrasound.

My dad is armed and ready with the camera, trying to capture

Finn eating his first birthday cake. Paige insisted Finn have his own. It's a crisp December day in Tennessee, but still warm enough that we can do this outside.

A picnic blanket is laid out especially for this moment. Finn is walking now, but he hasn't quite mastered walking outside yet, always wanting to stop and pick at the blades of grass. Using me as support, he stands.

Paige places the cake down before him as we all sing "Happy Birthday." It's not a big crowd, but big enough that he hugs my neck for reassurance.

"Make a wish," Paige says, holding the cake out in front of him as she and I blow out the single candle together.

He looks at both of us for encouragement. Paige sets the cake on the blanket, and I scoop the icing with my finger and take a lick to show him what to do.

He promptly turns around and sits down on his cake, and everyone bursts out laughing.

"Finn!" Paige cries, but she lets him sit there, mushing the cake between his fingers and then sticking his hands in his mouth. When it starts to go in his nose and ears, she scoops him up, rushing to throw him in the bath.

The party winds down after that, and everyone heads home. It's just about Finn's nap time anyway, so the timing is good. After some quick cleanup outside, I walk in the house, hearing Finn's little footsteps on the wood floors. I hear his giggle and see his belly enter the room before he does. Wearing only a diaper, he rushes toward me. He can't quite run yet, but he's getting there. His speed is now a fast waddle.

"Finn Albert Turner," Paige says, a playful tone in her voice as she chases him, her shirt covered in cake and water.

Picking him up, I toss him in the air a little, and he squeals. "Everyone leave?" Paige asks.

I kiss her on the head. "Yep. Just us."

She tickles Finn a little. "Sugar rush. He's never going to nap."

"I'll put him down," I say.

Finn is a great baby and an even better napper. He sleeps about as good as he eats, so that's saying something. It doesn't take long before he's out for the count. Paige's sleeping habits have improved as well. She still loves the Cooking Channel; she just doesn't watch it in the middle of the night anymore.

Looking for Paige, I grab a slice of leftover cake and stick a candle in the middle. I know Paige didn't have any except what got on her clothes. I wander to our bedroom, which is on the opposite side of the house from Finn. Paige isn't quite used to that yet, accustomed to him being close.

Opening up the door, I see her standing at the dresser in only a black bra and panties, changing from Finn's icing finger painting. Her little baby bump is in full view. My breath catches in my throat. I'll never get used to seeing her like this, finding her in my bedroom. I remember that first time I found her asleep in here, so beautiful. It's that same feeling every time.

"Stay just like that," I whisper.

She turns to me, her skin blushing. I just stand there, admiring her, so beautiful, growing our little baby. "Think I might need to keep you pregnant."

She raises an eyebrow at me. I know I'm pushing it. We are already going to have two kids less than two years apart. "I've actually been thinking about something you suggested," Paige says.

"What's that?" I ask, holding out the piece of cake for her.

"Clean baby food. Or as you like to call it, *green shit*," she teases. "I'm thinking instead of nursing, I'll maybe get a marketing degree and start my own company, helping low-income parents give their babies healthy options. The organic stuff is so expensive. There has to be a better way."

"How am I supposed to argue with that?"

"You're not," she says, placing the cake on the nightstand. "I know you don't expect me to work and are happy to provide for our family, but I need to do this."

"And I'm all about giving you what you need," I tease, taking her hands. "Paige's Promise. That should be the name."

She kisses me slowly, sweetly. "Thank you."

I reach into my pocket for a folded-up piece of paper. "A gift," I say.

"It's not my birthday," she says, smiling and shaking her head at me. I love spoiling her, giving her everything she never had before.

"I think the mother of the birthday boy should get a gift," I say, handing her the paper.

Kissing me again, she takes the paper and opens it. She looks up at me, confusion in her eyes.

"A picture of a beachfront bungalow?"

"We never had a honeymoon," I say, grinning.

"What?" she cries out.

"A week in the Caribbean," I say. "That's our room."

"Are you kidding me?" she asks as a smile spreads across her face.

"And before you freak out, Finn is coming with us. They have a nursery and full-time nannies on staff to watch the kids so we can have a romantic dinner or . . ."

"Oh my God, Slade," she says, bouncing up and down a little.

"I know the week of Finn's birth doesn't hold the best memories for you," I say. "But we are going to change that. We leave tomorrow."

She leaps into my arms, kissing me hard on the lips. She's in her underwear, and she's kissing me, so that's the only invitation I need. I tackle her to the bed as she laughs. Inspiration strikes, and I reach over to the birthday cake, grabbing some icing with my finger.

She gives me a don't you dare look, but I'm a pretty daring guy. Slowly, I use my finger to glide the icing down her neck, pulling her bra down and circling her nipple, my tongue following the same path.

It's not her birthday, but she is my wish.

ALSO BY PRESCOTT LANE

Ryder (A Merrick Brothers Novel)
Knox (A Merrick Brothers Novel)
Just Love
A Gentleman for Christmas
All My Life
To the Fall
Toying with Her
The Sex Bucket List
The Reason for Me
Stripped Raw
Layers of Her (a novella)
Wrapped in Lace
Quiet Angel
Perfectly Broken
First Position

ACKNOWLEDGEMENTS

Two little words—thank you. Hardly seem sufficient. But those two words and these few lines are what I have to express how much it means to me that you've read my book. Whether it's your first book or your tenth, whether you've been with me since the beginning or just found me. Thank you.

Thanks for loving romance, reading romance, and falling in love with the characters I write over and over again. It means more to me than I can ever express.

Thank you to Mary Dube and the team at Grey's Promotions for sharing my books and organizing this release. A special thanks to Lori Jackson for her incredible cover design. I love it so much. And to Scott Hoover for taking the exceptional photo.

A huge shoutout to Jenny Sims at Editing 4 Indies for polishing my words until they shine. And huge hugs to Michelle Rodriguez for being the absolute best beta reader in the world.

Lastly, thanks to my friends and family for sticking with me through all my crazy, which happens with each book. I love and appreciate you all so much.

Hugs and Happily Ever Afters,
Prescott Lane

ABOUT THE AUTHOR

PRESCOTT LANE is originally from Little Rock, Arkansas, and graduated from Centenary College in 1997 with a degree in sociology. She went on to Tulane University to receive her MSW in 1998, after which she worked with developmentally delayed and disabled children. She currently lives in New Orleans with her husband, two children, and two dogs.

Contact her at any of the following:
www.authorprescottlane.com
facebook.com/PrescottLane1
twitter.com/prescottlane1
instagram.com/prescottlane1
pinterest.com/PrescottLane1